The House Rules

Calvin Naraghi

First Edition: October 2024

ISBN: 979-8-9915614-0-2 (ebook)
ISBN: 979-8-9915614-1-9 (paperback)

Cover design by *Christian Storm*

Published by Cozy Manor Publishing

To my mother, who said I could be a writer, and to myself, for deciding to believe her.

Contents

Chapter 1

Portrait of a Boy

People always say there is no right way to act at a funeral, yet as Lonnie stood there watching his brother being lowered into the ground, he couldn't help feeling like everyone was doing it wrong. Standing beneath an old sycamore tree, Lonnie took quick breaths, trying unsuccessfully to get his rage under control as a hurricane swirled in his head. He watched the people perched before him atop the grassy hill dotted with white chairs, black suits, and frowns.

This is insane.

But no one seemed to notice him. Or if they did, they paid no mind to the crying ten-year-old boy.

The graveyard darkened as the afternoon sun slid behind a thick layer of tumultuous clouds. Lonnie flinched at the drop of water that suddenly planted itself on his cheek, and a snort forced itself from his mouth. *Finally a real tear*, he thought.

Peering between the supposed grievers toward the front, Lonnie spotted a portrait of his brother, which for a second made him smile before turning knots in his stomach. Approaching the image, he reached out and pressed his hand to the gilded-framed canvas, his brother's face meshed into it by a myriad of oil and brush strokes. On the bottom of the frame, a handful of words were neatly printed:

Benjamin Frederick Grambell
September 9th, 1995 - June 14th, 2015

Lonnie blinked back more tears, trying to wrap his head around those dates. *How has it already been two days?* Nothing about it made sense.

Nobody is making sense.

He moved from the portrait to let others by and caught a glimpse of his parents, who had managed to tuck themselves behind some trees, building a shield of people to hide among. Lonnie's ten-year-old mind supposed it was to hide from him, as they'd been doing the past two days. Every mention of his brother, Ben, seemed to frighten them, like it was something they weren't allowed to talk about.

Even the first conversation after the death had felt brief. They'd said his brother had gone to a party the previous night... and had been drinking. His parents hadn't even looked sad when they told him, which is probably why it shocked him the most when they finally added he was gone. If anything, they'd looked surprised, like it wasn't supposed to happen.

It shouldn't have happened, he thought.

As he wiped another stray tear from his eyes, a car pulled up alongside the grave site, its lavish black exterior drawing everyone's eyes. The man got out first from the back seat. His arm extended a hand for the woman to latch onto as she exited behind him. Lonnie recognized most of the guests from birthdays and lunches his father hosted at the house. But these people, he drew a blank. As the purring car rolled off behind them, the couple made their way to the crowd. Their bodies were wrapped in fitted black silk, and their faces were stretched and polished. Lonnie knew his parents were rich, but with these people, power wafted off them like a spray.

The guests had barely walked a step before Mr. and Mrs. Grambell appeared in his peripheral from the tree line. His parents' faces were stoic, though Lonnie noted an odd spark of fear in their eyes as they beelined across the cemetery. When they finally reached the wealthier couple, the four broke into a deep conversation that was too far away for him to hear. After a few exchanges, they each turned to peer across the hillside, with faces steeped in disdain. Shocked, Lonnie followed their gazes to his brother's college friends, who were standing separate from the crowd in a huddle by the chairs. Their demeanors were sullen and pitiful, and in that moment, Lonnie almost felt embarrassed by how much he used to idolize them, while another part of him now wondered if they had been there that night.

Are Ben's friends the reason he's dead?

Except as he looked back, he realized the couples weren't staring at the boys but at a girl standing behind the group, just outside their circle. Her interest seemed to wander in and out from their conversation as she tugged at the ruffles of her dress. It was Ben's girlfriend.

Why are they looking at Danielle?

Danielle was one of the first people who had shown up that morning, her eyes outlined in deep black liner and her brunette hair swirled into a bun. She looked nice, but it was obvious that beneath the surface she was unwinding at the seams. Lonnie tried to find a reason for his parents' and their friends' piercing stares, but nothing came to mind. She was always kind to him, in the same way she was nice to everybody, he supposed. There was a special kind of warmness about her that everyone seemed to like. He had met her a few times, starting when they visited his brother during Freshman Parent Weekend last year and then again when she came down to stay with them for holiday break. She had even brought him a present, which he thought was touching.

Now, he watched her across the grass, being propped up by her friends who'd just shown up to embrace her. With a cry, she'd thrown herself into their shoulders, the weight of grief clearly setting in. The sight made Lonnie nauseous, but he couldn't look away. Her outburst was entrancing, like her soul had been set ablaze. He had never seen someone love so hard yet look so lost.

Lonnie turned back to his parents only to find them and the new guests now staring at him. He swallowed, a ripple of nerves running down his spine. He looked behind him to see if someone was there, but it was only the trees.

What do they want?

Their gaze felt invasive. Frightening even. He wanted to shout for them to stop, but upon noticing him staring back, they immediately turned away and returned to talking discreetly among themselves. Just then, the officiant summoned them to the grave site. He stood with graying blond hair, tall stature, and deep bags extending from the corners of his eyes. A leather-bound book lay tucked under his arms, and a white collar straddled around his neck. Once people reached the grave, he requested they sit in the chairs, then began his speech with a coughing fit of words.

"Benjamin Grambell was a lovely young man, taken long before his time. And he will be remembered always by his parents and his younger brother, Leonard, who will miss him dearly."

Lonnie winced. He hated when people called him by his full name; it sounded so proper and high-class, things he thought himself too empathetic to be.

What makes this man think he knows my brother?

Neither him nor Ben had ever met this man, and quite frankly, it didn't matter what he had to say. However, he found himself sliding into his seat obediently as the man recounted lies to the crowd.

Lonnie tried to listen as the officiant talked, but his voice just melted into the wind. He couldn't understand how everyone else was soaking up the words being spit out. Lonnie looked for the strange couple in the crowd, but they had disappeared. Rolling his eyes, he continued to search around for them. He knew they were near; he could feel the goosebumps running up his arms. But before he could find them, an ovation erupted from the audience, telling him the speech had concluded.

A tall, silhouetted figure approached him from the side, quickly stuffing a pile of rose petals into his hand. Caught off guard, Lonnie frowned up at his mother towering over him.

"What's this?" he asked her.

"They're rose petals. We need to throw them on the casket."

"Wait, why? Ben didn't even like roses."

"Just throw them on the casket," she whispered, already drained from the conversation.

Lonnie crushed the rose petals in his hand, his forehead crinkling. "No. He didn't like roses!"

His mother spun on her heel and grabbed him by the wrist, her face turning from pearl white to an ugly vermilion.

"Hey! Do not raise your voice at me."

"You're doing it all wrong! All of this is wrong! Why can't you see that?" he screamed.

She stared at him for a moment, rubbing the arch of her nose. Then channeling a deep breath, she squatted down so they were face-to-face.

"Sweetheart, they're just petals."

"No, it's not!"

She stood and lowered her voice. "You need to stop fighting me on this. We are in public, Lon—"

"Why don't you care that he's dead?" he whined, trying to tug his wrist free.

People began to turn in their seats at the commotion. Their eyes peered out at Lonnie and his mother situated awkwardly in the center of the crowd. For the first time in days, he saw her facade fade, and emotions started to pour from her. Mainly annoyance.

"Of course I care," she hissed. "Why would you say something so horrible?"

"Because it's true," he wheezed under his breath.

She looked around, growing more flustered by the second as Lonnie noticed the rich couple who'd arrived late standing nearby. The man watched them, then he leaned over to whisper something into the woman's ear. Mrs. Grambell, Lonnie's mother, must have noticed as well, because she went quiet, her lip quivering.

"Fine, Lonnie," she whispered. "Throw them or don't, I don't care."

She wiped at her eye before stomping back to the safety of the distant trees. When Mr. Grambell went to chase after her, he was stopped by the rich couple, each placing a hand on his shoulders. With serious expressions, they led his father away from the crowd. Lonnie wanted to follow them but was interrupted by the line of people now approaching the grave. As they strolled by, their lingering eyes followed him. And when they finally passed, the couple and his father had vanished. Frustrated, he pushed through the chairs, making his way to the grave.

He hadn't seen the full casket up close yet. It was smaller than he expected, which made him feel sick. His mind wandered, picturing his brother's crumpled-up body lying on the other side of the wood. A sense of overwhelm rose within him until it became near suffocating. He dropped to the ground where the short, stiff grass poked him, and he pressed his face intimately close with the coffin. The outside of it was painted a metallic black with a nice green trim, which looked properly expensive.

Ben would have hated this.

"I'm sorry," he whispered as he pulled out the crumbled up rose petals and tossed them angrily onto the overpriced box.

How can someone so big fit in such a tiny space? The question niggled at him.

Is he even in there?

Raising his head, he faced a group of people standing at the other end of the grave, tossing their own petals into the ditch while glancing at Lonnie in pity. Climbing to his feet, Lonnie strode away.

He watched the rest of the service from a park bench at the bottom of the hill, half-listening to people stutter and mumble their way through speeches until his brother's friends began to share. Soon, he hung on every word they spoke as a collection of anecdotes flowed from their mouths. The stories seemed almost fictional, like bedtime tales. Except they said them with such conviction and meaning that they had to be true. The occasional chuckle from the audience set his teeth on edge, as if they remembered the stories any more than he did.

Why didn't he tell me these stories?

A calloused hand on his shoulder interrupted his focus. He flinched. On his right, a burly man in a long peacoat with kindly eyes had taken up residence beside him on the bench. Lonnie vaguely recognized him as one of his father's friends.

"How are you doing?" the man said bluntly.

Lonnie shifted his body forward, unsure how to respond to such a stupid question. "Fine," he finally sassed.

The man sighed, then shook his head. "Sorry, that was a dumb thing to say."

Lonnie rolled his eyes and went back to focusing on the service in front of him.

"My name is Michael. I'm an old friend of your dad's."

Lonnie stayed silent, causing the man to pause for what felt like minutes.

"I know how you're feeling right now. My older brother died last year."

Lonnie turned slightly to get a glimpse of the man, interest piqued by his statement. "He did?"

"Yes. Trust me when I say I know how much it hurts."

Tears unexpectedly welled up in Lonnie's eyes, making him feel quite embarrassed. Trying his best, he wiped them away, but they wouldn't stop rolling down his cheeks. "Everything is just happening too fast," he whispered. "And everyone just keeps looking at me. Why do they keep staring at me?" Lonnie said bluntly. "Was it like this for you? At your brother's funeral?"

The man paused again, his hand subtly swiping at his eye.

"Yeah, I suppose it was. Everyone was waiting for me to fall apart."

"Did you?"

"Not that day, but I did. Couldn't stop crying."

"Did you ever stop?"

His gaze now met the man's, and in return he saw two bright hazel eyes shining back. The man produced a handkerchief from his pocket and handed it over to Lonnie. In a brisk go, he took it and wiped his entire face, covering the rag in a mixture of snot and tears.

"Some days I still do, some I don't." He rubbed the edge of the bench awkwardly.

"Oh..." Lonnie said, a bit disappointed.

"It's just time, I suppose—" A beeping noise signaled from the man's pocket, cutting off his comment. He pulled out his phone, then stared at it as the corners of his lips shrank in.

"Shoot. I'm sorry, I have to run... It's a work emergency. But I am glad I got to finally meet you, Lonnie. And I'm truly sorry about your brother."

The man smiled once more, then rose to leave.

"How did he die?" Lonnie blurted to his back.

The man turned around, his phone still clutched in his hand. "Sorry?"

"How did your brother die?"

"Oh...he overdosed at a party."

Lonnie squinted at him. "At a party? What did—"

"I'm sorry, I really do have to go." Michael gave a sympathetic grin, then walked away. He stopped briefly by Lonnie's parents, giving Mrs. Grambell a hug and Mr. Grambell a firm handshake, before disappearing off to the edge of the graveyard. Lonnie watched him, his final words still churning in his head.

A party?

The crowd began to disperse, leaving only a handful of stragglers behind. Danielle and her friends were some of the last to leave, and as her friends escorted her to her car, she locked eyes with Lonnie, who stared back awkwardly. With her hand resting on the open vehicle door, she gave a sympathetic wave. And then she, too, left, leaving only Lonnie, his parents, a few guests, and Hilda the housekeeper, who had driven alone with him to the graveyard.

A chilled wind suddenly overtook the hillside, sending a shiver down his back. The trees started rustling above him, dropping an array of leaves onto the lowered casket. Feeling uneasy, Lonnie pulled himself up and strode briskly over to Hilda, who gave him a nurturing hug before leading him to the waiting car.

Chapter 2

Old Endings

Eight years later.

For the moment, he felt content.

The pit in his stomach from the morning had disappeared long enough for him to catch his breath. Lonnie sat, arm wrapped around Hannah, and with each pulse of her heart, he felt a wave of relief wash over him.

"Smile!" Jamie directed. His knee bent into a pose on the grass, his Polaroid camera latched between his hands.

"We are smiling," Hannah said, forcing a toothy grin beneath her graduation cap. "See."

As she bobbed her head jokingly, her cap's tassel fell into her mouth, causing her to cough and Lonnie to burst out laughing.

"Oh my gosh!" She pointed at Lonnie's exposed teeth. "Hurry, Jamie, take advantage of this rarity."

Lonnie went to object but got distracted as he felt her arm wrap tighter around his back in the playful way she did. Her body constricted against him like a pressed sweater, making his cheeks grow warm. Between that and the wind picking up her auburn hair and sending strands across his face, he had already forgotten what he was going to say.

A flash went off, drawing his attention back to the camera. The photo began to print, and Jamie straightened and jumped up, his fingers ripping the film from the dispenser and lowering it into the shade. He beamed as he looked at the photo, his other hand running through his thin, curly, blond hair, his body swaying as he danced to whatever noise was running through his head.

Buzz.

A muffled noise came from the nearby tree, causing Hannah's arm to tense before receding from Lonnie's spine. Running over, she plucked a black bag from the base of the tree and pulled out her phone.

Buzz. The phone rang again, but she just stared at it, the color draining from her rosy cheeks as her eyebrows folded into lines.

Buzz.

"I have to take this, I'll be right back," she finally yelled back to the boys, already walking farther across the courtyard.

"Okay?" Lonnie responded awkwardly.

Her steps grew quicker until she had put at least a few trees' distance between them. She was too quiet to hear, but from the way she held her stance, he could tell it wasn't a pleasant conversation. Giving her privacy, he turned his attention to Jamie, who was now tightrope walking across the rock wall, the film gripped in his hand. He was especially vibrant today. Maybe it was because they were about to graduate, or just because it was one of those days. Then again, Lonnie supposed it wasn't far off from Jamie's normal mood most days. He had that pure child-like fun that most people tended to lose around their age.

Jamie continued to shake the Polaroid, his face captivated by the developing picture as the sun slipped out from behind the clouds, illuminating the quad. The light reflected off Jamie's cheekbones, protruding his sculpted features as if to remind the world that Jamie Harken was quite handsome. He had the kind of looks that people painted and hung in museums for millions to ogle at.

Lonnie must have been staring too long because Jamie looked up and locked eyes with him. The clone of Dorian Gray smirked and jumped down from the little wall to run over and slap the Polaroid into Lonnie's hand. Before he could get a glimpse of it, however, another flash went off. Little lights flickered across his retinas, blinding him. He viciously rubbed his eyes, stumbling backward in an effort to regain his balance. When his vision finally returned, Jamie stood holding the camera inches from his face, taking a selfie of the two of them.

"What the hell, man? Warn a guy next time," Lonnie said. But his fuse quickly extinguished as he looked at the first picture Jamie had handed him. Hannah's cheek was pressed against Lonnie's, with the golden tassels resting on either side. A natural light shining down from the tree line projected the grins on their faces. He smiled and put a finger to her face, her freckles painting her cheeks like a constellation. Strands of wild hair stretched out from under her graduation cap as if they were each gasping for breath.

She was intoxicating.

Blushing at the photo, he heard her heels clicking in the distance, each step growing closer until she was in front of him.

"What did I miss?" she asked. Her face was covered in faint lines of mascara that she'd clearly tried to wipe clean.

Lonnie frowned. *Has she been crying?*

He wrapped his arm around her shoulders. "You okay? Who were you talking to?"

She caught her breath and looked like she might start crying again. "It was Carter... He said he isn't going to make it today."

"Oh, I'm sorry," Jamie and Lonnie both recited.

"I just really wanted to see him." She looked at Lonnie, and a sudden realization crossed her face. "Oh gosh, I shouldn't be complaining to you about this. I—"

"No, it sucks your twin won't be here." He wiped some dry mascara from her cheek. "And don't feel bad for me; I'm as familiar to no-shows as one can be."

"Hey, maybe they'll show up for this," she added in a hopeful voice.

"Yeah...maybe."

She pointed at the Polaroid resting in his hand. "Is this the picture?" she asked, a fake smile surfacing. She traced her finger over the photo in his hand as she rested her head on his shoulder. "Aw, I love this. Can I keep it?"

"Of course," Lonnie said.

"Gosh, I'm going to miss you so much." She hugged him tightly. "You should just stay with me instead this summer. My parents love you. They wouldn't mind!"

"Sorry, he is spoken for, lady," Jamie scoffed, sliding between them. "My parents already have his old room set up."

Hannah opened her lips to rebut, but Lonnie grabbed her wrist. Slowly sliding his hand down into hers, he murmured, "Hey...it's just for the summer, right?"

Hannah lifted her cheeks, but a look of sadness still caressed her face. "Yeah...of course."

"By fall, we'll all be at Hopkins, and then I'm all yours." He grinned, then pulled her lips to his, holding the ends of her face gently in his palms like works of glass. With it, an electric rush coursed through them, causing her skin to warm beneath his hands.

"Get a room," Jamie blurted.

"Shut up." Lonnie chuckled.

He leaned over to give him a playful shove when a sudden static crinkle filled the air. Looking up, they listened as an older woman's raspy voice rung from the nearby speaker:

"Good evening, Dreyaird Academy! The graduation ceremony will begin shortly. All students please report to the auditorium for line order and staging."

"No way. It's not even supposed to start until 4:00," Jamie argued.

"Actually, it's 4:17," Hannah said, plucking her phone from her pocket.

Lonnie's eyes grew wide. "Oh shoot."

The three grabbed their bags from the grass and started hauling them across the courtyard, with Hannah almost losing her balance as she stumbled in heels over the cobblestone.

"My robe is too long for this." She reached down to grab the hem.

Lonnie grabbed the tail of the robe from behind. "I've got it, just keep running."

Their stifled giggles floated through the school as they raced down the halls, their voices echoing as they began huffing from the weight of their bags. Beads of sweat formed under Lonnie's gown as the Virginia summer heat beat down on him. But he continued moving. As they approached the auditorium, the opening music flowed from the backdoor.

"Oh no, it already started," Lonnie gasped.

Carefully, he pried the door open a crack, making enough

room for Hannah and Jamie to scoot past. Then he proceeded to follow them in. Ahead, rows of parents sat, filling up the auditorium. Students hidden under robes and caps, stood amusingly in lines behind the stage curtain. Next to them, paper signs were planted on the floor. The first read:

A-M

And the other:

N-Z

Hurriedly, they shuffled across the floor to their respective lines just as a woman in a pantsuit and a clipboard charged at them from behind a curtain. "You're late!" she hissed. Her outfit said business professional, but the rest of her was being held together with hairspray and coconut-scented deodorant.

"Sorry, miss," Lonnie muttered. Before he could say more, she moved on to alternate between scrolling through her list and checking her watch as if waiting for more students to burst in late.

Minutes passed, and Jamie used the opportunity to take more Polaroids with other friends while Lonnie peeked between a slit in the makeshift curtain hanging between the graduates and the parents. The ceremony was intimate. Couldn't have been more than a couple hundred family members in the audience. But as he scanned the crowd, he felt that pit from the morning reform in his chest.

He turned away just in time to find a familiar face watching him from across the room. Hannah's eyes were starting to well with pity. Lonnie stood there frozen for a second, embarrassment causing his neck to itch. As he reached to close the curtain, a woman in a white pinstriped suit and curly black hair pushed past him and onto the stage.

"Hello, everyone. Hope you're having a lovely evening!

Before we get started with speeches and introductions, let me first present to you the 2023 Dreyaird Academy Boarding School graduating class!"

Starting with a delicate clap, she led the audience into an applause that hummed through the auditorium. Lonnie felt a cold presence behind him, only to find the frazzled lady with the clipboard had once again appeared. Her hair had begun to unravel from its tightly formed bun, and her brow was now painted with a thick coat of sweat. She looked at her watch. "Let's go," she seemed to shout beneath her breath. With a gesture, she directed their line towards the side entrance, where they met with the other line on the stage and crossed. From there, they walked down and found their seats at the front of the audience. With what little remained of his dignity, Lonnie made another attempt to search the crowd, scanning each row, until he found himself once again staring eye to eye with Hannah seated two rows back. He huffed and faced forward. She had always been very good at reading him, which he typically enjoyed. It allowed him to speak to her without needing to put his problems into words. However, at this moment, her eyes felt like screws winding into his skull, and he wanted it to stop.

"How long do you think this will be?" Lonnie whispered to Jamie.

"I don't know, maybe an hour."

Lonnie planted his head into his hands and slumped down in his seat.

Terrific.

He watched the clock tick, second after second, as the pinstripe lady's voice droned on, and then suddenly they were standing and walking single file to the stage, where he shook the lady's hand and faked a smile for the camera.

Once back in his chair, Lonnie watched the other hundred or so students who'd been behind him stride across the stage. Following them, Hannah stepped back up to give her valedictorian speech. She sounded so confident, spewing each word with such power and emotion that even the coconut deodorant lady stopped moving to watch. At the end of it, Lonnie stood and cheered, but his voice was drowned out by the uproar of the crowd. From the corner of his eye, Lonnie could make out Mr. and Mrs. Rodbloom, Hannah's parents, cheering.

They looked sweet, each sporting a pair of inch-thick-deep glasses with cable-knit sweaters and matching rings. Their rosy cheeks sparkled as they watched their daughter. Lonnie had gone on vacation to Aruba with them over winter break earlier that year. They were so put together. A warm family that did silly Christmas cards in matching pajamas and hats. And though he was happy for them, the sight of their cheerful expressions also threatened to boil his blood. He shook himself, letting the anger dissolve from his skin.

This is my day... Even if no one cared enough to come and acknowledge it.

Suddenly, his classmates stood up around him and lifted their tassels from one side of their caps to the other.

With an exaggerated pull, Hannah flung her cap into the air from the stage and yelled, "Congratulations, you graduated!"

The classmates followed suit, each squealing with joy as they tossed their hats into the mosh of people. Lonnie held his firmly on his head as he crept his way from the mass. Using the diversion as a chance to sneak out before having to talk, Lonnie had nearly reached the auditorium door by the time the congratulations died down. His escape was futile, though, as Mrs. Rodbloom called his name from across the room. He continued moving, pretending he misheard, but her footsteps grew closer across the floor. Finally, he succumbed to his fate and turned to face her.

"Congratulations!" she bellowed, wrapping him in a motherly hug.

"Thank you, Mrs. Rodbloom."

She looked at him, a mystified expression crossing her face. "Are you all alone?" she pestered. "Where are your parents, darling?"

Amazing question.

He gave an awkward chuckle. "I'm sure they're around."

"I see," she paused. "Why don't you come out to dinner with us then?"

"Oh no, I can't—"

Mr. Rodbloom and Hannah approached. "Hey, Mr. Graduate." Mr. Rodbloom gently punched him in the arm in an endearing and nonthreatening way.

"Hi, Mr. Rodbloom."

Lonnie's face grew hot. He suddenly felt surrounded, seeing Hannah's family form a wall in front of him. Taking a step back, a flash suddenly shot up from the side, nearly blinding him. A group of people had taken up residency there, using the space for their family photos. Seemingly trapped, he turned back to face Hannah's parents, his mind racing, looking for a way to change the subject.

"Sorry to hear that Carter couldn't be here. I know Hannah was excited about it."

"Sorry?" Mrs. Rodbloom responded, looking taken aback.

"Hannah said her brother wouldn't be able to make it today."

The parents shared a glance, followed by Mr. Rodbloom whispering something in his wife's ear.

"Yes, that's right," he blurted. "He got caught up with something last minute. Just wasn't able to get out of it."

"That's a shame."

Mr. Rodbloom nodded. "Just bad timing is all—"

"Ken, don't you think Lonnie should come out and celebrate with us?" Mrs. Rodbloom cut in. They exchanged words with their eyes, and whatever they were saying made Lonnie nervous.

Mr. Rodbloom turned and patted Lonnie's shoulder. "Of course! What do you say?"

"I actually can't. I have to finish packing for tomorrow."

"What's tomorrow?" Mrs. Rodbloom interjected. "Are you going to your parent's house?"

"No," he said forcefully. "I'm staying with my friend Jamie for the summer, so I really should go back and pack."

"Are you sure?" Hannah asked.

"Yeah, sorry. I haven't even gotten the boxes out yet."

"I can help you pack after the dinner if you want."

"No, that's okay. You guys have fun!" He gave her a kiss on the cheek, then waved to her parents. "Nice seeing you both."

After the quick goodbye, he rounded the corner of the building, then hesitantly looked back before breaking into a sprint across the campus. With his arms outstretched, he straddled his overhanging robe and ran toward the setting sun. A beautiful array of pink and orange silhouetted him against the auditorium wall.

Finally making it back to his dormitory, he noticed the hall to his room was completely abandoned. Doors were swung open as he walked down the corridor, each emptied of bedding and personal items. Now just bare twin beds were left elevated above the floor, and a tiny wooden desk and closet were tucked into the corner of each room. All the non-graduates had finished class earlier that week and headed home, and the rest were out partying, he supposed. Even the security had taken the night off, probably assuming no one would be lame enough to step back in here this soon after graduating. Lonnie's feet carried him across the floor in a broken sprint, driven by a mix of embarrassment for running and a desperate need to lie in bed and rid himself of this day. Reaching his door, he threw it open and dredged past the countless boxes along the floor and a giant suitcase resting neatly against the wall. He looked at the pile for a second before ripping off his cap and gown and dropping them to the floor. Kicking off his shoes, he jumped into his unmade bed and rolled himself in the raggedy old blanket that lay across the bare mattress top.

Before he'd taken two breaths in relief, a ring sounded from his phone, jolting him into an upright position. He looked down to see a new text message from Hannah:

We're getting dinner at Le Capri d'Armando. Join us if you finish packing early.

He began to type a reply, but no excuse seemed good enough to write. Erasing what he had written, he flung the phone onto the bed in frustration, then reached across the bridge of his forehead, rubbing it gently, before hesitantly reaching his hand back out toward the phone. After a few unwavering seconds, he finally pulled it back, letting his pride overpower his guilty conscience. The joy on their faces would be too much to handle, he repeated to himself.

God, why couldn't they have just shown up!

Rolling to his side, he faced the door, where he noticed an

envelope lying precariously within the door jamb. Was that there when he walked in? Climbing from the bed, he snatched the envelope up in his hand and rubbed the forest green binding between his fingers, his nail scratching across the border of a charcoal seal. Atop the wax, an unusual white symbol was pressed onto the paper. The outline sort of looked like a tree with human faces extending from the branches. Confused, he rotated the envelope in his palms and found his name plastered across the back in black ink. He looked for any clues as to the sender, but the exterior didn't even show his own address, let alone someone else's. Finally, he pried his hand beneath the seal, digging it up in aggressive fashion, and then he pulled out a papyrus letter with typed letters punctured into its frame:

Dear Leonard,

Mr. and Mrs. Grambell wish to congratulate you on your secondary school graduation, and with it, cordially invite you to their estate for the duration of time before the beginning of university.

Lonnie stumbled back into the bed, using the nightstand to catch himself from slipping to the floor. He felt faint as he continued reading.

We expect your response to be given posthaste, no later than noon of June fourteenth. If you do so choose to accept this invitation, a car will be provided to escort you directly to the premises. Keep in mind, no guests may accompany you.

If you decide, please send a call to (518) 227-3452

Lonnie flipped the page over in search of more words, but it was blank.

Sitting on his bed, he hesitated a moment before breaking into a slight grin, which quickly grew into a hysterical laugh as he began ripping the envelope and letter apart in his hands. A violent rage overtook him as his heel stomped into the pile of papers on the floor. His fingers curled into fists, letting the pain leak out of his palms.

"Seriously?" he yelled at the pile of paper.

Looking down, he again noticed the black seal lying face up along the ground. The mysterious symbol stared back at him like a curse.

With one last kick, he sent the pieces flying around the room, then hopped onto the bed. In a state, he pulled his phone out and looked up Hannah's number. Though as he reached for the call button, he caught himself.

"Damn it," he huffed.

Tossing his phone onto the nightstand, he collapsed onto the bed and pulled out a pill bottle that read:

Trazodone

Dropping two pills into his hand, he launched them down his throat. Then he let his limbs dangle over the edges of the bed frame as though he were an overgrown weed. Eventually, he felt his eyes glaze against the moonbeams shining through the window; it was a full moon so hypnotically bright he thought he might go blind by staring. But he refused to look away. Taking deep breaths, he let himself be taken by it, feeling each breath grow easier as his mind wandered away from the bitterness that scratched at his veins. It wasn't long before darkness encapsulated his room, and he found his thoughts harder and harder to hold together, until eventually he had none at all.

Chapter 3

New Beginnings

Fluorescent bulbs flickered overhead, sending waves of darkness across his blurred vision. Something was moving him, quickly shifting his body down a never-ending hallway. Meanwhile, strong chemicals burned the hairs from his nostrils as he caught each breath.

"Help," he opened his mouth to yell, but nothing came out.

This dream had grown quite familiar to Lonnie. A nightmare that he couldn't seem to escape, popping into his head every few weeks like clockwork.

Lonnie tried shifting his arms, but they lay frozen against something stiff and metal. In his peripheral vision, he spotted the edges of figures hovering alongside him, their bodies like shadows, whispering words he couldn't make out.

Help.

The figures suddenly stopped beside a door. Their voices quieted as something had begun shaking around from the other side, causing noise to expel into the hallway.

What is that?

Before he could get an answer, footsteps began running on the other side of the door.

Slam!

Something had smacked into it. The impact was like a fracture through his skull, making everything go dark and quiet.

———

Tap.

Tap tap.

What is that?

With his hand cupped over half his face, Lonnie lifted his head from the pillow and peered around the room for the source of the tapping. Beads of sweat covered his forehead, which he wiped away in minor distress.

Tap.

It sounded close. Wiping the gunk from his eyes, he turned to the wall. There, sitting on the windowsill, was a plump raven, its beady eyes observing him with a fiery intensity. Its talons pressed gently on the glass, making that annoying sound. Lonnie gestured for it to leave, but it continued to tap on the window. Its face pushed against the frame like it was trying to pry its way in.

"Shoo, go away." Lonnie gestured again.

When it didn't stop, Lonnie climbed from the bed to make his way to the window, but a ring chirped from his phone. The raven cawed at the newfound noise, seemingly taking it as a signal to fly off. Leaving the windowsill, it soared up into the nearby tree to join an unkindness of others perched along the branches. Lonnie slipped the curtain closed before tossing the blankets around in search of his phone.

"Where are you?" He fumbled the blanket up into the air, causing a loud thud to take place in the slit between the bed and the wall.

"Just hold on," he yelled at the phone.

Diving to his hands and knees, he reached under the bed and grazed the edge of the case with the tip of his fingers. Prying out the phone from the crack, he raised it to his face. "Hello?"

"Hey," Hannah chimed.

He drew himself back toward the wall, letting her voice warm against his ear.

"How are you doing?" she asked sincerely.

"I'm fine." As he paced the room, he came upon one of the pieces of envelope he'd ripped apart the night prior. Lonnie picked it up, staring at it as if it had materialized from a dream. His eye began twitching as he tried to slip back into the phone call. "Actually, can we meet up somewhere?"

"Like right now?" She sounded surprised. "Is everything okay?"

"Yeah, everything's fine. Just if you're free, I—"

"Sure. Is our normal spot good?"

"Yeah, see you." He hung up the phone, giving another foul look to the bundle of papers stuck to the floor. Then in a rush, he scooped them into a plastic bag and headed out the door.

Sitting in the cafe, Lonnie aimed his body toward the entrance. As he waited for her to show, he gently shook his cup around, unintentionally watching the frothy foam sink to the bottom. A shadow approached behind the glass front door, and then Hannah waltzed into the room, her messy hair pulled back into a ponytail over a fluffy peacoat and wrinkled pajamas. Spotting him, she darted across the coffee shop and plopped herself into the open seat before laying her phone and bag atop the table.

"So, what's up?" she asked, taking a light sip of his coffee.

Lonnie reached under his chair to reveal the bag full of envelope pieces. With a perplexed expression, she opened her mouth to speak, but he had already begun dumping the contents onto the table.

"Uh...it didn't come like this, I just—"

Hannah picked up one of the pieces, raising it so she could read it. "What is this?"

"My parents sent me a letter."

"Oh wow." She paused. "*Wow*... How do you feel?"

"Angry." He rolled his hands into fists before letting them flatten on the table. "I don't know. Maybe upset... Excited. How am I supposed to feel? Eight years of nothing and then this just out of nowhere."

"Well, what did the letter say?" Hannah asked curiously.

Lonnie lowered his lips to his coffee as he ran through the contents of the letter in his head. "They want me to come home for the summer," he murmured.

"What? Lonnie, that's amazing!"

"Is it?"

"What did you tell Jamie?"

"What do you mean?" Lonnie's brow raised.

"Aren't you both supposed to leave today?"

"Yeah, but there is nothing to tell. My plans aren't changing, because I'm not going back there." Lonnie sat back in his chair, retreating into his coffee cup.

As he raised it to take another sip, Hannah leaned in. "Are you kidding! You have to go home. You've been waiting for this for—"

"That's not my home!" he yelled louder than expected, startling himself and the few others nearby. He looked around the coffee shop, embarrassed, before returning to the conversation.

"I stopped waiting and I moved on," he said calmly.

Hannah ignored his response and instead started to put the pieces of the envelope and letter together along the table. "If that was the case, we wouldn't even be talking about this, so—"

"Except I didn't bring you here for that. It's just... God, the whole thing is so frustrating!" He accidentally smacked the coffee, causing a spill on the table and letter. "Dang it, sorry!" He plucked a few napkins from the dispenser and started to wipe up the spill.

"It's fine, don't worry about it." She grabbed his hand with an understanding stare that pulled him up short.

He sighed. "You know how many times I reached out and they never answered? I tried calling, I sent letters, hell, I even showed up on their doorstep. They ignored me every time because they didn't want me there, and...and that's fine. I learned to live with that. But then they skip my graduation like I'm nothing and invite me to come home all in the same day. That's insane, Hannah!"

Hannah's eyes scanned the letter she'd just finished piecing back together between them, the pieces now slightly damp but still readable.

"It says you have to call this number to let them know."

"Yeah, I know."

"No, it says you have to call them before noon today. Lonnie, it's already past eleven."

"Didn't you hear what I just said though? They are crazy."

She looked at him, coils of energy flashing from her eyes as her body faced him. "I heard you, and that's why I think this is something you have to do. But not for them. Do it for you."

"What do you mean?"

"You've been killing yourself to get them to see you, and for some unexplainable reason you finally have their attention. This is your chance to talk to them face-to-face, like you always wanted. So don't waste it."

She got up from her side of the table and scooted in next to him. Her palms grabbed the sides of his face. "I can't let you keep living in this purgatory, hoping they are someday gonna become amazing, emotionally mature parents. They won't. This is the best you're gonna get, so take it."

"Damn, Hannah." Lonnie rolled his eyes, trying awkwardly to pull his head away.

Buzz!

Feeling the vibration pass through his body, he took his hands off the counter, immediately noticing Hannah's phone shaking on the corner of it. He was about to alert her, but her eyes showed she was well aware of its presence. That familiar drained look shrouded her cheeks.

"Is that your brother again?"

"Yes, but I'm just not going to answer it."

"Cause of the graduation thing? Or is something else happening?"

"He has just been making my life really difficult lately..."

As a joke, Lonnie reached across the table for her phone. "Here, I'll talk some sense into him—"

"No, stop!" she yelled, swatting his hand from the phone.

"Geez! It was just a joke."

"Sorry." Her expression quickly flipped. "Can we please just drop it and go?"

What did Carter do?

Hannah briefly pulled out her phone, just long enough to grab the time.

"It's 11:47. If you're going to do it, you need to decide now. Are you going to go hide away with Jamie's family or go back and face your own?"

Lonnie chugged down what remained of his coffee and stared at Hannah. With a relieved grin, he took her cheek, giving it a wet kiss. "Thank you." He sighed.

"You're welcome," she laughed, wiping the coffee stain from her cheek. "And worse case, maybe you can guilt trip them into increasing your trust."

"Will do," he replied with a light, anxious chuckle.

Pulling out his phone, he slowly turned the slightly damp scrap of paper around on the table. Taking the numbers from it, he copied them into his phone. The ringer sounded as he raised it to his ear, his eyes still watching Hannah, who stared back at him.

"Hello?" Lonnie asked, flipping the dial to speaker.

The line was filled with static, which was growing a flutter inside his chest. He turned to Hannah. "I don't hear anybody—"

Before he could finish, a monotone voice possessed the other line. "Good to hear from you, Leonard. A car will be there soon to take you home."

That was all they said before the line went dead.

Hannah turned to him, raising her hands to form a little cheer. "Hey, you're doing it," she boasted.

"Yeah, I'm doing it."

"This is a good thing, I promise. Just swear you'll text as soon as you get there."

"Of course." He lightly grinned, pulling her into a hug.

A ray of morning sun made its way through the window to land perfectly in her hair, illuminating her like an angel. Even in her pjs and peacoat, with her hair a bed-head mess, she was the most beautiful person he had ever laid eyes on. Her eyes pierced into him, making him feel woozy but in the best way. She offered up a rogue smile.

"I love you," she stated, more serious than he had ever heard her say before.

"I love you too," he murmured nervously.

Her phone buzzed again, causing her to flinch. Without looking at it, she rose and patted his shoulder. "Guess it's time to face the future, eh?"

Chapter 4

Sheep and Wolves

Crackle.

Lonnie awoke to the somewhat familiar sound of tires rubbing on a gravel road. The day seemed to have gotten away from him, judging by the setting sun illuminating the side of his cheek. He didn't even know he had fallen asleep, but perhaps the morning had taken more of a toll than he realized. From the cafe, he had returned to his dorm to find a limo parked out front, its long frame appearing on the street as if materialized from thin air. A plump driver, who he later found out went by Angus, waved him down from across the street, his arm gesturing Lonnie into the now open back seat. The interaction was quite odd, but he supposed everything with his family was. Without another thought, he jumped in and watched his school drift into the distance.

His face felt flushed as damp air made its way around the back seat of the car. Struggling with the door switch, he rolled down the window, letting the fresh breeze waft over him. The Catskill forest wrapped around the car, dropping slivers of skylight from between the tree canopies. The branches of old oak trees spread out across the street, reaching out to him like beckoning hands. Following them up to their branches, his eyes locked on something in the distance. Through a gap in the leaves, he grabbed a glimpse of a structure basking in the glow of the sunset.

There it is.

A second-story balcony floated in the air and, atop it, a cute little wooden railing and a chair set to match. But that wasn't what Lonnie was looking at. At the end of the balcony was a door. His door...or at least the one he used to have. In its glass facade, he could see the long-gone shadow of a little boy as the car drew near the house, a vivid memory of a child staring out of his bedroom. Lonnie felt sick. His stomach began to churn as he crept closer and closer to his past.

Two thousand nine hundred and nineteen days.

Has it really been that long?

The limo came to a sudden stop, and Angus's window cracked open as he leaned over to the gate box and entered the code with ease, causing the fencing to split in two. Lonnie watched the rest of the giant mansion materialize ahead. And while the gate slid along the ground, Lonnie counted each second until it came to a halt.

One...two...three...four...five.

With each number, his chest squeezed his lungs. He clutched his backpack, as the limo made its way over the divide and across the smoothly laid asphalt. A few seconds of darkness passed before a warm glow shone through the window. Lonnie peered out just in time to see the house towering in front of him. His mouth dropped at the sight of it.

It's even bigger than I remember.

The side stretched back almost half an acre, and the front at least a quarter. The outside facade was a combination of French Renaissance and modern flair, all coated in a thick egg-white paint. As the limo pulled in, Angus came to a stop around a large fountain centerpiece taking up the center of the driveway. Compared to it all, the long limo looked dainty and small.

Slam!

Lonnie leaned forward enough to see that Angus had already evacuated the car. Stepping out himself, Lonnie found the driver standing by the trunk, heaving out boxes and dragging them along the ground to lay out along the entryway.

Is that my stuff?

It wasn't until that moment that Lonnie realized he never even loaded his luggage into the car. But as he stood there, his belongings continued to spawn from the seemingly bottomless trunk.

How did he manage to get all this from my room?

How did he even get into my room?

Lonnie wanted to ask, but before he knew it, Angus brushed past him, grabbing the final bag from the trunk and depositing it, too, onto the tarmac that was once a courtyard. With a wave, he bid Lonnie farewell and dove back into the car to speed off toward the gate.

"Even the chauffeur doesn't want to be here," Lonnie grunted.

He stood alone outside for barely a second before the front doors burst open. Four men in modest penguin suits came marching out of the Corinthian column archway, like gladiators expelling from the Colosseum. Each of them grabbed a pair of bags and conveyed them back into the mansion. Lonnie felt the need to help, but by the time he strode over to ask, they'd already finished and shut the doors behind them, leaving him to walk himself slowly up the stone steps.

The front entrance was still a pair of dark red French doors with a wooden frame and glass panel. He grabbed them familiarly but felt his hand start to shake at the thought of opening them. He let out a slow, harsh breath before pulling on one handle and stepping inside.

Marble floors glistened over the entryway, reflecting tapestries hanging from the walls. Above him, the roof elevated at least twenty feet and held a large diamond chandelier. Lonnie grew flustered by the sight of it all but tried to play it off. In front of him, a flight of stairs transcended from the center of the foyer, on top of which, the house staff had aligned themselves on either railing, arranged in single-file lines. On the base step stood a slender man in a tailcoat with white gloves and a black bow tie. He surged forward and greeted Lonnie at the doorway. He was rather old, but he gave off a vibe that made him seem quite spry for his age.

"Good evening, Mister Grambell. Pleasure to have you back."

"Hello," Lonnie said uncomfortably. "Have we met before?"

The man buffered for a second before responding, "Oh... no, afraid not. You can call me Rossi, sir."

"Nice to meet you, Rossi." Lonnie outstretched his hand. "You can just call me Lonnie."

Rossi stared at the hand before reaching out his own for a brief shake. Raising his head once again, he smiled. "Very well. Your room is the first one to the left from the stairs. Would you like us to carry your backpack up for you...Lonnie?" he said with a bit of duress.

"Thank you, but I'm good."

"My pleasure." Rossi gave another bow before walking himself out of the room. The rest of the staff stood frozen like statues, their eyes peering at him as if waiting for a command.

"Hello?" Lonnie muttered toward them.

"*Questo è tutto!*" Rossi yelled from just outside the room.

Suddenly everyone dispersed to different corners of the home so that, before long, Lonnie stood alone in the foyer. Freshly waxed tiles squeaked below his feet as he approached the stairwell in the middle of the room. His hand dragged along the wall, feeling for something familiar. Everything felt new, which made him feel even more out of place. The banister on the stairs was now a shiny matte black instead of epoxy wood. He ran his hand along the bottom, looking for the scratches he had made when he used to race down it with toy cars. But they were filled in, like they'd never existed. Even the walls had changed from an old maroon to a new dark forest green. And where the family photo once hung was now just a bundle of paint strokes wrapped in the same pretty gold frame. Lonnie stared at it in anger, wishing he could chuck it off the wall, but he refrained, instead, plucking his bags from the floor.

They changed everything.

Struggling with his stuff, he shuffled toward the stairs. Yet as he started to ascend, he noticed a face staring at him through the hallway mirror. It was a woman, her hair like chalk and her eyes sunken beneath a pair of loose wrinkles. Startled, he turned to face her, which must have given her a fright because, without a word, she fled around the corner. He frowned and wondered if he should follow her but ultimately decided to leave it. Repositioning himself back on the stairs, he made his way to his room, where he let out a sigh of relief as he approached his old door.

The white facade was exactly the same, and even the doorknob still jiggled when he opened it, like he remembered as a child.

They hadn't changed everything.

Except once he cracked the door open, his whimsical grin changed to horror. Lining the walls were plastic creatures and shelves with tiny trophies wedged atop them. On the floor, his old race-car tracks had formed a junkyard in the corner of the room, and his carpet looked like it had been blindly sewn together. Staring at the electric blue colored walls and amenity of toys gave Lonnie the sick realization that his room *literally* hadn't been touched in years. Had his parents hated him so much they couldn't even bear to clean his bedroom?

Sure, he wanted things to still feel familiar, but this didn't even feel like his anymore. It felt haunted by someone who had passed long ago.

Grabbing a stuffed animal off the shelf, he looked at it like it was a vague memory. Its button eyes were slowly coming loose from its stitches, and its arms were missing their filling. It looked properly loved, but still he felt nothing towards it. Throwing it on the boxes the men had brought up from the car, he approached the bed. Laying his suitcase on top of it, he undid the zippers to reveal a folded bundle of clothes, but a quick glance around the room made him grow anxious.

Where can I even put these?

Striding to the closet, he pried it open to reveal a bundle of children's clothes lining the hooks. Immediately he shut it, shaking the uncomfortable feeling from his shoulders.

"This is insane."

He reached into his pocket for his phone to text Hannah but it wasn't there. With a slight sense of panic, he grabbed his backpack. "Where did I put my phone?"

He rummaged through each zipped compartment until he reached the small pocket on the side. His hand grazed his phone, but something papery fell out as well when he pulled it out. It was the Polaroid of Hannah and him from the day before.

Lonnie put the Polaroid to his chest and felt his muscles uncoil beneath it, as if her hand were resting against him. With her in mind, he turned his attention back to the room. Rezipping his bag, he tucked it under the bed. Just then, his pocket started vibrating from his phone. The screen read:

HANNAH

A sigh of relief slipped from his lips.

"Hey. You make it home yet?" Hannah chimed.

"Yeah, I'm here," Lonnie sullenly replied.

"That bad?"

A crunch came from under his foot.

He glanced down to see he'd crushed one of the race cars that had slid over from the track. Its little wheels rolled around the room before flattening out on the carpet.

"My room looks like a shrine for a child," he stammered.

"Aw, that's kind of sweet—"

"No, it's... I don't think it was a good idea coming here."

The line went quiet, aside from the subtle sound of Hannah's breathing.

"Have you even seen your parents yet?" she asked.

"No..." he confessed. "I don't think they're here."

Lonnie's eyes met the bookshelf. Tucked in the corner, he saw a picture frame creeping out from behind a pile of books. Picking it up, his heart skipped a beat. The background was a simple red hue, like that of a studio. But in the front, he saw himself. He had to have been no older than eight, and his brother sat beside him. Both were rocking apathetic grins on their faces as their parents each rested a hand on either of their shoulders. They all wore matching attire. Black formal with dark green highlights.

"I need to leave."

"Okay, you need to relax," Hannah said. "It's going to take more than five minutes to undo eight years of problems."

"I guess."

She coughed sarcastically. "And on the off chance it doesn't work out, it's just a couple months and then you'll be back with me."

The thought of that made Lonnie smile.

She continued, "Anyway, I need to run but wanted to see how you were doing... Are you going to be okay?" she joked.

"Yeah, yeah, I'll be fine." He laughed embarrassingly. "Thank you for calling; I just needed to rant."

"Of course."

The phone beeped off, leaving Lonnie to his old room.

This is so weird.

Turning, he caught a pair of eyes staring at him through the door slit. It was the same lady from the stairs. Locking gazes, she immediately turned and began walking off again. This time, Lonnie didn't hesitate. He pounced from the room, bolting to the top of the stairwell. But even with his speed, she still managed to vanish below the steps. Lonnie glided his hand down the stair banister, this time following her shadow into the arched hall. As he rounded the corner, a stretch of closed doors appeared on either side, most of which he found to be locked until he noticed one hanging slightly ajar. Without thinking, he pried it open and stepped inside.

He couldn't recall ever stepping into this room before, but

it appeared to be some kind of office. The walls were a dark forest green, each bathed in awards and certifications. Lonnie felt drawn to the walnut desk planted in the center of the room, its top covered with tchotchkes, pictures, and folders. Curious, Lonnie picked up the first picture frame, holding a photo of Mr. Grambell giving a speech at a health summit. He vaguely remembered reading about that achievement online, but it was much more real to see it in person.

This is my dad's office.

Plucking a folder from a stack, he began to read:

Genetic Engineering: A Change to Modern Medicine

As he flipped it open, a bony hand suddenly descended on his shoulder. He let out a yip. Spinning on his heels, he found himself face-to-face with the old woman, her features cold yet oddly comforting.

"Why are you here?" she pressed, her accent a bit sharp. She looked distressed by his presence.

"What?" Lonnie frowned. "What are you talking about?"

Lonnie tried to squirm away, but she trapped him against the door jamb. Now able to see her clearly, he noticed her beady blue eyes and the maid outfit wrapped around her body, both of which dusted off a memory of her. It was Hilda, the house-keeper. The one who had cared for him so often as a child. Though she looked different, her face withered with age.

"Hilda?" he muttered.

Her expression lightened at the sound of her name, but her panicked intensity held. "You shouldn't have come back."

Lonnie glance around. "Why?"

She paused to peer back over her shoulder before lowering her tone. "They don't—"

She was cut off by the office door opening. The smell of

Grand Soir perfume instantly filled the room like a gas, followed by a soft-pitched voice.

"Hilda darling, there you are; I've been looking for you everywhere."

In the doorframe, she stood, her naturally curly, brunette hair now straightened and dyed blonde, her eyes shimmering like gold-dipped amber. From what he remembered, Monica Grambell never wore loungewear, so it wasn't surprising to Lonnie when this woman came in dressed in a single ruby necklace, a cream sheath dress, and wedges that made her even taller than she already was.

Upon seeing Lonnie, her plastic smile widened to reveal her whitened teeth before returning to the housekeeper. "Can you let Festus know to start preparing dinner?"

"Of course, ma'am," Hilda responded submissively.

The old maid quickly fled the room, her hands tucked down by her sides. As she closed the door behind her, Lonnie felt his airway constrict. Now it was just his mother and him in the room, her body standing between him and the only exit.

Is this a dream? Or a nightmare?

"Hello, Mom," Lonnie blurted.

"Sweetheart, hello!" She reached over to hug him. Her ring finger blinded him as it reflected off the ceiling lights. "You're here. How was the drive?"

With her arms wrapped around his shoulders, he impulsively began to squirm. Her sudden embrace felt like a numbing agent across his entire body. Unsure what to do, his hands began to sweat. With a light cough, he pulled away enough to face her. Her face looked foreign; the eyes were the same, but everything else was altered. It was like the wrinkles and crow's feet he remembered had been rubbed smooth, and all that was left was a tightly wrapped face coated in shiny plastic.

"It was good."

She noticed him eyeing her skin. "What do you think?" She turned toward the wall mirror, pawing at her frozen face. "It's amazing what Portello can do to faces; he's like Van Gogh with a scalpel."

"It's...nice. I'm happy for you. I was just surprised is all," Lonnie stammered.

She turned from looking at herself in the mirror to pinch his cheek. "And as am I. Look at you! You've grown so much." She returned her attention to the mirror and smoothed a hand under her chin. "Someone ought to take a photo before you become unrecognizable."

"Actually...my graduation picture should be coming in later this week."

She stopped rubbing her neck and lowered herself onto the desk edge. "Oh my gosh, your graduation. I'm sorry, darling, we wanted to be there, truly, but it just wasn't in the cards."

"It's fine, really. Don't worry about it. I know you're both busy."

"No, it's horrible! We're horrible. What parent misses their child's graduation?"

What parent misses their child's whole life?

"It's not a big deal, honestly." He sat himself beside her, his hands balled into fists behind his back. "It was a small graduation. Not many parents came."

"Really?" she said through choked back tears as she slid into the desk chair.

He tried not to roll his eyes.

Eventually, the color seemed to return to her face, and her

eyes reignited. She gave him a slight nudge with her shoulder. "Well I am excited to see your pictures. I bet they turned out great! I mean look at you, you're just so handsome."

Embarrassing as it was, the comment made Lonnie blush. And for the moment, it somehow seemed to wash away the whole graduation debacle. They shared a friendly exchange of smiles. Genuine smiles.

Lonnie opened his mouth to ask if she'd like to catch up, but he was cut short as his mother abruptly rose and made her way to the door.

"So glad you're back, sweetheart," she almost sang, her eyes already drifting from their conversation as though it were a hundred miles away.

"Wait, where are you going?" Lonnie gave a confused nod.

"Sorry, dear, I can't stay and chat. I have an errand to run. Your father wanted to give you his condolences that he couldn't be here for your arrival, but he is excited to see you at dinner tonight. So just make yourself at home!" Her arms went up into a flaccid hurrah before she closed the door behind her. Lonnie listened as her clacking footsteps departed down the hall.

Is that it?

He had pictured that interaction so many times, so many arguments he had narrated in his head, so many scenarios he had planned out. But now smelling the lingering perfume in the air, one thought trumped the rest.

What was Hilda trying to warn me about?

Chapter 5

The Man of the House

Harold Grambell was a medical geneticist, which in simple terms meant that he cured people by rewriting their genetic code. But what it also meant was that he was smart...

Terrifyingly smart.

Lonnie's foot tapped repeatedly against the floor as he stared at the empty chair at the end of the long dining table. His hand twisted a spoon in circles around the soup dish in front of him. Mrs. Grambell, who had already started in on her lobster bisque, offered him a quizzical smile. "Eat your soup, sweetheart. It's going to get cold."

"But he isn't here yet—"

"Oh nonsense, he's always late from work. It's quite alright."

She gestured for him to eat, and with a shrug of surrender, he dipped his spoon into the soup, pulling it out slowly as though it were molasses. Lonnie was starving; however, no one had told that to his roiling stomach.

When a door shut in the distance, Lonnie abruptly dropped his spoon and turned his gaze to the window, where a silver

Bentley now rested by the old fountain. His breath caught in his throat at the sound of the front door opening followed by shoes scuffing across the marble floor. Eventually they stopped just on the other side of the dining room door, making Lonnie's entire body freeze.

A few seconds later, the door swung open, and Mr. Grambell stood there, his back to the dining room as he continued some conversation with the head chef. They looked crazed, both steaming at the tips like betta fish about to rip each other apart.

"Fine! Lobster bisque and cod," his father growled. "Is there any more seafood I should expect tonight?"

"That is it, Mr. Grambell," the chef murmured. He returned to the kitchen, and Mr. Grambell slowly turned.

"My god. He knows I hate seafood. He knows—"

"He just must have forgotten," Mrs. Grambell sympathized.

"Clearly." Mr. Grambell paused mid-step at the sight of Lonnie seated at the table. They exchanged an awkward glance. He wore a tan linen suit with a white button up that covered a muscular frame. His dyed black hair sat gelled in place, while patches of gray grew from his lightly shaved beard. "You're here..." he said, his face still red from yelling.

Lonnie gave a hesitant nod. "You invited me."

"And you came."

Lonnie turned to his mother, who seemed utterly ecstatic to see her two men in the same room together. With a perplexed look on his face, Mr. Grambell took a few steps forward, and without thinking, Lonnie rose from his chair. His father now stood inches away, his presence like a well-built tree with branch-like arms extending into the air. Suddenly they wrapped around Lonnie's torso. Shocked, Lonnie contorted his body like a wild animal in a trap, and for a minute, he thought he was being strangled, but the pressure soon eased. He surrendered himself, raising his own arms back out in a similar gesture.

Lonnie couldn't remember the last time his father had hugged him. His beard hair brushed the edge of his cheek, and his thick cologne stung his eyes like freshly cut peppers. It felt strangely nice.

"We're so happy you're back," his father exclaimed.

"You are?" Lonnie coughed. "Then why did you wait so long to invite me?"

Mr. Grambell turned to his wife with a glare. "You see, I knew he was going to ask that. Didn't I tell you?"

"You did tell me that." She laughed in defeat.

"Lonnie, look at me. That had nothing to do with you. This...this was just not a place for a child...it never has been. We wanted someplace—something—better for you, so we sent you away. We had to. You see that, right? You would have been miserable locked away here all alone. No one's ever here; you would have grown up alone. Trust me, this was the right thing for you and for us."

"So why did you invite me back now? What changed?" Lonnie muttered.

The two parents exchanged a glance.

"Well, you're not a child anymore." His father squeezed him around the shoulders. "You're a man now. Look how grown you are. Just trust me when I say that sending you away was the best thing we could have done for you. But now you're back, so let's not dwell on the past. Let's get excited about the future!"

Lonnie stared at him uncomfortably, his brain shifting in a panic.

"Can't wait," he blurted out.

His parents seemed satisfied by this as he reclaimed his seat. His father even took a ladle of soup, though his curled mouth couldn't hide his utter distaste. Lonnie started in on his soup as well. Not because he was hungry, but to avoid saying something he would regret. But even with his head glued to his bowl, he could feel the occasional glance of his parents.

Mr. and Mrs. Grambell held up small talk across the table, their words bouncing back and forth like verbal ping pong. Lonnie tried to listen, but an off-beat ticking lay just under the tone of conversation, keeping him on guard like a silent whistle. The noise taunted him as he scoured the room for the source until eventually he noticed the old grandfather clock hanging by the window.

That's still here? Of all the things they kept.

Tik. Tik. Tik. Tik.

"So, Leonard, I hear you're going to college," his father announced from across the table.

Like a sobering punch, Lonnie fell out of his daze. He looked up from his lobster bisque. "I'm going to Johns Hopkins actually."

"Really?" His father sat up straighter. "Quite impressive."

Lonnie bit his tongue. "Thank you."

"I guess that makes you a legacy."

"You went to Hopkins?" Lonnie asked.

Mr. Grambell nodded.

"I didn't know." Lonnie shrugged. "My friends are going and I just decided to apply."

Lonnie quickly returned to his soup, which he hoped would give Mr. Grambell the clue that the conversation had ended. The room grew quiet, aside from the occasional clank of a spoon. Lonnie listened again for the ticking. However, as he turned to the old clock, he realized it was coming from somewhere else.

How strange.

The more he tried to ignore it, the louder it seemed to grow in his head until he anxiously began his search again. His eyes took in every iota of the room and eventually landed upon Mr. Grambell's left wrist. There, a stainless steel, blue-faced watch sat, its second-hand rattling like a locust.

Lonnie attempted to refocus on the meal, but the dining room door suddenly opened, and two members of the kitchen staff strode in to switch out their soup for the next course. Before he could thank them, they'd already hurried away, leaving the door to swing behind them. Through it, Hilda could be seen dusting one of the wall paintings. She briefly turned to Lonnie and gave him a pitying look before the door swung closed. For his own sanity, Lonnie paid no mind to it. Instead, he put all of his energy into getting through the rest of dinner.

After a final course of macarons and eclairs, Mr. Grambell's phone rang. He stared at the caller ID with a look of importance.

"I have to take this; carry on without me," he insisted, pulling himself from the table.

"Is it okay if I go as well?" Lonnie requested of his mother. "I need to lie down." At her agreement, he left the room and made his way to the stairwell. However, as he reached the bottom step, he heard his father's deep voice drift out from his study. Slipping round the corner, Lonnie peeked through the door.

"Yes, my wife is with him now," Mr. Grambell muttered. He held the phone to his ear as he spun a glass of whiskey in his hand. The person on the line had a lot to say, because his father didn't speak again for a solid minute.

"That doesn't seem necessary," he eventually added.

The voice grew louder from the receiver until he was forced to hold the phone a good five inches from his ear. "Right, of course..." he responded.

When Mr. Grambell hung up the phone, he took a few deep breaths into his chest. Pouring himself another shot, he tossed it back before setting the glass down and scooping his jacket from the desk chair. Noticing him moving to the door, Lonnie retreated to the hallway. However, he only made it a few feet before he heard the doorframe's hinge open behind him. His father gave a surprised glance that turned on a dime into a grin.

"Leonard!" he said jovially. "I was just going to come find you."

"Why, what's going on?" Lonnie asked skeptically.

"Would you like to accompany me to the country club tomorrow for lunch?"

"The country club?"

"It'll be fun!" Mr. Grambell slapped him on the back.

Lonnie tried to think of an excuse, but nothing came to mind. And while the question had seemed genuine, the decision felt already decided upon.

"Yeah, sure then," he said.

"Fantastic. Dave and Mike will be excited to see you." Mr. Grambell walked back into the dining room, tossing out behind him, "We leave at 10:00."

Lonnie made a stammering sound. *Who are Dave and Mike?*

The idea of acquainting with strangers made him a little

nauseous, but he hadn't been to the club in years, and the thought of reuniting with that succulent, brunch buffet table made the whole experience somewhat more appealing. Making his way back to his room, he hopped in bed, but the contents of his childhood room kept him from falling asleep. Reaching into his bag, he pulled out his pill bottle and took one, then returned to his lying position and slowly let it serenade him to sleep.

Quiet voices filled his dream like chirping crickets, each one compounding on the other until they formed one giant note. They were saying something, but the words sounded unreal. He looked for the source of the noise but found his eyes impossible to open.

What are they saying?

Their voices grew more excited, the tone rising around him like helium filling a balloon.

Bang!

Just then, a gunshot rang past his head, searing his ear with a light ringing. He tried to get his bearings, but a woman's scream quickly followed. Her banshee-like wail made his arm hair stand on end, jolting him from his slumber.

"Ah!" he screamed.

Lonnie shot up in his bed, wrapping his arms tightly around his torso. He took deep, strenuous breaths, trying to calm himself from the nightmare, but the strange woman's scream still rang in his ear.

Not again.

Of all the dreams that seemed to haunt him, this one was always the worst. Each time, it followed him for hours. The sound of the scream chased him like a ghost, forming permanent goosebumps on his skin. Who was that woman?

Jumping from the bed, he ripped off his sweat-soaked T-shirt and began picking up the pillows and blanket he'd apparently kicked to the floor. Noticing the sunlight shining in, he grabbed his phone.

9:30 AM

He tossed it on his bed, where he eyed his pill bottle resting on the side table. Looking at it with disgust, he pushed it into the drawer and then dressed for the day.

By 10:00, Lonnie was being further awakened by gusts of wind to the face. He didn't remember his father being lead-footed. However, as they rode the winding highway through the tree lines, he doubted his prior assumptions. They reached the country club in record time, his father screeching to a stop at the front entrance.

He must be in quite a hurry.

As they walked to the front, Mr. Grambell tossed his keys to the valet, then made for the door at the top of the stairs. There, a vested salt-and-pepper-haired man walked down to meet them. He looked weary but tried to hide it through face lifts and clumps of makeup.

"Welcome, Mr. Grambell!" the man said through dabs to his furrowed brow.

"Hello, Stephen, how are you today?"

"Very good, sir! Very good. Shall I get your usual table?"

"Let's get the one with the view today. I have my son with me."

"Your son?" he said. He looked curiously at Lonnie. "Ah, your son! Of course, terribly sorry! Pleasure. Right then, follow me," Stephen announced as he led the way up the stairs.

Lonnie followed Stephen up the stairs to the entryway. As his father and Stephen made their way to the dining facility, Lonnie lagged behind in the hallway. It was more gorgeous than he remembered, with redwood-paneled walls and white furniture accented by linen tablecloths. Gold chandeliers straddled the ceiling every couple of feet, and lavender diffusers were planted on every shelf from the door to the check-in table.

Lonnie attempted to walk with grace as he doubled his steps to catch up with his father. Upon entering the dining facility, he saw his dad already seated at a round table by the sunlit corner window. With him sat two suited men—one tall and lanky, and the other short but riddled with muscles from his neck to his calves.

Mike and Dave, I assume.

Lonnie made out whispers as he approached the table. He saw his father's eyes dart from one man to the other, his eyebrows furrowed, with a vein wrapped around his forehead. Lonnie had only walked a few steps before one of the men noticed him and gave a quick tap to his colleague's shoulder. Their conversation halted, and suddenly they were all staring at Lonnie, his father included. A moment longer, and Dave and Mike stood from their chairs in acknowledgment.

The muscular man was the first to offer his hand. "Hello, Lonnie, I don't know if you remember me, but we met long ago. I'm Michael."

His soft eyes did seem familiar, but Lonnie couldn't place him. It wasn't until he shook Michael's calloused hand that the memory hit.

"Yes," Lonnie stated uncomfortably. "From the funeral."

"Glad to see I made an impression," the man responded.

"And this is Dave." Mr. Grambell gestured to the other man.

"Hello." Lonnie again offered his hand.

"Hi, nice to meet you," Dave responded, giving a firm shake.

Like on cue, the waitstaff came out of the kitchen in droves, each with a silver tray resting in their hands. They set them down at a table by the grand window, then retreated back to their door, through which a man in a white double-breasted jacket emerged and approached the first tray. He opened it in a dramatic flair to reveal fresh baked chocolate scones crammed inside. One by one, he walked down the line, whisking open tray after tray, revealing crepes, lobster scrambled egg, country baked ham, crème brulée, French toast, and more. Lonnie started to drool.

After the man had finished his lap and returned to the kitchen, Lonnie rampaged the line, cutting off countless canes and walkers in his path. The waiter handed him a plate as he approached the first tray. He grabbed pastries by the trough-full, among other snacks and treats, as he made his way back to his seat. The three men stared at his plate.

"Got enough there, champ?" Dave chuckled.

Lonnie's glow faded. "I suppose I went a little overboard."

"No, it's fine, you enjoy." Mr. Grambell grinned magnanimously.

Whatever surprise Lonnie felt at his dad's casual acceptance was overridden by his hunger. He dove in the moment his dad and Dave went off to get their own food, while Mike stayed seated and simply asked for a refill of his red wine sangria.

"You don't want any food?" Lonnie asked, covering his full mouth.

"I don't seem to have an appetite today." Mike nodded. "But I hear you just finished up school. You excited to be back home?"

"Yeah, sure," Lonnie replied politely.

"That was very convincing." Mike chuckled, sipping his drink.

"Sorry, I'm just not used to all this. I was at the boarding school so long, and now I am just here again like nothing happened."

"I can understand that. I went to boarding school for a while."

"Really?"

"Yeah. It's an unusual feeling. Like you're split in half. There's the half that used to live here, and the other that lived there. And now you feel like you don't know which you are."

"Makes sense," Lonnie agreed. "Except in my case, I think I never had that other half. Which is probably why they sent me away in the first place."

Mike gave him a pointed glance. "Or maybe they sent you away because they hoped you'd turn out better than them."

Lonnie considered this. "Better in what way?"

"In all the ways that are important."

Dave and Mr. Grambell returned to the table, each carrying their lightly filled plates. Lonnie ate and listened as his father laughed with his friends, something Lonnie hadn't seen much of as a kid, and by the time it was time to go, the adults had finished off two entire bottles of champagne. He watched his father walk down the front steps, his face a little red from his light buzz. Lonnie wanted to ask if he was okay to drive but decided not to ruin the moment.

It was a nice morning.

"Your friends are nice," Lonnie said when the valet pulled the car up.

"Yeah, I've known them since college. Did you know that? Been around thirty-eight years now."

"Wow."

"Yeah, we met in the medical program together. Started as first years and then worked at the same hospital for our residency."

"So you guys really stuck together." Lonnie laughed.

"It just happened that we had the same goals. We all wanted to revolutionize gene editing. Cure diseases and disorders at a code level." He cackled, then sighed. "We were definitely ambitious; I'll give us that."

"Isn't it good to be ambitious?"

"Not always." Mr. Grambell's smile suddenly faded, and he climbed into the driver's seat.

Did I say something wrong? Lonnie thought.

"By the way, do you enjoy parties?" Mr. Grambell asked.

"Me?" Lonnie glanced at him.

Mr. Grambell looked over so their eyes would meet. "Yeah, I'm asking if you ever enjoyed any parties at that school of yours."

"Yeah, but they weren't anything too—"

"Good," his father cut him off. "How would you feel about attending the Blythorne's annual gala with your mother and me tonight? It's always a fun time."

Lonnie bit his tongue. He had been hearing about the Blythorne's house parties ever since he was a child. He remembered the nights his mother would come home with confetti wrapped in her hair and his father wobbling across the foyer. Those were the only nights when he really saw his father piss-drunk. They would serenade themselves across the hallway to invisible music as he watched from between the upstairs railing.

"Really?"

Mr. Grambell turned onto the frontage road. "I figure you're not a child anymore. Things are different now. You're eighteen. You're going to college. They won't mind," he emphasized.

"Won't it be weird if I'm the only young person there?"

"Who said you would be the only young person? It was packed to the brim last year. You remember my friend Ron? His son that goes to Hopkins was there just last year. If he goes again, I'll introduce you," he said optimistically.

Lonnie didn't know what to say. He wasn't one for big parties, especially with this kind of crowd. But how could he refuse—it was the Blythorne's gala. The most exclusive party in the Catskills, hell maybe even in all of New York.

"Yeah," he stuttered. "I would like to go."

"Amazing, Angus can take you to get a suit. We leave at 8:00."

Chapter 6

Royal Blue

"I'll take this one," Lonnie said to the clerk who was straightening out Lonnie's suit collar.

"Wonderful choice, sir. I can ring you up at the counter. Just the navy blue plaid three-piece suit, white dress shirt, belt, red tie, and shoes for you today?" the clerk asked.

Lonnie felt his father's card cradled in his hand and couldn't help drifting his eyes toward the display of watches behind the counter.

"Can I try that one on?" he said, pointing to a black leather wristwatch hidden to the side.

The clerk handed it to him; Lonnie felt an instant connection and knew he had to have it immediately.

It's the least Dad can do, right? Lonnie thought to himself.

"I'll take the watch as well," he said, handing over the credit card.

The clerk nodded. "Excellent choice."

Lonnie walked out of the store with his bags and approached the limo parked out front with Angus propping open the back door for him.

"Did you find everything to your liking, Mister Grambell?" he asked.

"Sure did." Lonnie smiled, giving the bags a slight shake in the air before he got into the car.

Driving back from the shop, Lonnie gave Hannah a call to tell her about the past day. But as the limo pulled out of the parking lot, only a single ring sounded before sending him to voicemail.

She must be busy.

Opening his contacts, he then dialed Jamie, but to his surprise, he was met with another single ring followed by voice-mail. He tried again, getting the same result.

Everyone's busy today.

With no luck, he tossed his phone onto the seat next to him and admired his new watch in the box. He took it out of its case and let the sunlight wash over it.

It's beautiful.

At the house, he put back on the suit, and between that and the new watch, he felt more confident than he ever had before. Staring in the bedroom mirror, he attempted to run a clump of gel through his thick wavy hair. Then he sprayed a dash of cologne he'd snagged from his parent's bathroom. It smelled woodsy, which he didn't expect to like. On his bedside table, the clock read 7:55 when a knock rattled his door.

Click. Click. Click. Click. Click.

Monica Grambell walked through the door like Daisy Buchanan. A fur shawl was wrapped around her outstretched arms, and she wore a glittering gold dress with a matching purse that blinded Lonnie if she moved too fast under the light.

"What do you think?" she asked, giving a twirl.

"Looks great," he halfheartedly responded, still messing with his hair.

Mrs. Grambell finished her twirl and sat down on the bed. Looking up, she suddenly noticed Lonnie's suit.

"Oh wow," she fawned. "You look stunning!"

"Thanks." His cheeks warmed.

A sniffle escaped her nose, and she quickly dabbed at her eyes with a tissue.

"Are you okay?"

"Of course. Of course... Just look at you. My gosh, how the time flew." She reached for his face, to which he recoiled. She watched him for a second, then like a flip of a switch, her stiff smile returned. She checked her tiny, bejeweled watch and looked out the door toward the stairwell. "Your father is waiting downstairs, so don't be long."

After she had exited the room, Lonnie noticed her purse lying open on the bed.

"Wait, Mom, you forgot your—" He hastily grabbed one of the straps, causing the contents to spill out onto the floor. "Crap!" he spit out under his breath.

He began shoving credit cards and lip balm back into the purse when he suddenly noticed a bright orange bottle under a tissue.

On closer inspection, the label seemed like it had been scratched off in a hurry, but a handful of white oval pills remained inside the cylinder. Lonnie only had a second to process before a gentle honk sounded from out front.

"Angus is here. Come on, Leonard!" Mr. Grambell shouted from the bottom of the steps.

Lonnie quickly tucked the bottle into the bottom of the

bag and ran down the steps, where both of his parents stood impatiently, his father staring intently at his phone.

"Here, Mom, you left your purse in my room." Lonnie handed it to her as if it was glass.

"Oh, thank you, sweetheart!" she fawned, reaching for the bag.

For a moment they both held it, with Lonnie hesitant to let go. He stared up at her glossy eyes, unsure of what to do next. Then Mr. Grambell looked up from his phone and noticed Lonnie standing next to him.

"Look at this guy!" he marveled.

The excitement made Lonnie lose his grip on the purse, and his mother pulled it in and straddled it over her shoulder.

"Who knew you could dress yourself so well." Mr. Grambell smirked, giving the lining of the jacket a feel. "Nice material."

Lonnie propped up a smile. "Thanks," he responded, looking past his father to the door. "Are we set?"

"Absolutely."

They grabbed their things and made their way to the door. As they entered the limo, his parents took the back bench, leaving him banished to the side seat. Once all in, the car made its way down the cobblestone road. Seemingly settled, his father went right back to texting on his phone, and out of the corner of his eye, Lonnie noticed his mother riffling through her purse.

Best to leave it.

Minutes passed and Lonnie grew tired of watching the tree line. He turned to his parents, who were both preoccupied, his mother with applying her eyeliner and his father with whoever he was texting on his phone. Lonnie pulled out his own phone and began to swipe through his graduation photos when an alert popped up letting him know his battery was low. He decided to reserve it for later, in case the party didn't turn to his liking. Shoving it back in his pocket, he turned back to his parents.

"So how do you know the Blythornes, Dad?" he asked.

Mr. Grambell briefly looked up from his phone. "Patrick was my professor at Hopkins, before he recruited Mike, Dave, and I to become his research fellows. Then after a few years, he decided to leave Hopkins and went on his own to create one of the largest genome research labs in the country. They cure hundreds of patients a year with the procedures he invented. He is utterly brilliant. As is his wife, Ophelia. She runs the business end of his program."

"That's amazing. Are Dave and Mike going to be at the party tonight?"

Mr. Grambell gave him a confused glance. "Of course they are. This is the biggest event of the year. Nobody misses a party like this."

"So, what's the party for?

His father frowned. "Sometimes you just need to celebrate life. Does there need to be anything more than that?"

Lonnie shrugged but didn't reply. He had no idea what to expect, but he knew this wouldn't be like the school parties in the dorm.

How do rich people party?

Chapter 7

Aristocrats

The house was the most breathtaking thing Lonnie had ever seen. Trying to get a better view, he pressed his face to the car window. In the distance, the bright reflection of fireworks lit up the night sky. And the house... The house was nothing like he imagined. A veritable castle had materialized where the forest once stood. Its exterior displayed at least a hundred windows across the multi-story facade, with beautiful gothic balconies edging every floor. Each was filled to the brim with people over-hanging the handrails as champagne slipped from their glass flutes, creating a waterfall over the terrace. A circus of animals, they were. All happy and bubbly.

Once the limo came to a halt, Lonnie threw himself out the door to get a better look. He tried to number the rooms but lost count just at the top floor. It would take days to explore this place, maybe even weeks.

How does one find enough furniture to fill such a place?

Behind him, Mr. and Mrs. Grambell exited the limo.

"Thank you, Angus," Mr. Grambell said.

Mrs. Grambell stepped down onto the draped red carpet

and reached for the floating curtain of twinkly lights in the entryway. "They out do themselves every year."

"Shall we go inside?" Mr. Grambell extended his arm out to his wife, and Mrs. Grambell excitedly wrapped herself around it to walk up the marble steps toward the front door.

"You coming or what?" Mr. Grambell asked Lonnie.

"Yeah, sorry." Lonnie glanced away from the upper floors long enough to follow. However, for as beautiful as the exterior looked, the inside gave him chills. Gold-trimmed black walls were matched with even darker marble floors. Greek busts lined the sides, each unguarded as people bumped through to get to the dance floor. The busts were so raw and exposed, as if knocking one over would merely be a minor inconvenience to replace.

Each piece of furniture looked as if it belonged there and nowhere else. Made of this same blood-red fabric with gold-painted wood frames, while appealing to look at, it also gave Lonnie an unnerved feeling. One he just couldn't place. He knew his parents had money, but this house was different... This life was different. These people weren't just rich; they were aristocrats.

Just as they surrendered their coats in the foyer, a clapping chant began to echo in the next room. Lonnie took a peek around the corner, where he saw an older couple descending down dual sides of a double staircase. They were ravishing. The woman started down the left, carrying the lacing of her red ball-gown in either hand. She moved with such grace that her feet seemed to float above the ground. Her silver-blonde hair was curled and bounced flawlessly on her shoulders with each step she took, and she waved to the crowd in such a way as to make every person there feel seen.

The man followed at a leisurely pace down the right staircase. He wore a matching red tuxedo with a black vest and a gold chain strung from his lapel to his pocket. His silver hair was slicked back, with matching stubble lathered across his face. He, too, gave a brief wave to the crowd and showed his dimpled smile in an otherwise plasticky, stitched-up face.

Lonnie suddenly froze.

It was them.

He'd never forget their faces; they'd been burned into his mind. The couple from his brother's funeral.

This is their party?

He looked to his parents, but they just clapped with the rest of the audience, applauding the couple now at the bottom of the steps. As they reached the floor, they met in the middle, where a magnificent marble statue stood. Lonnie had never seen anything like it. The bodies of five men pulled out in all directions but fused together at the spine. Their arms stretched out as if reaching for the crowd. Looking closer, he noticed the faces didn't look fully human but rather like they'd been melted off. It must have been designed that way on purpose, though, because their mouths still hung open as if screaming and their eyes had been so delicately carved that they felt haunted. A chill ran down Lonnie's arms. He could have sworn the one positioned toward the audience was staring right at him. Its eyes like pitch-black orbs. They all looked a bit different: one strong, one thin to the bone, one with cut-out eyes, and the last two identical and each wielding a small blade.

The man stepped forward to the crowd. "Thank you all for coming out to our...*little...soiree!*"

Everyone let out an obnoxious chuckle.

"I am honored to spend this grand anniversary with you all.

My friends, still after all these years, I am eternally grateful for the support you give. None of this would be possible without you. So please grab a drink, some hors d'oeuvres, and enjoy the party! And wait until you see the show I have in store for you tonight." He lifted a champagne flute off a server's tray and held it out. "Cheers."

The crowd broke into a roar of applause as the music erupted from the speakers. Guests filled the floor and began to dance as the couple sipped their champagne and began walking in Lonnie's direction. Lonnie's head swiveled around anxiously, looking for a way out of their path. But before long the man was right in front of him, reaching out a hand. Lonnie looked at it, confused.

"Patrick, thank you for having us," a voice said from behind.

Lonnie turned around to see his father inches behind him, reaching out his hand to shake the man's. His body had become tense.

"Glad you could make it, Harold." Mr. Blythorne smirked, which pulled at the tight skin around his lips.

Mrs. Blythorne approached his mother, who had been standing a few feet away. She grabbed her fingers, cupping them with her own, then whispered something that made his mother's face flush. But after a moment, she nodded and gave a debutante smile. They proceeded to walk off together, meshing into the crowd of people.

"You really outdid yourself this year, didn't you," Mr. Grambell shouted over the music.

"Oh, I've been planning this night for months!" Mr. Blythorne grinned. "It should be the best one yet."

Their conversation muffled into the background as Lonnie

watched the other people in the room. Most of them were his parents' friends, some of whom he vaguely remembered from his childhood, but their faces were like discolored Polaroids in his head. It was odd, like he was in a room of people who have looked at him through a one-way glass his entire life.

"Leonard," Mr. Grambell said.

Lonnie tuned back into the conversation, where he noticed a hand had been presented in front of him.

"You must be Lonnie. I've heard so much about you," admitted Mr. Blythorne.

Lonnie shook his hand in surprise. "You have?"

"Of course! I hear you're starting Hopkins in the fall. What a genius you must be," he said through a beaming smile.

"I suppose. Yes, very excited. This party is amazing, by the way," Lonnie added.

"Ah, I'm glad you enjoy it. I try not to get too carried away." He winked. "Well, I better continue mingling, but truly it's wonderful to have you here tonight."

As Patrick Blythorne walked away, Lonnie had the brief sensation of being starstruck. The man he remembered from that funeral day as a child was not anything like he expected. He was charming and attentive and good with a toast.

Why had his parents been so afraid of them?

"Come on, Leonard. I have more people I want you to meet." Mr. Grambell gestured for him to follow.

Mr. Grambell and Lonnie made their way through the ballroom and out onto a terrace balcony overlooking the pool. Leaning against the guardrail was a heavyset, middle-aged man talking to a woman who seemed absolutely disinterested in their conversation. He clinked his drink to hers, causing her to give an uncomfortable laugh. Just then, he noticed Lonnie's father approaching, which gave the woman an opening to drain her drink and run back inside.

"Ah, you spooked her, Harold."

"Hello to you too, Marty. Ah, look at your head, did you get work done?" Mr. Grambell asked.

"My gosh, how could you tell?" Marty chuckled sarcastically.

"How could I not." Mr. Grambell waved at the man's full mane of hair.

"Turkey is amazing; you should visit!" Marty rubbed a hand through his hair. "All this for a couple grand! It's unheard of."

"Incredible. I'll have to check it out." Mr. Grambell turned toward Lonnie. "By the way, have you met my son?"

"So, this is the infamous son!" The man patted Lonnie's arm. "Benjamin, isn't it?" Lonnie felt a part of him chip off at the sound of his dead brother's name, but he tried to brush past it. His father's face crinkled, but he seemed to let it go as well.

"No, Marty, this is Leonard, my youngest."

Marty turned to face him. Up close, he had a warm glow to him, most likely from the champagne.

"Ah, apologies, Leonard." He aggressively shook his hand. "Well, it's a mighty pleasure to meet ya!"

"You as well," Lonnie said tightly.

A firework exploded over the pool, and Lonnie jumped back.

"Your first time here, I take it?" Marty asked.

"Yeah." Lonnie looked down, embarrassed.

The man paused for a moment, then grabbed him by the shoulder.

"Where's your drink?"

"I didn't get a drink yet."

"Harold, get your boy a drink! It's a party, for God's sake. Let him enjoy it!"

To Lonnie's surprise, his father nodded and turned to him. "Would you like a drink?"

"Sure?" Lonnie said.

"Fantastic. I'll just be a second." Mr. Grambell walked into the ballroom, subtly whistling to a server nearby. Taking two flutes from her tray, he returned and handed one to Lonnie.

"Bottoms up then," Marty cheered. He dramatically clinked his drink against Lonnie's, spilling bits of champagne onto the floor and his shoes, but it didn't seem to bother him. He started chugging his drink while simultaneously lifting the bottom of Lonnie's, which resulted in more liquid spilling out of the sides of their mouths until both glasses had emptied. Marty then seized Lonnie's empty flute and set them both on the handrail.

"Shall we get you both another?" Mr. Grambell asked, still clutching his mostly full glass.

"Definitely. Now it's a party!" Marty hollered.

Lonnie shook his head no, but it was ignored. Reaching over and grabbing another pair of drinks from a passing tray, Marty propped one into Lonnie's hand, then took his own and earnestly threw it down his throat like he had a funnel for a mouth.

"I'm going to go explore the house, if that's alright," Lonnie said, weakly holding his full glass.

Mr. Grambell nodded, which Lonnie took as his opportunity to get away from this creature.

The ballroom was a circus when Lonnie reentered. Couples might as well have been swinging across the room like trapeze acts, each finding new, exciting ways to steal the attention from the last. One couple caught his eye. They wore matching leopard print suits and had broken into a dance routine in the middle of the floor. Others watched as the one swung their partner over his head like the man was lighter than air, spinning him around until they'd both broken into a heavy sweat.

Lonnie noticed a door at the other end of the room.

I need to escape.

Setting his drink down on a table, he carefully made his way through the crowd, trying his best to blend in with the background. An old lady met his gaze, and in a panic, he tried to keep moving, but she grabbed his hand.

"Come dance with me, sweetheart," she said, her grip like a bear trap.

She wore an uncomfortably low-cut sequin dress, and her orange hair had been recently dyed, based on its chemical perfume. She dragged him to the dance floor like a siren serenading a sailor to his death. He looked around for someone to help, but no one seemed to notice. Eventually he twisted his wrist, giving him enough room to escape. She reached back out for him, but he moved fast until he cleared the door.

The hall behind the door was like a subway car. Rows and rows of people stood crammed together in the corridor, perusing the wall art through the arches leading to rooms like windows. Lonnie wound his way between them, taking each step like it was a minefield while avoiding rogue elbows and drinks spilling from glasses. He, too, couldn't help peeking into each archway, discovering what rooms made up this house. The first was a reading room or library. Piles of books towered to the ceiling like a twenty-foot wave of paper, washing the floor in shadows from the moonlit window. Across the hall sat a bathroom with emerald-encrusted floors that spanned back the length of a football field. Lonnie was in awe. The rooms continued in just as gawdy a manner the rest of the way down the hall, each more remarkable than the last, until he eventually shot himself out of the crowd at the end of the space, and coincidentally, the end of the party.

He paused to let the air fill his lungs again, then looked up at the final door filling nearly the entire wall in front of him.

All the other doorways he had been able to peer inside, but this one was closed. He reached out cautiously to the handles, giving them a pull, and to his surprise, the other side wasn't another elaborate hallway of doors. Instead, it was just an oval-shaped room with leather chairs and a corner fireplace that someone was standing in front of stoking. The space was quite intimate and calm, a haven that existed outside the atmosphere of the party. Only six people occupied the room, including himself, the majority of whom lay spread out in the chairs, enjoying a cigar and talking among themselves. The people on the couch looked up when the doors slammed shut behind him, but their faces showed a lack of care as they returned to their conversation. The man by the fire threw in a final log, then turned.

He frowned. "Lonnie, is that you?" the man sputtered, rubbing his eyes in disbelief.

"Yes?" Lonnie responded, trying to place where this guy knew him from.

The man moved into the light, revealing his hazel eyes.

He grinned. "Hi, Mike!"

"What are you doing all the way down here?" Mike questioned.

"I got turned around."

Mike plopped himself down on the couch. "How are you finding the party of the year?" Mike joked.

Lonnie joined him on the sofa. "Overwhelming, to say the least."

Mike nodded. "Actually, I am glad you found me. I had something I wanted to give you." He reached into his pocket and pulled out a rusty, silver pocket watch. The top was detailed in random arrangements of spirals and lines. He placed the watch into Lonnie's hand. "Here, I wanted you to have this."

"That's very nice of you, but...I don't really understand. Why give it to me?"

"Flip it over."

On the back side of the metal, engraved in tiny print, were the initials *L.G.*

Lonnie Grambell.

"Leonel Gulligan," Mike explained. "My brother designed it."

"Wait, this was your brother's? Why would you want to give it away to someone you barely know?"

"I think I know you quite well, Lonnie." He smiled. "Or at least the things that matter. I'm giving this to you because I know you'll appreciate it more than any of those people out there ever would." He reached his hand back out, rubbing over the initials on the watch, then he patted Lonnie on the shoulder. "From one grieving brother to another."

"Well, thank you then. This is wonderful."

"Well then, you're very welcome," he mocked.

Lonnie rolled the watch around in his hand, feeling his way through the cut grooves. It wasn't until he felt across the lines on the top with his finger that he realized they weren't random at all. Looking closer, he noted they'd begun to form shapes. Carved images stretched from the face of the watch, each reaching out toward the edge of the frame.

Is that the same creature as the statue by the stairs?

"They represent fortune and vitality," Mike blurted as if reading his thoughts.

"I see." Lonnie continued looking at their gaping mouths. His stomach tightened. They looked horrifying. He slid the watch into his inner jacket pocket.

"Do you want a cigar?" Mike asked.

"I probably should get back actually," Lonnie replied.

"Alright, well, I'll let you get to it. I'm sure someone is looking for you by now."

"I doubt that but thank you." Lonnie started for the door, then turned around. "Thanks again for this." He pointed to the lump in his jacket pocket. With that, he made his way back to the main wing of the house, where the dancing raged on and the fireworks continued through the windows. It seemed just as he thought; nothing had changed in his absence.

Or so he thought. In the corner of the room, he saw his mother, who now seemed in a frantic state by the bar, her legs jittering across the floor as she rotated the ring on her finger. Lonnie walked over and tapped her on the shoulder. "Hey, Mom."

A look of relief washed over her distressed face. "Lonnie, my gosh. I have been looking everywhere for you."

"What, why?"

"You disappeared without telling anyone."

"What do you mean? I told Dad I was going back inside earlier—"

"Please don't argue, sweetheart. Just...stay by me the rest of the night. I don't want you wandering off anymore."

Lonnie opened his mouth, then closed it. He planted his feet and imagined the floorboards wrapping around them.

"Here," she said, handing him the drink in front of her. "Enjoy." She looked quite proud of herself for this exchange and proceeded to go back to talking to her friend at the bar. Lonnie grabbed a seat next to his mother, who immediately seemed to forget his presence. He felt like a purse dog. Disgruntled, he sipped his drink in an attempt to stop any irritated comments from spilling out of his mouth. Before he knew it, he had drunk his glass dry.

Cheers rang from the other side of the room, piquing his interest. Lonnie swiveled in his chair to find the dancing had stopped. Next, the music came to a halt, leaving all the noise to the crowd that had formed around the front of the room. Leaning back, he attempted to see what was happening, but the heads in front blocked his view. He looked to his mother, who stayed completely distracted by her conversation. She hadn't noticed the commotion, or if she did, she didn't seem to care. Just then, packs of party-goers began to flock in from the corridors. Lonnie saw his opportunity and waited for the perfect moment. Looking once more to his mom, he snorted, realizing how oblivious she was to what was happening.

Diving into the stampede, he found himself both walking and being carried across the dance floor. Lonnie shoved his way to the front, itching through gaps between people like water leaking through a dam. Getting on his toes, he could just barely make out the front.

The first thing he noticed from the band was their gray hair and matching set of black suits. There were four of them on the makeshift stage. They were musicians, all holding their instruments close to the chest. A guitarist, a bassist, a drummer, and him, the singer.

He looked so familiar to Lonnie. He couldn't stop staring

73

in the hopes that the memory would call out to him. The band began to play, slowly at first, letting their energy captivate the room, and the crowd fell silent.

When the familiar-faced man began to sing, his angelic voice sparked through Lonnie like a jump-start to his mind.

This man was dead.

It was so obvious, but the idea seemed impossible to imagine. Everyone knew that. It was on every station, every corner, every paper. The singer was gone, yet here he stood. Lonnie tried to tell himself he was an imposter. That he was just a fake like they have at carnivals and small festivals. But he couldn't deny it. There was only one man who could sing so beautifully and with so much *suave*. But how was he here?

The thought made Lonnie sweat. *How rich are these people that they bought out death?*

He tried not to focus on it as the crowd lulled him with its synchronized swaying, until soon his mind got lost in the music. If he was honest with himself, this was the first time he'd actually felt happy all night. Just him and the crowd, all the same. No more watching acrobats take to the floor or getting lost in endless hallways with enough rooms to house a small town. He felt equal to everyone at this moment, and that felt nice. He didn't even know he could dance, but the music brought something out in him. A perkiness. And to his surprise, a smile had crept up his face.

But it wasn't long-lived.

As the concert continued, the fireworks began to go off again, sending blinding lights in through the balcony doors. The first came in like a strobe, hitting Lonnie with a splitting headache. He held up his arm to block the brightness, but looking around, to his surprise, no one else seemed bothered by it. He heard the whistle as another rose into the sky, that faint hissing sound as it sprung into the air. But instead of being followed by a light crackle, it erupted in a bellowing explosion.

Boom!

This one knocked him to the ground. Looking up, the faces around him continued dancing, but the music had gone silent, replaced by a light ringing. His head was cracking. He managed to get to his feet but was instantly shoved back down by the adoring fans. The audience had turned on him. What was once gentle swaying now morphed into rip currents slamming him against the ground over and over. Lonnie knew if he stayed still, he would drown. Reaching for the shirt of the person next to him, he pulled himself up from the floor.

With every passing second, his surroundings intensified. The sounds and lights felt like they were ripping at his skin, and his legs became heavier with each step. Seeing he was near the balcony door, he fought his way through the crowd, stumbling over all the body parts in his way until he reached the handle. Opening it, he dragged himself onto the balcony.

Once outside, he took a big breath of fresh air, but to his surprise, he felt nothing, like the wind had gone right through him, and he found himself gasping for oxygen that wasn't there. His stomach lurched in panic.

What is happening to me?

He leaned forward just as his sight started to blur, shooting black dots across his vision. He felt sick. Like every cell in his body was dying one by one, which was when he heard a slight whistle in front of him. He looked up to see another white dot rising into the sky.

Oh no.

Bang!

A medley of green and blue lines erupted, knocking him back like a landmine. He lay paralyzed on his spine, staring up at a narrow awning. The lights from the party danced across it, but he was finding it harder and harder to see them. As his field of vision slipped away, he saw a shadow walk in front of him. The body moved closer, and then everything went black.

Chapter 8

The Silver Box

A faint humming awakened Lonnie.

Dazed, he wrestled his eyes open and was immediately blinded by the fluorescent bulbs above him. Against his face, he felt the cool tile floor, and for the moment, it was the only thing helping subside the thumping in his skull.

"Hello?" he whispered.

He tried to pull himself from the ground, but an invisible force shoved him back down. After a couple more attempts, he curled up into a ball and noticed his lower back graze against the wall. With his last bit of energy, he sunk his palms into the ground and used the wall as a crutch behind him to throw himself into a seated position.

Where am I?

He ran his fingers along the wall, searching for a handle or crevice, but all he felt was metal. They were like sheets of titanium propped together, with small bolts running along the interconnecting pieces. There was nowhere to grab and no door in reach. With a cupped hand, Lonnie covered his brow from the bright light, giving him just enough cover to squint his eyes without feeling nauseated.

The room was suffocatingly small.

Around him, the four silver metal walls came together to form a room no bigger than a prison cell. Lonnie's heart picked up its pace. The metal ceiling couldn't be a foot taller than him, and the black tiles lining the floor made it feel like he was floating over the edge of space.

"Is anyone there?" he slurred around another wave of dizziness.

Oh god, did someone roofie me?

Across from him, the wall held a small plaque with some text that he wasn't in any state to read. Upon closer inspection, a second plaque hung across from it beside an envelope-sized vent, which continued humming as it pumped stale air into his cage. Otherwise, the room was completely empty, which gave Lonnie room to fill it with a truckload of panicked thoughts.

However, as terror set in, so did his adrenaline, giving him enough strength to bring himself to his feet. Once stable enough, he started running his hands along the walls in search of a way out.

There has to be a door somewhere. There has to be something. And how the hell did I get here?

The thought floated around his head, making his skin crawl. But he couldn't place it.

Anything before this moment was a blur. Pieces of the party came to him like fragments of a puzzle, but the overall image was missing. He remembered music spilling through the house as he made his way through the party. The sight of fireworks going off over the pool. And he felt the soreness in his bones from dancing in the ballroom. But that was it.

What happened next?

Tears stung Lonnie's eyes. "Hello? Is anyone there? Please let me go!" he cried out.

Curling his hands into fists, he suddenly felt a sharp pain course through one of his fingers. Lifting it up, he noticed dried blood had gathered at the tip, and beneath it, a tiny hole stood out as if pricked by a needle.

What is this place?

Goosebumps riddled his arms. Lonnie wanted to scream, but when he opened his mouth, only a gasp emerged. Anything stronger made him lightheaded. He bent over and immediately felt the jab of something in his pants pocket. Fishing his hand in, he pulled out his cell phone. Relief washed over him.

7:20 AM was plastered at the top of the screen.

Was it already morning? Lonnie rubbed his eyes. "That's not possible..."

Suddenly a notification popped up.

LOW BATTERY WARNING

Panicked, he dialed the police, but as he looked around the room, he hesitated.

What would I even tell them? He didn't know where he was or who took him. He was nowhere. Before he could consider it further, though, the phone to the police was already ringing.

"Come on, come on," he muttered.

Seconds passed and the ringing continued. He waited a few more until the phone beeped twice and the no signal bar flashed in the top right corner of the screen.

"Are you kidding me?" his strained voice yelled at the phone.

He pounded the wall and let out a muffled scream, but rather than fix anything, the reaction just made his eyes start to blur again. His adrenaline was quickly wearing off. The headache slipped back in, and his eyes struggled to close. Through willpower alone, he managed to remain on his feet, but he could no longer move with the grace he had just taken for granted.

"Damn..."

He stumbled to the wall, using it for support as his fingers slowly followed the outline of the box in search of an exit. He touched each panel, hoping for a hidden door handle to appear. But as he made his way from one section to the next, he came up empty. Until the fourth wall.

Framed directly in the center, he squinted at the black plaque that sat no bigger than a picture frame, with white words carved into it. By this point, his vision was so bad, he had to place himself barely an inch away to read it:

The path forward must always begin with the first step.

"What..." Lonnie rubbed his forehead with his thumb and index finger. "Is this a riddle? Are you kidding me?"

A path forward is a step. A step.

He tapped his feet on the tile floor below. Falling to the ground, he moved his fingers along each one, looking for a button or a clue. But after minutes went by, he could only conclude it was nothing other than just a floor. Defeated, he rested his head on the tiles. Maybe the box didn't even have a door. What if they just built it around him like a tomb? Just locked him away forever, with no way to escape. Like a joke.

Where were his parents? Did they even notice he was missing?

This is all a big, sick joke.

"Please," he screamed at the air. "Just let me go!" Hot, frustrated tears smeared his cheeks. Whatever the hell was going on, it was terrifying. He brought his arms to his knees and held himself on the cold ground as dark thoughts flooded his mind. He tried to calm them, but they were growing chaotic.

"Why did you put me in a box?" he tried again. "Did you just want to drive me mad before you kill me?"

If that was the case, they were succeeding. Lying out on the ground, he listened for a response, but all he got was the hissing of the air vent, which now carried a tune to the rapid beating of his heart.

Clunk. Clunk.

Leaning closer to the vent, he heard a rattling mixing into the whooshing of air. He wiped the salty tears from his eyes and put his ear inches away. The distinct sound of metal scraping repeated.

What is that?

He pressed his eye to the bars in search of the source of the clinking. Except, all he found was darkness beyond and a dry eye from the blowing air. He sat back. Then he remembered his phone. Leaning back in, he turned the camera flash on and shone it through the slits. This revealed a tiny black cube bolted to the bottom of the vent. One of the bolts had half unscrewed, causing it to shake against the washer.

But what is the black box?

Plastered to the side of it, the tiniest red light blinked on and off—so small that someone would miss it if they looked too fast.

"What are you?" He frowned quizzically.

Scanning it again, he noticed the glass-like piece on the front with little bits of metal wrapped around it. His breath caught.

It was a video camera.

The red light meant it was live. Watching him. Recording him. Lonnie felt disgusted. "You're sick!" he screamed at it.

What were they doing? Watching him spiral into madness like it was their own personalized television show? He ripped at the steel grate, pulling over and over until he realized it wouldn't budge. Without another option, he jammed his longest nail into one of the little screws on the vent and began to twist. The first turn was the hardest, ripping at the edges of his skin until it began to bleed, but he kept going. Once it was finally loose enough, he ripped the screw off, but by this point his nail had filed down to the nub. Letting out a pained sigh, he moved onto his next finger, continuing like this until he had four screws and four filed down fingernails.

With the vent loosened, he flung it off, then thrust his arm in and wrapped his hand around the mounted camera. However, another set of screws locked it to the duct, and his nails weren't going to cut it.

He stared at the camera, letting the gears in his brain click, spurred on by the anger boiling up inside him. Walking over to the now slightly bloody steel grate, he picked it up, and with a final glance at the camera, he raised his middle finger and then began ramming the grate in.

"Screw you," he huffed.

The first thrust made a devious clang against the camera. He continued to hit it, grunting in between each swing.

Clang!

"How do you—"

Clang!

"Like that?"

After seven hits, each more dramatic sounding than the

last, it occurred to him that there was nothing left to hit. The camera lay broken into a hundred pieces on the bed of the vent.

Lonnie relished the sense of control returning.

"There, now we're both blind," he said, out of breath.

Celebrating his small victory, he sprawled out on the ground. His lungs struggled for breath. After a moment, he stretched out even further and flung his arms above him on the tile floor.

Thud.

What the?

His hand had slammed against something hollow-sounding. He sat up and looked at the mundane tiles spread underneath him. Once again, he ran his now-bloodied fingers along each one, feeling for anything different. But they all sounded the same. Putting his hand into a fist, he lightly started knocking on the floor, then laid his head down to the cold tile to listen for the noise again.

Knock.

Knock.

Thud.

The sound resonated from the floor, making Lonnie's eyes widen. With what remained of his nails, he tried to sink them into the grout around the tile. But to his surprise, they dug in as though it were butter. Getting a grip around the edges of the tile, he gave a tug, which made the fake grout material stretch like cheese. Then, like the release of a button, the tile flung off with a pop, causing him to fall to his back. His head hit the edge of the wall.

"Aw!" He rubbed at it.

He lay there a moment, pain flowing and stacking on top of

his already horrible headache. Once it subsided, he straightened and looked at the piece of tile still gripped in his hand.

It was odd. The topside was normal and matched the rest of the floor. But the bottom was a completely different story.

"What the hell?" he muttered.

Wires were lined across it, each connected together like a motherboard. They stretched across the floor and back into the hole the tile had once covered. The knobs and connectors glowed blue, as if bioluminescent, each bit vibrating as though they were alive.

Crawling back to the opening, Lonnie discovered a snake pit of wires sitting in a tiny hole no deeper than a foot. Most of the wires shot into the side walls of the hole, but a few ran directly into a panel.

"The path forward begins with the first step," he mumbled to himself.

Without hesitation, he reached his hand into the hole and tugged the wires out of the way. Seeing the bottom, he noticed the panel was lined with unlabeled buttons. The left side was covered in six square green buttons, and the right had a giant rectangular dial on a track. On the top, a switch read ON and OFF.

He looked at the tile lying next to him on the ground. This had to be it.

"The first step," he said hypnotically.

He smiled with the first ounce of hope he'd felt so far in here as he analyzed the face of the panel. But the reality of the situation quickly shifted it to fear. *There are too many options.*

"Which one do I pick?" He looked for a hint around the room, but he already knew there was nothing else.

I guess we start with turning it "on."

He slowly reached inside the box, letting his hand hover over the switch. Trying not to overthink it, he quickly flipped it, causing a little light inside the switch to illuminate the word ON. Lonnie analyzed the room to see if anything had changed, but nothing moved.

"Did that work?" he spoke out loud.

Suddenly a faint hissing sound started. Confused, he turned to see a sliver of smoke spewing out of the air vent. *What the hell?*

Leaning in, his nose met the putrid smell of chemicals. He tried to take a breath in but immediately fell into a coughing fit. The air was toxic. He pulled his shirt over his nose and took short, raspy breaths as he dove down to the panel and tried to flip the switch back to OFF, but it had locked in place. Meanwhile, the gas continued flooding the room.

"Come on, turn off!" he yelled. With each passing second, Lonnie grew more lightheaded. His eyesight blurred again as he stared at the other buttons. *What if they're even worse?*

The thought scared him, but the continued hissing of toxic air scared him more.

Going down the panel, he clicked the top left green button, causing it to turn red.

Swoosh.

On the wall in front and behind him, the middle sections of metal slid to the side, revealing toggle switches. Lonnie didn't even have to think. Climbing to his feet, he ran to the closest one and held it down.

Swoosh.

The metal panel where the plaque once stood shifted halfway to the floor. To his astonishment, it revealed a dark abyss that let in fresh air. However, it was barely enough to counteract the toxic gas still coming in from the vent. Releasing the switch, he walked closer to the opening but was surprised to find it shut in his face.

"What the hell!" He slammed his palm against the metal.

Behind him, the toggle had flipped itself back upright. Unsure what to do and quickly running out of air, he ran back to the switch. *What do I do?*

Noticing the second toggle across from him, he decided to reach for it while his hand still pressed the first switch. Lonnie stretched himself and found that his fingers were just barely able to reach both. He simultaneously pulled them down. "Please work."

The opening began to move again, this time growing wider until it created a door now reaching all the way to the floor. A light breeze flooded into the room, cleansing it of the gas.

Thank god.

Lonnie lapped up the clean air, briefly alleviating the effects of the gas. Though as he felt both his arms growing heavy, he quickly realized this would not be a long-term fix. "I need something to hold it down."

Seeing the grate he'd tossed in the corner, he shuffled his foot over and bumped the metal closer until he could grab it. Taking the grate, he slid it on the one of the metal toggles and let it hang.

Please be heavy enough.

The toggle tried to flip up, but the grate held it down, and Lonnie let out a sigh and dropped his arms. Scooting to the door, he peered out into the blackness on the other side.

Frazzled, he remembered his phone in his pocket. Pulling it out, he turned on the flashlight, shining it out into space. The light hit dark only to reveal more black. He waved the phone around, but there was nothing. Even the ground was black. Not black tile, or ground, just black. Like he was nowhere.

Tears stung his eyes again.

How is there no top or bottom? I don't understand. "I should have never come back home," he stuttered. "I had friends and a future, and I threw it all away for this." His nostrils flared as he stared at his prison. "But if someone wants me dead, they're going to have to do it with their own hands."

I'm not dying in this box.

Taking his slight boost of confidence, he swung one leg over the wall, forcing him to straddle it. Then with both hands, he leaned into the void. Reaching as far as he could, he continued to feel for something to grab hold of, while the flashlight continued shining on nothing.

There has to be something here, I know it.

Then it hit him. Sliding his hand into his other pocket, he pulled out his wallet. Without hesitation, he dangled it directly over the edge of the door and dropped it down. Then waited. He stood quietly, listening carefully for a sound to echo off the floor. A second passed. And the longer it fell, the wider his eyes grew.

"One, two, three...." he counted.

It hit at four with a soft thud. Doing the math in his head, Lonnie knew it had to be at least a few hundred feet. He crawled back into the box and moved back by the panel.

Staring at the buttons, he debated if he should dare press another.

He decided to slide the rectangular dial instead. Placing his hand on the small rectangle, he moved it all the way to the bottom, where it stopped with a click.

Gears started churning in the walls, and Lonnie waited for

another door to open, but no more did. Disappointed, he went back to fidgeting with the board, and suddenly the room began to shake. The wall opposite the door began to vibrate. It continued until he realized it was actually moving. At first it passed only millimeters, but soon they had added up to a foot. His gut clenched. It was going to push him out the door. Slamming himself against the wall, he attempted to stop it, but the wall kept moving, causing his shoes to slide backward across the floor. Sweat built across his forehead. He had no way of holding the wall at bay. With the door quickly approaching, Lonnie retreated back to the panel, which was close to being covered up. He grabbed the rectangular dial but, like the switch, it had locked in place. Pulling as hard as he could, he tried to muscle it back, only to snap the slider clean off.

"No!"

The wall wouldn't be stopped. He glared at the panel, visualizing the cords stemming from each button and where they might go to, but it was impossible to decide.

What if the next button turns out the light?

He couldn't breathe. Everything was too important; how could he possibly decide?

"Crap," he muttered under his breath.

Time was running out as the wall was now only inches away from covering the hole. He had seconds left to decide. He looked down at all the buttons just as the wall covered a portion of the hole, meaning his time was up. He looked at his choices once again and, in a rush, he pushed one of the middle green buttons, causing it to go red. Out of time, the wall covered the hole, causing his hand to get cut as he withdrew it.

"Ah!" he gasped, reaching for the side of his palm.

Clutching his hand, he looked around in hopes another door might open.

"Come on!" he yelled, pounding the walls with his non-bleeding hand.

Suddenly, a louder vibration noise surrounded the room, and the whole thing started to tilt. Bit by bit, Lonnie found himself elevating as the opening lowered beneath him. He slid across the floor and wrapped his leg over the half open door edge to support himself.

He planted his fingers into the metal, trying to hold his ground, but he knew he was going to fall soon. As the wall reached the center of the box, it slid over the toggles, permanently flattening them and, in turn, fully opening the doorframe. Lonnie shifted his feet as his anchor sank to the floor, leaving him with only the outer frame as support. He needed to find a place to land fast.

There has to be some spot near the door.

He reached into his pockets, looking for something else to throw, but all he had left was his phone. He held it up in his hand, hesitantly aiming it out the door as his arms and legs each wrapped around a different corner of the door. He paused.

There has to be something else.

Just then he noticed the watch strapped to his wrist. "Perfect! Yes!"

He managed to rip it off with his right hand, while his left supported him. With the watch curled up in his palm, he stared out at the blackness, his feet on the edges of the base and his remaining hand on the top. Then in a grand pitch, he underhand tossed it about ten feet out ahead of him.

Thud.

It landed after barely a second, which was all Lonnie needed to hear. Feeling the wall push against his back, he set his heels into it. Then with a burst, he used it to propel himself into the darkness. He glided through the air, feeling a dampness hit him. Behind him, he could sense the final glimpses of light go out as the wall reached the door. Then with a crushing noise, the light completely extinguished, and he was falling in emptiness. He braced himself, ready to land, but a part of him thought *what if I miss?* What if the watch had hit a pipe, and he was now falling hundreds of feet to his death? Before he could panic more, however, he slammed against the ground, his body rolling over and over until every bone felt like it had been ripped apart.

He couldn't get up. It was like the wind had torn through his lungs. He allowed himself a moment to compose himself and reached for his chest to make sure it hadn't ripped open and spilled all over the floor. He began to cry again for reasons he wasn't sure of this time. Possibly relief or just that everything hurt. He didn't think anything was broken, but he wouldn't be surprised if he had cracked a rib or two.

Thankfully the ground felt soft, like foam, which must have eased his fall. Confused, he pulled out his light and shone it at the floor. A yellowish green hue met his eye. It was moss. The entire floor was covered in a thick layer of moss. He picked up a handful and held it up.

Am I outside?

"This can't be outside. Wouldn't the sun be out by now?"

Getting to his feet, Lonnie traced back the way he jumped from. Shining his light along the floor, he quickly stopped as he came to the edge of a cliff. It was a dead end. As he turned to go the other way, the light began to reflect off something shiny to his right. He reached his hand out and found a metal bar. Feeling more closely, he realized it was a handrail. He pulled himself closer, shining the light alongside it to reveal a seemingly never-ending metal staircase and a stand beside it with a glass button on top.

He eyed the button, feeling a bit less confident after his previous trials. However, maybe it was the adrenaline, because he figured what else did he have to lose? He slammed his hand against it and instantly found himself lying back on the ground.

Chapter 9

A Whale's Throat

Light flooded the room like a hundred suns, touching each crevice and snuffing out every inch of darkness. Completely blinded, Lonnie clutched his face as though it had been burned off. Spots filled his vision, causing him to stumble backward, until ultimately falling flat back onto the moss. Gasping for breath, he ripped off his tie in an attempt to let air back into his lungs. To his surprise, a couple dozen feet above him, through his blurry vision, he could make out a rock ceiling which had been finely smoothed. Thousands of floodlights hung from it, each inches apart and held together with piping and metal rungs. Even just looking at them felt like staring directly at an eclipse.

As his eyesight returned, Lonnie was shocked to discover he appeared to be trapped inside a dome-like cave. The rock ceiling trailed down to the walls, which were covered in broken stalactites and more piping systems all running and interconnecting throughout the space.

Leaning on the button stand behind him, Lonnie pulled himself up. In the light, the thing looked quite odd. A petite pedestal with a large yellow button printed in the middle. Beside the button was that giant, industrial metal staircase. Tracing his gaze up the steps, he saw what he was looking for. Dangling at least ten feet above him was his prison cell. The silver box hung from a system of wires and pulleys, holding it in place like a fly in a web. The wall was still buried against the door, but the cube had finally ceased spinning. An air duct connected to the back vent, as he suspected, stretching down until it disappeared into the face of the cave. To the side of the cube was the top of the staircase. Just a few meters away from the doorframe.

What is the point of that?

It would be impossible to access the stairs from any portion of the cube. That's when Lonnie noticed the dolly track planted on the ground in front of him, running from the stairs to right in front of the door.

It was a test.

The whole cell, every part of it. The panel, the vent, the door. And he clicked the wrong button. He didn't make the stairs move in front of the door like he was supposed to. No, he was meant to fall. He stared over the edge of the cliff, looking for a safety net or something at the bottom, but even with the light illuminating the room, all he saw was a bottomless black pit.

Someone set me up to die.

Someone had tried to kill him, and he didn't even know who. He didn't even know why. The thought made him start to gag. His body convulsed as he dry-heaved over the edge of the cliff. Lumps of champagne rose up his throat and expelled into the black void, making him lightheaded.

"Why are you doing this!?" he screamed at the room.

He covered his face, immediately regretting his outburst. Whoever this person was had clearly spent a lot of time planning this. Perhaps it was best not to anger them. He waited timidly for a repercussion, half expecting the cliff ledge to start tilting or to be sentenced to darkness once again. Thankfully, nothing happened.

After waiting almost a minute, he heard a speaker ring, even though he couldn't see a radio system anywhere in the room.

It must be coming from the walls.

As the feedback cleared, a deep voice approached the mic. *"Please Proceed."*

The speaker went silent, and Lonnie looked around, confused. His eyes still burned from the burst of lights. "What do you want from me?" he called out.

"Please Proceed," the speaker rang again with the same cadence.

"Proceed where?"

"Please Pro—"

"Gahhh!" Lonnie stomped the ground, kicking up moss and dirt into a cloud around him. "I don't know what that means!"

His face grew hot as drops built on his forehead. He kept looking around the room for the speaker, but the voice sounded like it came from everywhere. As if it surrounded him, crushing him down.

With an abrupt click, the speaker shut off, leaving Lonnie alone with his growing anger. He continued stomping on the dirt when he heard a crunch. Looking under his shoe, he saw his watch buried under a thin layer of moss. The face had shattered, and little pieces of glass sprinkled over the ground. Under the broken glass, the hands stood still, 7:30 forever frozen on the dial.

"Of course..." He sighed.

With the watch in his fist, he considered tossing it over the ledge, but he stopped. Planting his feet into the dirt, he gave the watch another stare. He wasn't able to get rid of it. It felt wrong. He didn't want any part of him left behind to rot in this horrible place.

He rewrapped the watch around his wrist and gave a slight polishing to the shards of glass that remained. As he adjusted the strap, he couldn't help giving a pathetic smirk.

"A broken pair, we make," he said sincerely, eyes now glazed over.

Giving himself a second, Lonnie prepared his wits. Deciding to follow the voice's instructions, he proceeded away from the cliff. Facing opposite to it, he saw a hundred-meter stretch of moss and boulders leading to a wall. Hesitantly, he walked over to find himself at the base of a tall wall. This part of the cave wasn't like the rest. It had been carved out and replaced with a giant slab of metal, giving it an eerie similarity to the silver box.

Great, he thought. *Now I'm in a bigger cell.*

To his left, he noticed a tiny red sign burrowed into a pile of rocks and moss. On it someone had typed in tiny letters:

Please Proceed.

The side of the sign was shaped into an arrow that aimed directly at a portion of the wall. Lonnie strode to it, looking for a door handle or other panel switch. To his surprise, he immediately came across an extruded piece of metal at the height of his torso.

Was this a door handle?

He reached for it with both hands, giving it a heavy pull. A pop sound came from the wall, as if it was air-locked, allowing the door to swing out in front of him. Peering inside, he found a thin hallway just larger than the width of the door. The ceiling was illuminated by evenly spaced fluorescent lights, each filling the room with a dim orange hue. Carefully he stepped over the threshold and into the hallway. The weighted door shut behind him with that similar popping noise, letting him know he was not going back the way he came.

"That can't be good."

Lonnie didn't normally consider himself nervous around tight spaces. However, between the small box and the idea of his arms touching both walls simultaneously, he just couldn't shake the unsettling feeling from his stomach. It was like walking down the throat of a whale. With each step, the hall grew more narrow and more humid until the air became quite hard to breathe. So much so that he tried to inhale as little as possible, as it was beginning to hurt.

I hope this isn't a dead end.

Running his hands along the walls, he noticed they were different than the panels outside and in the box. What had been metal out there had become slabs of cement slathered from the ceiling to the floor, which didn't help the suffocating feeling. His heartbeat raced, making an echoing sound inside his chest, one that mimicked that of his shoes clicking against the concrete floor.

At the end of the hallway, it split into two, with one corridor to the left and another to the right.

"For the love of..." he cursed to himself.

A ball of nerves nested itself in his stomach as he scrambled to decide which way to go. On the wall between the two passages, there was a sign with the same font as the one inside the silver box, this time reading:

Come Hell or High Water.

It had a two-sided arrow drawn below it. Following the first arrow, he looked down the left hallway to see an upward spiral staircase at the end. Feeling confused, he turned to the right to find an identical hallway, only this one ended in a downward spiral staircase. The thought twisted his brain.

Am I above the ground?

With uncertainty, he followed the arrow to the downward staircase. He found it to be even darker than the corridor. A single bulb hung from the top, spreading light down until it faded to darkness. Lonnie hugged the wall, avoiding the sizable hole that gaped within the center of the spiral stairs. After a few steps, he pulled out his phone light. Squinting his eyes, he noticed a wooden door tucked away at the bottom of the steps. Carefully, he continued descending, each step causing him to wince as his bruised ribs jostled up and down.

As he approached the final flight of steps, his phone light went out. Raising the phone to his face, he watched in horror as the screen went black. He mashed the button on the side of the phone, but it was no use. The thing was dead.

Stupid battery.

Giving it a shake, he tried to get the power to turn back on. "Come on!" But in doing so, the phone slipped from his hands and fell down the flight of stairs into the darkness.

"No!"

The phone hit the ground below with a cracking sound, letting Lonnie know it was gone.

"Damn it," he hissed at the black void.

With his back pressed against the wall, he used his hands to guide him down the remaining steps. Briefly looking up, the faint lights from above made him wonder how high off the ground he had been in the first place. Or if he was even above the ground at all...

Reaching the last step, he jumped onto the floor, landing with a splash. Lonnie let out a yelp. A puddle had formed along the floor, filling his shoes with cold water.

"What the hell!" he shouted.

He didn't even bother to look around, seeing as he had no light aside from the small glow above and a bit creeping out from under the wooden door beside him. On his tiptoes to avoid the puddle, he walked over to the door and felt around for the handle. He pushed it open with a large heave, and a draft of warm air and light consumed him. He basked in the heat for a minute before approaching whatever hell awaited him inside this new hallway.

Like the previous space, rock and cement lined the walls, though this was a darker shade than before. Like it had been tinted. The long ceiling had fewer lights than the prior, only one every sixty feet or so, but it was enough to illuminate the area. Aside from this, Lonnie felt hopeful about this tunnel.

The air has got to be coming from outside, he thought.

Maybe following it was a chance to get out. It wasn't a very sound idea, but it was enough to keep him going down the path. After walking a bit, he realized it had been a lot longer than he'd expected. About a mile in, he thought about turning around but saw a wall a couple hundred meters ahead of him. His walk turning into a jog, he quickly closed the space, but to his disappointment, the wall had no door. It was just covered in a large grate, which he realized had been the source of the warm air. Being this close, Lonnie noticed a rank smell wafting out of the grate. Like heated sewage. He gagged, putting his hands on his knees as if he was going to hurl.

An idea suddenly hit him. If this was a sewer line, then it could lead him away from here. All he had to do was get in. Repulsed, he reached for the grate, aiming to pull himself up. On his toes, he managed to get a good grip and tug at it, but the thing was a lot more locked down than the vent grate had been. There was no way to pull it off. Disappointed, he sat on the floor to catch his breath. The thought of walking back down the tunnel and up the stairs felt so frustrating. He'd just be wasting all that energy for nothing.

"Damn it..."

Before he could force himself back to his feet, a droplet landed on his head. He swatted a hand to wipe it when he heard the sound of rushing water echo through the grate. It began growing, and it didn't take him long to figure out what it meant.

"No...no...no...no..."

He sprung from the ground and started sprinting down the tunnel. The sound picked up behind him, and before he knew it, a line of water had passed him on the ground. Peering over his shoulder as he ran, he saw a power jet of water shoot out of the vent. It filled the corridor behind him like a wave. He kept running, aiming for the wooden door off in the distance. His lungs began to burn, but it didn't matter. He had to push through it.

Behind him, the wave of water was gaining. He could feel it without looking. Though he should have been afraid, the only thing he could think of was Hannah. Images of her drifted through his mind. Her contagious laugh and pearly teeth, the warm feeling he got when near her, and the way her hair always smelled like coconut. The idea of her at Johns Hopkins next school year flooded his mind. She stood by the dorm entrance, patiently waiting on her phone. Texting him no doubt, asking when he was going to arrive. She was wearing her favorite green sweater, the one that he bought for her when they first started going out. The one she only wore when she was in a really good mood.

At this moment though, all he could picture was her standing there. Waiting and losing patience for a person who was never going to arrive. Because he had drowned that summer in a sewer, and she would never know. She would go on thinking that he left her, without a goodbye, without a word...

He never even got to introduce her to his parents. Not that he cared what they thought, but it just seemed like the thing normal people with happy families did. Something he had hoped this homecoming might result in.

I won't leave her. I can't.

A second wind rushed through him, and he picked up his stride. Now feet from the door, he lunged and tumbled through it before turning to see a streaming river of sewage flying towards him. With a large yank, he pulled the door shut.

Thud.

"Ah!" he screamed, as his body jumped back from the door.

His head hit the ground, just barely grazing the base of the bottom step. The sound of a running faucet filled the room as the water poured in through the underside of the door. Even in the darkness, he knew the wood wouldn't hold long.

"Get up," he whispered to himself.

The initial wave hitting the door had already caused a piece at the top to chip away, exposing little holes like breaks in a dam. Water sprayed in, smearing Lonnie's face with a warm texture. He gagged.

Feeling around with his hands, he looked to get his bearings, but all he noticed was that the entire floor was now covered in water. He attempted to stand, but as quickly as he did, he fell back to the ground. The water eventually overtook him, carrying him to the wall behind the stairs. Reaching out, he looked for something to pull himself up, and to his surprise, his hand wrapped around the cover of another grate.

The rushing water flowed under him, into the grate. His hands held tight against the wall as water slid around him like a stream against a pebble.

Another crack screamed out from the door as the sound of water intensified. Time was running out. With water pushing against him, he climbed his way along the grate, feeling out with his foot for the base of the steps. Eventually finding it, he realized the grate was blocked by the underside of the stairs.

How do I get in front?

A bigger crack sounded from the door, this time seemingly at the bottom, while the water level continued to rise.

With a sense of urgency, he turned his back to the grate. Resting one foot on the ground, while the other pushed into the metal like a springboard, he held his arms outstretched at an angle and prepared to jump.

You can do this. On the count of three.

One...two...three... He kicked off his back foot, throwing his weight just above the rushing water. His hands reached out, wrapping around the outer edge of a step, and with a swing he threw himself over it, landing face down onto the staircase.

He had made it to the steps.

Without hesitation, he tried to climb, but his legs stiffened under the rushing water. Unable to move them, he instead jammed his fingers into the stair above him and pulled his wet body up the next step. He proceeded to do it again, and again, until he had reached what must have only been the fourth step. Exhausted, he wanted to stop, but another creak bellowed from the door. He crawled on, his mind numb to the pain. After about ten more steps, his body gave out, and he laid there on the stairs, hoping he had made it far enough.

Below him, the door completely shattered from the wall. Water poured through like a jet, flooding the floor in a matter of seconds. The grate rattled as the blast pounded against it. Lonnie prayed he was beyond reach, but just by listening, he knew the water was rising faster than it could flow through the grate, causing the backup to fill the room.

"Please..." he muttered.

He felt the water touch his toes, and his stomach dropped. He sunk his fingernail nubs into the stairs, waiting for the fight of his life, and soon enough the water had reached his ankles, causing him to brace. He waited for the next stream of water to rip him off his perch, but to his surprise, the water stayed level. He was in the eye of a hurricane, holding himself steady as water warped around the room like a whirlpool. With hope renewed, albeit small, he opted for one final push and managed to pull his feet out of the water and curl up in a ball on the step.

The damp air plastered the water to his skin, leaving him freezing. Shivering, he waited another fifteen minutes for the water to stop rushing through. And as his feet began to regain their feeling, he once again started working his way up the stairs. He crawled from one step to the next until the faintest light began to dance across the wall above him. Never did he think he would be so happy to see that worthless bulb again. He continued on, soon managing to pull himself to his feet. At some point, the pain had gone away, and a numb layer had replaced it over his entire person.

The next thing he knew, he found himself at the top of the stairs, staring out at the old hallway. To his disappointment, the humid air did not warm him up as he hoped. Instead, it made the suit stick to his skin like a layer of weighted sweat. He ripped off the suit jacket, which clanged against the floor. Shocked by the noise, Lonnie picked it up, patting his hand over the fabric. There was a lump.

He reached into the suit sleeve. Suddenly the memory came to him—the pocket watch. He slid it out and eyed it. The top case had a deep crack split through the middle and little splotches of splattered glass surrounding it. Taking a closer look though, he noted the second hand monotonously spinning around the dial. Surprised, he raised it to his ear and confirmed it with a faint ticking.

It worked. To Lonnie's surprise, it read 1:55.

Perhaps it didn't work as well as he thought.

He put it into his pants pocket.

"I hope this is entertaining," he said sarcastically, talking to the air in case anyone could hear him. Just then, he noticed a tiny blinking red light tucked above the lights, peering down on him, like a predator waiting for its next meal. Lonnie's insides churned.

Turning to the camera, he gave a wave whilst displaying the snarkiest smile he could. Then he lifted his hand and aggressively jabbed his middle finger towards the sky. In the moment, a spike of confidence came over him. But it was quickly followed by a fit of fatigue. Losing his footing, he walked over and leaned on the right-side wall for support.

Creak. The edge of the wall inched open, causing Lonnie to stumble. Mid-fall, he reached for a solid bit of wall to catch himself on, and as he did so, he noticed scrape marks etched around the wall's base. A perfect semicircle stood out, ever so faintly, from previous times the wall had spun. Lonnie couldn't help kicking himself for being so distracted. It was another stupid test.

A bright light shone out of the wall crack. Eager to escape the hallway, he gave the wall a hard push, forcing it to do a ninety-degree turn and reveal a third passageway. Without batting an eye, Lonnie stepped through. Anything had to be better than sewage water and cold cement.

Chapter 10

Six Feet Under

After taking his first step into the new tunnel, he found the concrete floor replaced by mud and dirt. His foot promptly sunk into a layer of soft earth. With a strong tug, he managed to free his leg but could already feel his other foot beginning to sink as well.

Clang.

The wall he had passed through made a sudden clicking sound, then swung itself back to its original position. Lonnie threw himself at it, but it was no use. The wall held solid, giving him nothing more than an achy shoulder and another dead end. The lights flickered brighter above, illuminating a plaque on the backside of the wall. It read:

Trial #1 Completed

Lonnie froze. *Trial?*

"A trial for what?" he yelled into the void.

Beep! A blaring siren filled the room so loud it forced Lonnie to cover his ears.

When it stopped after a couple seconds, Lonnie hesitantly removed his hands from his head, his heart beating hard against his chest. He waited for it to start again, but instead he heard the crackling of a speaker.

The monotonous voice from earlier rang from the walls. *"Please Proceed."*

"I'm never getting out of here." He sighed.

"Please Proceed," it eagerly repeated.

He thought about yelling back at whoever it was, but so far that hadn't seemed to influence anything. Instead, he turned slowly to face his new prison. Made with faded chunks of brick, the walls were covered in thick layers of cobwebs and an odd smelling liquid stain that ran down to the floor. Something about it ricocheted through his bones—as if evil had painted the walls in blood. The sensation was so strong that a shudder ran down the length of his back.

This looks like hell.

Holding his nervous stomach, he ventured out into the catacomb, stepping lightly across the muddy floor. Overhead, a cord was strung along the ceiling, carrying dim lights covered in mold and webs, and alongside him, bricks were pushed in varying degrees from the walls, as long worms wiggled themselves free of the blockade.

"Gross." He gagged and shook his foot when one fell from the wall and onto his shoe.

But at the same time, he found it oddly motivating.

I refuse to get eaten by them.

Powering through the next couple blocks, the hallway suddenly opened up into a grand lobby. Archways spanned in all four directions, creating a handful of new corridors separate from the one he'd come from. Lonnie slowed.

This is going to be impossible.

Unsure which way to go, he picked the closest one to his

left, which led him into another lobby with more archways. Trying to keep his cool, he continued going left, each time expecting a new result and each time ending up back in a similar room of exits.

It all looked exactly the same.

With no way to organize anything, he couldn't even tell how far he'd gone. It might have been ten rooms or a hundred. All he knew was that each had brick walls and a formidable smell of iron. But no real exit. Just rooms that branched out into more rooms like roots.

Frustrated and exhausted, he continued walking straight for a while until he finally came across a metal gate hanging across one of the archways.

"Yes!" he cheered. *Finally something different.*

Approaching it, he leaned his arms against the cold rusty bars and peered inside. To his surprise, it wasn't a gate at all. It was a cage. One that spanned the length of the room. Unnerved, he walked to the edge of the bars to where a pile of bones was spread out in the corner. His gut clenched. Chunks of crushed up bone lay half embedded into the dirt, each piece looking as though it had been picked clean by whatever buried them.

"What the hell?" He pried up one of the bones with a nearby fallen brick.

Following the trail of bones, his eyes wandered to the open gate at the other end of the cage. It was lightly swinging on its hinges, as if waving to him from across the room. A sense of horror gradually dawned on him. The gate was moving. Meaning, whatever was in this cage had only recently gotten out. He swallowed and scanned the room. He had no idea what it was, but he certainly wasn't about to wait and find out.

Keeping his eyes locked on the gate, he slowly backed to another tunnel opening behind him. It led down an identical set of hallways, and he took the right until he came upon a large square room that finally appeared different from the rest. The room was about twenty square feet with no other exits aside from the one he'd just come through. Exhausted and in need of catching his breath, he dropped to the ground and positioned himself with his face toward the open arch.

Sitting there, he immediately noticed the bricks in this room had a yellowish-white stone instead of the previous brownish red.

That's weird.

As he backed into the wall, he felt something metal hit the back of his head. Looking back, he realized it was another one of those tiny signs plastered against the wall. Unable to read it in the flickering light, he crawled closer.

"We thank you ... for your ... sacrifice."

Grrrr.

A metallic sound grated through the wall, like metal being ripped apart. Lonnie jumped to his feet and felt as though the blood started to empty from his limbs. But even with that, he began scooting back toward the exit.

Zit. The lights in the hallway three rooms down went out.

"That can't be good," he whispered.

The gears grinding behind him turned deafening, like a bundle of engines being blended together.

Zit.

The light's two rooms in front of him went out next.

What the...?

Lonnie tried to analyze the situation, but so many things were happening all around him. One thing he knew for sure, though, was that he had to move. Breaking into big strides, he rounded the room's left side corner as the sound of churning gears and flickering lights stayed hot on his trail.

Zit.

The next second passed and the light in the room adjacent to his went out, making it clear which room was next. Turning his run into a sprint, he tore as fast he could toward the light. Without even looking, he could see the darkness growing row by row behind him. Every room he passed through, the darkness and churning gears were quick to follow. Feeling he had built a lead, he looked over his shoulder, when he suddenly felt a hard surface against his skull.

Bam.

Still looking back, he ran face first into the wall, flattening him out onto the ground. Gasping for breath, he lay spread out, his forehead bleeding down his face, with the wind knocked out of his chest.

I need to get up.

But as hard as he tried, he couldn't move. Delirious, his head turned on the dirt to see an open path to his left. But as quick as he saw it, the lights above him disappeared, and the churning sound of gears started to blanket his ears. Fueling on straight adrenaline, he was able to pull himself to his feet and broke into a run. Diving into the black void, his shoulder brushed against the wall as he made it down an open path he'd only briefly gazed upon.

His thoughts raced. *Now what?*

A faint light still flickered in between the walls in front of him. He ran forward, but with every step he took, the light moved a little faster. Always just slightly out of reach. As he scurried back and forth through the labyrinth of tunnels, slivers of light shone through cracks. Occasionally, he would lose the light, and other times it was clearer than the sun. But he couldn't afford to stop. Occasionally, he would look back for the source of the whirling gears, but in the darkness, all he saw was a black hole. And if he was honest with himself, he was scared for the moment that it was anything different.

Going between hallways, the archways began to vary in size, some spanning the entire wall and others barely the width of a door, making it hard for him to navigate his way. On multiple passes, he found himself slamming against the edge of the smaller archways, but all he could do was bite his tongue. Holding his shoulder, he inhaled the crushing pain, his arm feeling like it had been ripped from his body. He wanted to stop, but he didn't have time. Chasing the light was the only thing he could think of.

Shuffling from one tunnel to the next, the light grew closer in front of him, and he began to regain his vision. With only two rooms standing in the way, he kicked into high gear, cutting the distance in mere seconds, until suddenly the light stopped.

Behind him, the sound of crunching gears continued forward, but the lights no longer disappeared. Scared it was a trick, he continued moving, but a weird feeling had popped up in the back of his neck, and as he entered the well-lit room, he gasped.

A crevice loomed in the middle of the dirt floor. Without enough room to stop, he skidded across the ground until his legs flung over the edge, and he was left with only his hands to support him from falling in.

"Crap!" he yelled, as his fingers dug into the hardened mud.

He held on, the dirt slowly slipping out from under him. His shoulder began to burn from the sudden stress of his body weight. But he was not going to let go. Below him, the crevice dropped a good distance before shrouding into darkness. Terror filled his mouth along with the sweat dripping down his face. Swinging his leg up, he managed to dig the heel of his shoe into the dirt and used it to fling his body back up onto the ground.

With his dirt-covered fists, he gave the floor a good punch before returning his attention to the ten-foot-wide canyon that had split the room in half. The sides of which were covered in a jagged, rocky surface spanning down as far as he could see.

There is no way I can cross that.

He tried to go back into the dark to find another way out, but that mechanical abomination continued growing closer. There was only one way across. He would have to jump.

"This is crazy..." he muttered, desperately shrugging off his jacket.

Please let this work.

He placed a sleeve in either hand, wrapping them tightly round his wrists. Then he broke off into a sprint toward the cliff, making a long stride before his inevitable jump. Flailing through the air, his lungs rose into his throat, but all he could do was think about the fast-approaching rocky facade. With only a foot to go, he began to drop faster than expected. Reaching his arm out, his fingers grazed the top of the edge before sliding down. Panic surged, his arms now flailing for something to grab.

Before he could think of a new plan, the rest of his body slammed into the cliff side with a thud. His jacket sleeves had caught on an extruded rock. The whiplash ripped the sleeves in his hands, causing his palms to burn. He yelped in pain, but the sound of tearing fabric jolted him from his agony. Sinking his feet into the wall, he shifted the jacket higher, using it to grab onto the ledge with his hands. Specks of loose dirt crumpled under his hands, falling down below. He tried to ignore it and kept his focus on the top of the cliff.

Moving one hand at a time, he pulled himself out of the crevice and onto the edge of the canyon. Lying down, he winced, revealing the blisters etched into his hands. But already the pain had begun to fade away as they grew numb like the rest of his body.

What happened to the noise?

Lonnie listened carefully, but the grinding of metal had stopped. Rolling to his side, he looked back across the canyon. There, hiding in the shadows, a pair of green lights towered over him. He couldn't see what they were attached to, but he was happy not to know any more than that. Staring at him, the creature made a gut-wrenching noise. If Lonnie didn't know any better, he'd say it sounded as though it were screaming. Its voice ripped through the air like a buzz saw. Then, just as quickly, it stopped, and the lights slowly faded into the darkness until they were no bigger than stars in the sky.

Buzz.

As if on cue, the above lights began turning back on, row by row, and where the creature had stood sat an empty room. In its place, a set of large footprints were pounded into the dirt.

I hope I never find out what made those.

Lonnie turned back to the side of the room he'd landed on and took a deep breath. The new pathway he'd ended up on was similar to before. The brick archways spanned the halls, and dirt covered the ground. However, something caught his eye. Bending down to his knees, his finger grazed over two pairs of shoe prints receding into the coming corridor.

Were there other people in here?

A gripping sense of hope surged at the idea of no longer being alone. He jumped to his feet. "Hello!" he shouted.

His echo carried through the tunnels, replaying a few times before evaporating into the air. He stood in silence, listening closely for a response.

Nothing.

Again, he bellowed, "Hello, is anyone there?"

The echo continued, repeating over and over, and then for a moment, beneath his own ricocheting voice, he thought he heard something. Turning his head, he listened again until he made out the quietest stomping of feet in the distance.

People were here!

"Hello!" he repeated optimistically.

The footsteps started running, and without thinking, he broke into a sprint. Following the noise, he chased after whoever was making it, his body winding around archways and corners with determination.

"I know you're there; please stop running!"

But the people ran on, the sound of their heavy stomping covering the halls.

"Stop please, I'm not going to hurt you!" he yelled again.

Based on the noise, the gap between them was closing but not fast enough. Lonnie cut to the right, making a beeline through a string of archways. Speeding up, he attempted to do a slow loop around them, like a sheepdog in a pen. With a hard turn, he cut to the left, throwing himself through the archway and into the people on the other side. They all fell to the ground in a series of groans. Lonnie blinked.

"Get off me!" a voice yelled back, jamming his elbow into Lonnie's rib.

Lonnie fell onto his back, his hand clutching his side as he looked over at them. His mind raced.

I know that voice.

With their backs to him, the guy raised his arm to help the girl up from the ground. Her hair was tangled in a way he knew all too well, and the faintest aroma of coconut wafted up his nose.

It isn't possible.

Then with a flip of her hair, the girl turned to him, revealing a pair of bewildered emerald eyes.

"Lonnie?" she asked, shock taking over her face.

"Hannah?" Lonnie choked. "Jamie? What are you both doing here?"

Chapter 11

Three Musketeers

Ten months earlier.
   Everyone needs a hand.

Lonnie stared intensely at the picture, a slight ringing in his head. The poster showed the text in bold letters just above a hand flailing in the water. The fingers curled down begging for help while waves splashed over the knuckles, slowly pulling whoever they belonged to under.

"Lonnie, you're not listening."

Startled, Lonnie turned in his chair to face the lady sitting at the other end of the room.

The name plaque on the desk said ***Ms. Kollig: Guidance Counselor***. She stared at him with big, beady eyes. Her hair hung like strands of hay atop her head, and her sweater was littered with small holes.

He frowned. "Sorry. What?"

"I said," she adjusted her glasses, "how has this week been?"

"Fine," he said defensively. "Just perfect." Lonnie's gaze drifted behind her to the bookshelves on the wall. There had to be at least a thousand tomes there. Each one was bound in leather and stitched with a signature cover and alphabetized. Cheap trinkets lined her expensive oak desk, as if a purposeful contradiction. The smell of burning wood drifted from the tiny fireplace in the corner of the room, giving a cozy feeling that Lonnie was too nervous and annoyed to enjoy. His hands sunk into the couch cushion, which morphed into his imprint.

"I always say, life is too crazy to express in such a mundane adjective." She smiled to herself as though she said something profound. "Don't you agree?"

"I suppose."

"What other word could you use to describe your week?"

"Tiring…"

Silence held the room as Lonnie grew restless in his seat. Ms. Kollig seemed to pick up on this and reached for his file from her cabinet.

"I read here that your psychiatrist put you on trazodone," she said, pivoting the conversation. "How has that been making you feel?"

"Better, I suppose."

"In what ways?"

"Um, I guess everything feels a little slower. A little less gray."

"That's wonderful! Have you been having any side effects?"

"No."

"None?" she pried.

Lonnie kept his mouth shut, and Ms. Kollig let out a disappointed sigh as she fumbled through his file once again, pulling out a thin piece of paper.

"I received a note from your resident advisor. She said she's been having complaints from other students. Saying they've been wakened in the middle of the night by screaming from your room. Have you been having any side effects lately? Nightmares perhaps?"

"What? No."

"It's a perfectly common side effect, but it just means your doctor might have to adjust your dosage. Which could affect how you're feeling." Ms. Kollig looked like she was fishing without a line, but Lonnie had already zoned out of the conversation. Setting the file down, she stood from behind her desk and strode around to crouch in front of him.

"I know these things can feel overwhelming, but from where I see it, you're doing so much better than you think you are, especially compared to that scared little boy who first walked into my office."

She stared at him with pitying eyes. Ones that always made him feel like a sick puppy at the pound. Lonnie's brow twitched, and he shot up from the chair.

"Thanks," he said blankly. "Am I good to go?"

She sighed. "Yes. Of course. See you next week."

Freed from the conversation, Lonnie headed to the door. He'd just grabbed the handle when she called him back.

"Lonnie."

He slowly turned, kicking himself for not exiting faster.

"It all just takes time. Don't be discouraged."

Lonnie nodded, then managed to slip out the door before she could say more, still feeling her stare piercing through him. Relieved that it was over, he walked away.

Crash.

He found himself lying on the concrete. A bit dazed, he looked over to see he had taken another person down with him. Her red hair was spread along the floor.

"I'm so sorry," he stammered. He reached over to help her up, but she was already halfway to her feet.

"Don't sweat it, I'm fine." She glanced down. "Are you okay?"

A hole had ripped across his pants knee, showing blood dripping down the leg.

"Yeah, of course," he fibbed.

She helped him up, brushing a bit of dirt from his shoulder. He couldn't help staring at her like she was a dream. A sweetness flowed off her that made his heart rate rise, and the drive in her eyes intimidated him in the best way. She looked like she took no crap from anyone.

"Hey, do you know where Libby Hall is?"

He snapped back to reality. "Yeah, it's right over there." He pointed off in the opposite direction. "Why?"

"It's my first day," she grinned, "and I got a bit lost trying to find my dorm."

"Oh, welcome!"

"Thank you." She paused. "Sorry, you said that way?"

"Yeah...you go around the corner and—"

She watched his hand with extreme detail, which for some reason made him smile. "Here, actually, I'll just show you if you want. It's a bit far."

"Thanks, that would be great!"

"I'm Lonnie, by the way." He stuck out his hand.

She chuckled, shaking it. "Nice to meet you, Lonnie. I'm Hannah."

Present day.

Hannah's arms knitted a straitjacket around Lonnie's chest as she pressed her head against his.

A fresh tear fell down his cheek and onto her hair. "How did you get here?" He listened as her heartbeat drummed through him.

"I don't know..." she sullenly replied.

Suddenly Lonnie felt his body lift into the air. Before he realized what was going on, he was slammed into the ground, and Jamie was on top of him.

"What are you doing!" Lonnie yelled, shoving him to the side. He scrambled to his feet, puffing his shoulders back in a defensive motion. Jamie looked crazed, his face bright red and coated in layers of tears and dirt.

"This is all your fault!" Jamie howled, swinging his fist at Lonnie.

"What are you talking about?"

"I overheard them. They said this was all for you! That we were here because of you!" His glossy eyes twisted into daggers.

Lonnie shook his head. "I don't know what you're talking about! I just woke up here."

"That's a load of crap! You're lying."

"Why would I lie about that? I don't even know what the hell we are doing down here, let alone who put us here." Lonnie looked to Hannah for support, but she dropped her gaze. Confused, he took a step back, feeling suddenly claustrophobic.

"You put us here, just admit it!" Jamie growled.

"Okay, seriously. I don't know what you're talking about," Lonnie stammered. "One minute I was at a party, and then I woke up here in a cage."

"Liar!" Jamie ran at him, shoving Lonnie into the wall, and

then they tumbled to the ground. Jamie pinned Lonnie into the dirt and drove a knee into his chest.

"Stop!" Hannah ran over to break them apart, but they were like two feral dogs going at it.

"They said this was all for you!" Jamie muttered, digging his knee deeper. "What does that mean?"

"Who? I swear, I don't know what you're talking about."

Although fairly the same size as Jamie, Lonnie found it impossible to move. Jamie's strength was fueled by a rage that Lonnie was no match for.

"Tell me!"

"Get off of me."

"What are the trials?"

"Trials? I don't know! What—" Lonnie's mind flashed back to what the plaques had said. "Wait, hold on."

The pain from Jamie's knee started to make Lonnie dizzy. He could hear Hannah's screaming, but it did nothing to stop Jamie. Lonnie grabbed a handful of dirt and chucked it into Jamie's eye. With a bellowing scream, he fell back, giving Lonnie enough time to roll over and pin him to the ground. With a knee on either leg, and hands pressing down on Jamie's palms, Lonnie held him to the floor as he squirmed and tried to free himself.

"Just stop, Jamie!" Lonnie said sternly. "I don't know anything, I swear."

Jamie arched his back as if possessed and swayed frantically from side to side. He let out a scream so visceral that Lonnie began to wonder if Jamie had lost his mind.

"Jamie, please. You know me. I would never do this to you."

Jamie went lax, his limbs suddenly light against Lonnie's.

Is he done?

Lonnie waited for another outburst to occur, but instead, Jamie's face contorted and hot tears shot from his eyes.

"I was in there for two days," Jamie stuttered hysterically through a waterfall of tears.

"Two days?" Lonnie's chest tightened. "Two days in where?"

Hannah rested her arm on Lonnie's back, startling him.

"They kept us in a cage," Hannah explained. "It was horrible and full of discarded bones and rats."

"They treated me like an animal," Jamie whimpered.

Lonnie recalled seeing a similar cage earlier with the pile of discarded bone fragments sticking out of the ground. Just the thought of it made him feel sick. Turning to Hannah, he rested a hand on top of hers and gave it a squeeze. Brushing himself off, he rose to his feet and offered a hand to Jamie, who was still crying on the floor. Through blurred vision, Jamie reached out and took it, to which Lonnie wrapped his arms around him.

"You're okay," he whispered.

Jamie fell apart onto his shoulder, letting snot run down the side of Lonnie's back. The smell of feces lingered on his clothes, which made Lonnie momentarily gag, but he kept it down.

"I'm sorry." Jamie sighed.

He took a step back, placing himself in front of them. The light overhead shone onto their faces, giving Lonnie a proper glimpse at the state they were in. To his shock, Hannah's hair was caked in dirt, and so were the insides of her nails. Bits of her jeans had been torn near the knees, and the purple sweatshirt she wore was bloody at the elbows like she had taken a tumble. Similarly, mud was plastered against Jamie's grey joggers, and his eyes looked red like they had gotten infected. A ripped piece of his black long sleeve was wrapped around his arm, which showed a red blotch blooming through. And like his own, Lonnie caught the prick marks on both of their fingers.

Why do they want our blood?

Nothing about any of this made sense. Lonnie took a lap around the room, as Hannah consoled Jamie. His mind raced from all this new information.

Trials. What do they know of these trials?

"So you saw them? The people who said they sent you here because of me?"

"Yeah, but they wore these dark green cloaks," Hannah said. "I tried to make out their faces, but the cage was so dark."

"This is unbelievable."

"I'm sorry," Hannah said.

"No, it's not your fault." He stroked his chin. "Wait... so then how did you get out of the cage?"

Jamie looked up and gave a coarse cough. "It opened on its own."

"What do you mean?" Lonnie stared. "They just let you go?"

"There was a loud alarm, and then the door shot open."

"Yeah, I heard that too." Lonnie looked up at the ceiling and suddenly noticed another one of the little red dots shining above him. "Jamie, what did they say about these trials?"

Jamie looked frozen as he tried to recall. "They said the trials wouldn't be possible without us and," Jamie peered up at the camera, "then they said thank you for your sacrifice."

Clink.

A noise echoed off in the distance, causing them to jump. Lonnie covered his mouth, ushering them all to the corner of the wall. Carefully, he peered into the archway just in time to hear a chain rattle across the ground.

The three of them stared at each other, all sharing the same horrified expression. The sound of a gate rising echoed as pieces of rusty metal rubbed against each other. Then silence.

"It stopped," Jamie remarked.

Lonnie peered down the tunnel to see a tiny white blur in the distance.

Is that what I think it is?

He slowly stepped back. "We have to go."

Hannah grabbed his arm. "Why, what's going on?"

A deafening roar ripped through the tunnel.

"Run!"

Lonnie, Hannah, and Jamie bolted down the tunnel as, far behind them, the sound of paws stomping on the dirt erupted.

"Which way?" Jamie pointed to the three archways surrounding the hall.

"This way!" Hannah took their hands.

Running down the rightmost path, their feet kicked up clouds of dust that made it hard to breathe. Hannah grabbed her neck, slowing to cough.

"We can't stop." Lonnie grabbed her wrist and ran. Behind them, a crash echoed. Like something had slammed into a wall.

"Don't look back!" Lonnie begged.

The sound of paws sprinting started up again, only a hundred or so yards away, if he had to guess.

"We can't keep running!" Jamie yelled.

"What else do you suggest we do?" Lonnie asked.

"It's a dead end!" Hannah slammed her hand against the wall, and looking around, Lonnie realized she was right.

We're so dead.

The room they had just entered was covered in brick from

head to toe, with no more archways except for the one they just came through.

"We have to go back!" Hannah yelled.

Lonnie stared back at the entryway. "There's no time."

His heart froze in his chest as he watched their pursuer creep into sight from a few feet away.

"Oh my god," Jamie yelped.

"Shhh. Don't move," Lonnie whispered.

Standing under the archway was a white tiger. Its fur hung mangled, with patches missing in clumps along its body, and a metal collar wrapped tightly around its neck. Drool fell from the tiger's mouth, and Lonnie noticed its ribs protruding from its chest. It was clearly starving, but it stood still as if waiting for something.

"Why did it stop?" Jamie whispered.

"It's blind," Hannah stuttered. "It's because it's blind."

She's right.

Where its eyes should have been sat two silver pools above burn marks that spread down to its nose. Like the beast had been dunked in acid.

"They took its eyes," Lonnie said, disgusted. *They burned them out.*

"To make it fair." Hannah shuddered. "For us."

Jamie shook his head. "That's sick."

The tiger let out another roar as it slowly paced into the room. Its head cocked to the side, intensely listening. It swatted out its paw and missed the three of them by only a few feet. Lonnie prayed that his friends' pungent smell of feces and mud would blend them into the walls. But either way, it wouldn't make a difference. If the animal swatted them by accident or on purpose, they'd still be dead.

"Blind or not," Jamie hissed, "we need a plan."

They backed into the wall, but the gap was still closing fast. As Lonnie hit the bricks behind him, he felt an object in his pocket. Slipping his hand into his pants, he pulled out the heavy pocket watch.

This could work.

The tiger now stood face-to-face with the three, its breath hitting their faces like hot garbage. As it primed to charge, Lonnie bent his arm back and tossed the watch as hard as he could through the open archway.

Crash.

With a bang, it slammed into the wall in the next room, shattering as it fell to the floor. The tiger paused, now only inches from their faces. Then in a quick turn, the beast leapt into the next room, then out to the hall.

Lonnie let out a slight sigh.

"Oh, thank god!" Jamie relished, wiping sweat off his brow.

"Shh," Lonnie gestured to his lips. "We have to move."

Slowly, they crept from the room and into the open hall. On the ground, Lonnie leaned over and picked up the remaining pieces of his pocket watch from the floor. Apparently, the tiger was hard of hearing as well as it had seemed to run right past the broken watch. Lonnie turned it over, and to his disappointment found the top completely destroyed, with both hands dangling from the now open glass.

"Come on, let's move," he said, shoving the broken watch in his pocket.

Swiftly, they made their way in the opposite direction of the tiger.

"Where do we go?" Jamie whispered.

"As far away from that cat as we can," Lonnie answered.

They continued walking straight down the hallway. Hannah took to the front, leading them on at a steady pace. Her hands rubbed along the walls as if searching for clues, as Lonnie and Jamie drudged along behind, trying to support their aching limbs.

"You've been gone this long. So, your parents must be looking for you by now, right?" Lonnie asked Jamie hopefully.

"No, they aren't." Jamie sighed. "When the people kidnapped us, they made us text our parents that we were coming down to visit you for awhile. You know—to help you settle in."

"I see." Lonnie watched Hannah walking ahead of them, her arms swinging with great stride through the tunnels, her pace never slipping. "I thought you said you slept in a cage," Lonnie whispered to Jamie. "Where does she have all this energy?"

"I don't know. Except she wasn't in there for very long."

Lonnie slowed and gave Jamie a questioning look. "What do you mean? You said you were in there for two days."

"Yeah, I was." Jamie glanced toward Hannah. "But they took her the first morning, and I didn't see her again until today."

"What?" Lonnie said. "Maybe they just kept her somewhere else."

Jamie shook his head. "All I know is that she didn't seem the same when she came back. And she wouldn't talk to me about it."

A faint roar sounded in the distance, reminding them to whisper even quieter.

Lonnie glanced around and squinted. "Hey, what's that?" he said, pointing.

In front of them stood a gated archway. Getting close, Lonnie looked through it to see a similar cage to the one he found earlier, but this was more decrepit in every way. In the corner lay a worn-out mattress slathered in dirt and mud. Beside it was a metal bucket propped in the corner along with crushed water bottles scattered about. Similar to the other cage, bone chunks were embedded in the dirt and the gate door was open.

What kind of animal would they keep in here?

"This is where they kept us..." Jamie sputtered out.

"They kept you in here?"

Jamie put his palms to his face, letting out a muffled scream. "How am I back here again!" Banging his head against the bars, he fell to his knees and let out a silent sob as Lonnie patted him on the back.

"It's going to be okay—"

"No!" He shoved Lonnie. "It's not. This is the third time I've walked back here!"

"Jamie, you need to be quiet!"

"Are you kidding? I'm done being quiet! I'm done playing their—"

The tiger roar echoed from only a few rooms away, causing the blood to drain from their faces.

"Hurry, get inside!" Hannah whimpered.

Running to the front of the cage, they jumped through the gate and slammed it closed behind them, but it immediately swung back outward, leaving the entrance open. The sound of paws approaching made the hair on Lonnie's neck stand up.

Crap.

"Give me your belt," Hannah demanded.

"What, why?" Lonnie replied.

"Just give it to me, now!"

As Lonnie ripped off his belt, he saw the white blob emerging from the far shadows. One by one, it passed through rooms in seconds on its way to find them.

"Here." Lonnie handed the belt to Hannah, and she threaded it through the gap of the gated door, then attached it to the bar of the cage. She then looped it as tight as she could before diving away.

Bang.

The tiger threw itself at the bars, pushing with all its force to break through, its claw only inches away from the leather belt. All it would take was one calculated swing to rip the leather in half. Just one. The three watched from the middle of the cage as the beast paced around them. Occasionally, it would throw its paw through the bars and leave claw marks along the rods.

It let out another roar, this time so close it made their ears ring. Covering his head, Lonnie grabbed a bone from the ground and tossed it at the tiger. He hit it in the eye, and the creature let out another screech, its mouth snarling out drool.

"What do we do?" Jamie said.

Hannah grabbed a sharp bone from the dirt and placed it firmly between her hands like a sword. "We have to kill it."

Lonnie tried to grab her. "Wait, don't!"

"We don't have time to wait. It's the only way!" Running at the tiger, Hannah wielded her weapon and aimed for its head. But with a swipe of its claw, it knocked the bone from her hands and sliced the edge of her calf. With an agonizing scream, she flew back toward the boys, gripping her leg, which was dripping blood.

With a loud curse, she cuffed at her leg to block the bleeding, then stared at the tiger.

"Stop moving," Lonnie stated.

Sliding off his jacket, he held out one of his shirt sleeves and ran over it with a jagged bone between his forefingers, like a blade. Once the sleeve had ripped off, he wrapped it around her shin and tightly knotted it, which thankfully made the blood stop dripping. "This will have to do for now, but it's going to get infected if we stay here too long."

"Well, that didn't work like I thought," Hannah muttered.

"Maybe we don't need to kill it," Jamie argued. "What if we can trap it."

Dodging the extended paw, Jamie grabbed a bucket sitting in the corner of the room, a plan visibly forming across his face.

Leaning over the bucket, he gagged, then, taking its contents, he tossed them through the grate.

"Don't," Hannah whispered, her face frozen.

With the bucket propped in one hand, Jamie grabbed a handful of bones and handed them to Hannah and Lonnie.

"I'm not going to chase it with bones, Jamie. Didn't you see how fast it is?" Lonnie jabbed.

Jamie dug through the dirt, looking for the biggest bone he could find. Then raising it in his other hand, he looked up at Lonnie.

"We're not going to chase it. When I say so, undo the belt."

"What? You're crazy!"

"Just do it, when I say." Walking toward the tiger, Jamie raised the bucket like a shield and aimed the outstretched bone like a jousting spear. Lonnie briefly eyed Hannah's startled face before watching Jamie cross to the other side of the cage. Then, unexpectedly, a loud clanging sound filled the room. Jamie was bashing the bone into the bucket, creating the most gut-wrenching metal scraping noise. With it, he shouted, his voice cutting through the noise like a primal scream. The words were incoherent, but it was clear he was fueling the fire with his rage.

The tiger began shaking, jumping from left to right, trying to find the source of the noise. It backed away slowly, blindly throwing its claws out in front of it.

"Now!"

Running forward, Lonnie undid the belt and hastily pushed the gate wide open. Turning around, he grabbed Hannah's arm and dragged her out alongside them. The tiger was cowering on the other side of the room, but Jamie didn't stop. Walking briskly behind the tiger, he began banging the bucket again, drawing it back toward the cage. Realizing what he was doing, Lonnie and Hannah ran to either side of the door and began hitting the metal poles with the bones, creating a resonating noise.

The tiger, terrified, continued falling back until they had corralled it all the way into the cage.

"Hannah, refasten the belt!" Lonnie yelled, still hitting the bar.

Pulling herself from her daze, Hannah reached up and attached the belt back to the door. She then ran to the wall as fast as she could while Jamie continued to scream like a madman, his eyes a shade of red that Lonnie barely recognized. It was like looking at a different person. Finally falling to his knees, Jamie threw the bucket and bone to the side, completely drained, but as the noise dissipated, the tiger began to stir from its cowered position. Rage appeared on its face, and a few seconds later it charged at the gate, where it hit its head against the bars. The gate shook, but thankfully it held.

They'd trapped it.

"Oh my god, Jamie, that was amazing!" Lonnie cheered. "How did you know to do that?"

"I read that predators are afraid of loud noises," Jamie gasped. "I hoped a blind tiger wouldn't be an exception."

Their momentary relief was immediately cut off by the tiger once again charging the gate, and this time its paw descended on the belt, causing it to splinter at the edge.

"We shouldn't stay here," Lonnie said.

They hightailed it out of there, running until the tiger's hungry roar grew quiet in the distance.

"We need a plan," Jamie announced once they'd stopped.

"Yeah, no kidding," Hannah scoffed.

"I'm serious. This place takes you in circles. We could be walking around indefinitely, and I don't want to bet my life on that belt holding that tiger in for very long."

While the two nagged at each other, Lonnie reached into his pocket and pulled out the pocket watch. Tinkering with it in his hands, a bit of the broken glass sunk into his palm, causing him to yelp. "Damn it!"

He grasped his hand, letting the watch fall to the floor, and as it hit, the clock face shot off, revealing another layer hidden carefully underneath.

"What the..."

Lonnie plucked it from the floor and stared at his new discovery. Beneath what had once been a clock sat a compass.

"Hey, guys? Come look at this."

They stopped arguing and walked over in time to see the compass dial spinning around the track. Hannah snatched it from his hand. "Where did you get this?" she demanded.

"It was in my pocket."

"They let you keep this?" She raised it in the air, confused.

"They must have missed it. I don't know."

The dial continued to spin until suddenly coming to an abrupt stop on North. Lonnie tapped it with his finger, but it stayed unwavering. "I don't see how it would help though," Lonnie sighed. *Why did Mike insist on giving me this?*

Hannah looked perplexed and handed the pocket watch back to him. Stepping forward, Lonnie followed it north to the wall, where he began to push against the bricks with his hand, tracing it back toward the hallway they just came through.

"What are you doing?" Hannah asked. "And where are you going?"

Lonnie continued to stare at the walls, trying to map out the route through his head.

"What if we should follow it?"

She threw up her hands. "Follow it north? We don't even know what's at north."

"What if it's a false north? You know how big metal objects can sway the magnetic pole?" He smiled, an idea was forming in his brain. "If we follow the north, maybe it could take us to something big and metal. Like a stairwell, or an elevator, or—"

"Or another metal room filled with more horrible things to torture us," she said.

They both turned to Jamie as if he was the tiebreaker. He stared at them uncomfortably. After a long pause, he shrugged. "I think we have nothing to lose. We're going to be walking aimlessly regardless. Might as well be heading toward something."

"Fine," Hannah folded. "Let's just get a move on then."

Leading the way, Lonnie directed them down the path while staring intently at the compass in front of him. He followed the little red dial as it directed him north, and his friends trailed behind, winding around from tunnel to tunnel.

Lonnie was beginning to feel confident in this plan. The tunnels seemed newer. The group was now crossing through sections he hadn't seen before.

Maybe this was actually the right—

"Wait, what are those?" Jamie pointed to the ground and effectively cut off Lonnie's thoughts.

Along the edge of the wall were footprints. Lonnie recognized them as matching the ones the creature with whirring gears and green lights had left earlier. Seeing them closer now, they were even creepier. At first glance, the prints appeared human, but they were much too large and deep.

"I don't like this," Hannah whispered.

Crouching down, Lonnie stuck his finger into the indent it made. His hand went down to the knuckle before it reached the bottom.

"They're deep," he said in a hollow tone. Looking up, he followed the footprints with his eyes. They continued onward into the coming rooms, creating a trail that zigzagged along the floor.

"I don't like this at all," Hannah blurted. "We need to move."

Zit.

Crap, not again.

The sound froze them in their tracks. Jamie and Hannah looked around, confused, but the noise was all too familiar to Lonnie. Grabbing their shoulders, he broke into a sprint.

"Come on," he hissed.

Without questioning, they chased after him just as the lights started going off behind them. Same as before, they blinked out, one row at a time, as if driving them back section by section.

But back toward what?

Next came the gear churning sound that sent a chill across Lonnie's spine.

"Guys!" Hannah pleaded.

Lonnie and Jamie turned to see that the distance between them and Hannah had grown considerably. She was beginning to limp, and red streaks started growing on the white shirt bandage. In unison, they jumped toward her and threw her hands over each of their shoulders before continuing moving toward the light. With the added weight, their speed slowed marginally, causing the darkness to nip at their backs.

"Just leave me, I'll be fine," Hannah pleaded.

"Don't say that!" Lonnie snapped. "We are all getting out of here."

Passing into the next room, his toe dug into an embedded rock, causing them all to tumble to the floor. He grasped his knee in agony, waiting for the light to cut off around them. But it didn't.

"What happened?" Jamie said, his head swiveling around the still bright room. "Did it stop?"

"I think so," Lonnie responded, puzzled.

Behind them, the darkness barricaded them in like a wall. And in the midst of it, Lonnie noted those same green lights from earlier staring back at him. But this time, the silhouette of a tall man floated behind them.

"What is that?" Hannah covered her ears to block out the churning noise.

Lonnie stood up to face it, watching it as it faded back deeper into the darkness, its gears scraping together with that same animal cry. Then suddenly the lights began turning back on, one row at a time, revealing nothing where the metallic creature once stood except those same tracks.

It stopped again.

When Lonnie stepped hesitantly toward the new footprints, something crunched beneath his shoe. Kicking aside the dirt, he uncovered a thin wire. He grabbed it and pulled. Dirt flung off of it as the rest of the wire tugged in a line from the earth, extending out to his left and right. Following it to the nearby wall, he noted it ran into a tiny black electrical box hidden between a pair of bricks. "Why is this here?" he muttered.

Letting the wire drop, his gaze went back to the footprints, which ceased just inches from the other side.

It's not allowed to cross the line.

"Oh my gosh." He let out a gasp. "I think I understand!" He turned to look at his friends, a confident expression on his face. "It's a guard dog."

Chapter 12

The Guard

Taking the bone fragment from his pocket, Lonnie traced it through the dirt, first making a wide circle and then putting an "X" smack in the center of it. Hannah and Jamie sat behind him, staring in confusion at the drawing he had just made on the floor. Jabbing his finger, he poked a hole in the outermost ring of the circle.

"Here is where we are," he began. "And next to us is the first cage—the one you guys were in. The one the tiger is currently in, we hope."

"Okay," Jamie responded.

"Now you both have been walking around the outside ring this whole time. Which is why, when I found your footsteps, they were by the edge of the ravine. And why you ended up going around in a complete circle."

With the bone, Lonnie drew two more circles, both getting smaller and closer to the center.

"This outer circle is like a perimeter fence. You see, the first time I saw the lights turn off, I thought it was a fluke—that maybe it only stopped because I passed over this crevice." He raised the bone, drawing a zigzag line on one end of the outer circle. "But this time, it stopped without any warning. The lights remained on, and that thing stopped with it. Which means we must be here."

Pointing with the bone, he aimed at the other end of the outer circle.

"So, it works in sections?" Jamie pitched in.

"Yeah. The outer section was the tiger. That's why it had the metal collar on, to keep it from crossing the wire barrier and leaving its zone. Kind of like those shock collars they put on dogs. Then the middle section is that guard dog thing back there. It also can't cross between zones, which means it's stuck between this wire and whatever is on the other side."

"So then the inner circle is what—the finish line?" Hannah asked.

"I think that the zones have a trigger. Like a warning alarm, that we are getting too close to the exit. As soon as you walk too far, the lights start going off. Always from the center. It's like a wave. No matter how close we get, the water will keep pushing us back to shore."

"So that means the compass was leading us the right way." Jamie smiled.

"Yeah, but we can't read it if we are in the dark," Hannah interjected.

"Yeah, that's going to be a problem." Lonnie sighed. "Do either of you guys have a phone or anything with a light?"

Jamie and Hannah both reached into their pockets.

"I have half a pack of gum, my ChapStick, and an old restaurant receipt," Hannah said. "I didn't have my phone when they grabbed me."

"What about you?" Lonnie gestured to Jamie.

"I have my wallet, my dead phone, and...a lighter. I have a lighter!"

Lonnie snatched it from Jamie's hand. "This is perfect!"

"Why do you have a lighter?" Hannah accused.

Jamie gave her a deadpan stare as if the answer was obvious.

"Ah..." she redacted.

Lonnie flickered the lighter on, revealing a small flame. Shining it over the compass, he was able to read the tiny N even though the reflection of the light made it hard to see. "Good enough. This will have to do."

"And what about the guard?" Hannah swallowed.

"Run fast, I guess."

"Uplifting plan..." she said sarcastically.

Lonnie led the way, using the compass as his guide, with Hannah close behind resting one hand on his shoulder and her other hand on Jamie's. Fresh, large footprints appeared near his own, but he did his best not to alert the others. A weight was already growing in Lonnie's stomach, but if everyone was panicking, what good would that do? If he let the fear take over, they were as good as dead.

Just keep moving forward.

They traveled deeper into the middle ring, waiting nervously for the lights to abandon them. A drop of sweat trickled down Lonnie's neck as he continued forward, cruising down each corridor, expecting that metal monstrosity to be waiting just around the corner.

Zit.

The light in the next room went out, bringing them to a static halt.

Crunch.

The gear noise churned loud enough that his ears began to ring. "Go now!" Lonnie screamed.

They ran straight into the darkness. Lonnie flicked on the lighter and shone it carefully on the compass. With Hannah's hand on his shoulder, he continued going.

Making sharp turns around walls, he kept as straight of a line as he could toward the compass' red arrow. But as the light grew farther away behind them, the gear noises only continued to move closer. Lonnie briefly turned to look back and saw the green lights tailing close behind them.

"It's gaining on us!" Jamie yelled.

"We're almost there," Lonnie yelled back. *At least I hope we are.*

The compass suddenly began spinning out of control, letting Lonnie know that whatever they were running towards was getting close. But which way was the right way? He waited for the North to stop turning, but it just kept going.

"It's not stopping, I don't know which way to go!"

"Just pick anywhere!" Hannah yelled.

Without time to choose, he ran straight, clipping his shoulder on the edge of a wall, which shot the lighter from his hand, extinguishing all the light in the room.

"I dropped the lighter!"

They all fell to the floor, hastily moving their hands over the dark floor, acutely aware the gear guard was merely yards away. Reaching his hands out, Lonnie scrambled and dug into the darkness, coming up empty over and over.

"Come on, come on," Lonnie mumbled. The stubs of his broken nails filled with dirt.

"I found it!" Jamie cheered.

He raised it up to the sky and gave it a flick. A tiny hollow light filled the room, and Hannah let out a muffled shriek. Reflecting off the light, Lonnie saw the monster towering inches behind Jamie's head. It was unlike anything he had ever seen before.

Wait, is that a man?

Looking past the nightmarish details, a man materialized in the mess of rotting flesh and metal.

What have they done to you?

Patches of his skin peeled back from his face, revealing a metal frame underneath. And where eyes should have been were two metal tubes radiating out a green glow. His jaw had permanently locked, exposing two rows of blades spinning where his teeth should be; they repeatedly entangled with each other, creating that terrible grinding noise Lonnie had been hearing. Black gunk collected around the creature's hard lips, like dried blood, giving off a pungent smell of melted metal.

Like the face, the body was a metal skeleton with straps of what appeared to be diseased flesh sewn on in patterned splotches. Chunks of exposed veins nestled between metal ribs and plates of steel. Each of those plates were whirling around to pump blood to a beating heart that hung exposed in the center of the chest. On top of the rotting skin, the creature wore a torn-up beige jumpsuit with the number "1" embroidered into the right sleeve. The thing had to be at least eight feet tall, with legs oddly elongated like a praying mantis.

In the faint light, Lonnie noticed the trail of footprints behind the abomination. They were made by a set of large metal human feet, with claw-like nails stemming from where the toes should be. Attached to his body were two weathered metal arms, each breaking out into long, thin claws with ends like sharp needles, each delicately clinking against each other.

"Jamie, don't move," Lonnie whispered.

"Trying not to," he squealed.

One of the hands delicately walked along Jamie's shoulder, feeling him with his claws. Lonnie reached out a hand to grab him, but his friend was out of reach. Sweat rolled down Jamie's face. He looked like a deer in headlights, waiting for something to happen.

Without warning, the claws wrapped around Jamie's chest and punctured into his skin before lifting him off the ground.

Jamie let out a bloodcurdling scream.

"Jamie!" Hannah and Lonnie jumped forward to grab him, but they were too late. In one swift motion, the cyborg dragged him off to the nearest tunnel, the lighter in Jamie's hand flickering on and off as they went until it was just a dot in the distance. With it went Jamie's bloodcurdling scream.

"No!" Lonnie shouted.

He tried to sprint after them, but how could he? He couldn't even see his hands in front of his own face. Hannah grabbed for his arm, pulling him back. "What are you doing? We need to go."

"What!" Lonnie threw her hand off him. "We can't just leave him."

"Did you see that thing? Even if you manage to find them in the dark, what are you going to do then? It would kill you!"

Hannah was terrified. Lonnie didn't need to see her to know that. He could hear it in her trembling voice alone. Grabbing through the dark until he located her hand, he wrapped it in his. He could feel her pulse racing.

I don't know what to do, he thought. His eyes weren't adjusting to the dark, making him panic even more. His mind was racing so much that he felt he might throw up all over the floor. He jolted his hand from Hannah's and held it to his stomach. A deep pain ran through him that nearly brought him to his knees. His eyes began to water, and his breathing grew shaky.

"I don't know what to do," he said through rapid huffs of air.

"Screw it," she said. "Give me the compass."

With a reluctant face, he felt around for her hand and slipped it to her. "It's no use; it's pitch black in here."

"Just give me a second," she spit, shaking the compass in her hand before eventually lowering it down in defeat. "There has to be a way."

All Lonnie could think about was the image of Jamie's body being lifted into the air like a doll. It repeated over and over, alongside his echoing cry for help.

I'm so sorry, Jamie.

"Wait, look over there!" Hannah shouted, twisting Lonnie's body toward a spot in the darkness.

"What am I looking at?"

"There is a light. Come on!"

Hannah placed Lonnie's hand on her shoulder, and before he knew it, they were running toward a faint glow way off in the distance.

"Are you sure this is the right way?" he asked.

Suddenly the gear noise sounded again, going off somewhere. Both their heads turned briefly before the two picked up the pace.

"It's definitely better than staying here," she spat.

Lonnie thought the sound of the monster would strike fear into him, but in the moment he found he just was exhausted. After a few more hallways, the faint glow grew into a beacon. *Hopefully we aren't running toward another guard.*

Swinging through the remaining opening, they finally burst into a new room. A dangling bulb hung from the center, which at this point might as well have been the sun. It buzzed quietly.

"What is this?" Lonnie looked around in sudden alarm.

They had walked into a cylindrical room, with the ceiling spanning at least a hundred feet high. Archways spread around the whole exterior wall, flooding in the darkness from the outside. In the center of the floor stood a square pillar that spanned up to the ceiling, its exterior covered in a newer color of brick than the rest. Hannah pulled out the compass from her pocket and watched as the dial spun around infinitely.

"This has to be the right spot." She carried it around the room, disappearing behind the pillar.

Lonnie looked out past the archways. A growing feeling set in that he was being watched. Backing to the pillar, he swiveled his body in an effort to keep an eye on all the openings.

"I don't like this!" he said, attempting to keep his tone calm. Nobody answered.

"Hannah?" he whispered.

Again, no answer. Slowly he made his way around the pillar, his feet digging into the ground with each step.

"Hannah, where are you?" He started to turn the corner when a hand reached out and grabbed his shirt. He opened his mouth to scream, but a second hand covered his mouth. It was Hannah.

"Lonnie, look!" she said, tugging him by his collar.

In front of him, tucked within the brick and mortar, was an

elevator shaft that spanned up to the ceiling. Though instead of a metal door, it was paired with a rusty gate that swung open with a handle.

"Come on!" Hannah opened the door and gestured back to Lonnie.

Lonnie went to step in when he heard something. That familiar gear sound played quietly in front of him. Scanning the darkness, he heard the creature moving. He was fast. The noise spun around him, starting in the front and then creeping its way to the back of his skull.

"Hurry!" She pulled at his arm, but he didn't budge.

"Just a second," he stammered.

Hannah found an old battery-powered lantern on the ground and turned it on, sending light flooding through the elevator. Next, she looked for the button panel but was unable to find any. She searched every wall until she came across a crank. Giving it a slight turn, she got the elevator to rise. "Lonnie, come on. I got it working."

He squinted. In front of him, he could have sworn he saw a pair of green lights, but they quickly vanished. His gut was hurting, like he knew he should leave, but he couldn't bring himself to move. Then the green lights appeared again, only for a moment. This time two archways to the left.

"I see you!" Lonnie yelled. "What did you do with Jamie?"

For a second, silence fell. Lonnie tried to appear confident, but his eyes darted back and forth as a wave of nausea ran through him.

Where are you?

The silence was followed by a sudden shattering of glass. Pieces of bulb fell on the floor, leaving the only light source coming from the lantern. Feeling exposed, Lonnie stepped into the elevator and slowly reached for the gate. The gear churning noise turned on, and that distinct burnt metal smell reappeared in the air. With a swift motion, he threw the gate closed in front of him.

Crash!

Out of the shadows, the monster threw himself against the elevator, his claw-like hand slipping through the holes in the gate.

"Go, go!" Lonnie screamed.

Hannah began turning the crank, lifting the elevator off the ground and dragging the monster up with it. With the light from the lantern shining on him, Lonnie got a clearer look at the creature's face. The skin was rotting and old, like it was worn down under a heat lamp. The green eyeholes stared aimlessly at the wall, with bits of liquid leaking from his tear ducts.

"Do you think he can get in here?" Lonnie asked nervously.

As if on cue, the monster started filing his razor-bladed mouth along the gate, shredding through pieces of rods and opening more room for his body to slide in.

Noticing the ceiling above the elevator quickly approaching, Lonnie ran back and jumped to Hannah's side. Grabbing the crank, he took over. With a boost of energy, he cranked it as fast as he could, hoping desperately that the monster would get knocked from the edge.

"So close," he whispered to himself.

"Lonnie!" Hannah screamed

A clanging sound followed. Still cranking, he turned his head to see a giant hole had been cut out of the gate, and the monster now stood in the center of the elevator with one hand hanging on and the other wrapped around Hannah's waist.

"Please, don't!" Lonnie begged.

Lonnie let go of the crank and dove onto the mechanical man's arm. He pried at the claw, slowly loosening his grip on Hannah's waist. But it was no use. Raising his other arm, the monster slammed Lonnie against the wall. Then with what only could be described as a grin, he looked through Lonnie with a blank stare as he dragged Hannah to the opening. She kicked and screamed, trying to get free, but each time she only made the claws sink in deeper.

At Lonnie's feet, he noticed a sharp piece of metal that had been ripped off the gate. Unsure what to do, he grabbed it. "Hey!" he shouted toward the monster.

The creature turned to him, his body now more than halfway out of the broken gate. With a charging sprint, Lonnie launched forward and jabbed it into the monster's chest, causing him to flail. A black liquid spurted out onto the elevator floor, and his grip slipped from the elevator, causing him and Hannah to fall into the black abyss.

"No!" Lonnie shrieked.

Jumping to the edge of the elevator, he slammed his body against the broken gate, his hand catching hers as the monster fell to the floor below.

"Ah!" Lonnie screamed out in pain. His arm had landed on the torn gate metal, which sliced deep into his skin. But he didn't care. He tightened the grip of his other hand, keeping Hannah dangling in the air.

"Help!" She tried to pull her other hand to the bar but couldn't reach.

Lonnie's left hand was in more pain than he ever thought possible, and the weight of Hannah's body sunk the bars deeper into his skin. Feeling his arm go numb, he used his legs to push on the gate for leverage, then threw down his other hand to grasp her wrist.

"Hurry, I'm slipping!"

With one big pull, Lonnie lifted Hannah back into the elevator, ripping his arm from the pole in the process.

"My god, ah!"

His arm gushed blood all over his clothes and the walls, and his head immediately grew fuzzy. Without anyone turning the crank, the elevator passed the outside ceiling, then came to a hard stop, trapping them in a rocky cocoon.

Hannah picked herself off the floor and moved over to look at his arm. "Oh my gosh...hold still."

She reached for the remaining sleeve he wore and tore it along the stitching with both hands.

"Hannah..." he mumbled.

"Hold on."

Wrapping the sleeve around the gash in his arm, she tied it into a knot. But the blood continued leaking out.

"Crap, it's not tight enough!"

Untying the previous knot, she stretched out both ends again, this time giving a tighter pull. Lonnie let out a whimper before she tied it off.

"Thanks..." he whispered, knowing he was losing his focus.

"Hey, stay awake!"

Lonnie grew faint as he leaned against the wall. In the light of the lantern, he saw his blood splattered along every wall and the floor. It looked like someone had died here.

Am I going to die?

He huffed, blinded by the hot tears and blood in his eyes. Suddenly a loud beep blasted their eardrums. The same one as in the tunnels. Covering their ears, they waited for it to stop as the elevator shook, causing bits of dust to fall on them. They waited as one long melancholy chord continued for seconds, until it cut without warning.

"Is it over?" he asked quietly.

"I think so."

"Good."

Lonnie lay against the walls, resting his tired eyes toward the exit to the shaft. The elevator now sat still in a sort of purgatory between the two floors. In the center of it, he noticed a familiar-shaped plaque placed against the concrete. Even though his vision was blurry, it wasn't hard for him to guess what it said:

Trial #2 Completed

But of how many?

His bandage was now dripping from the amount of blood it had absorbed, making his head spin. Over and over, he tried to focus on something to anchor himself, but everything was moving so fast.

"Hey, Lonnie?" Hannah grabbed his shoulders.

Lonnie's eyes began to drift, coming in and out of consciousness.

"I'm going to get us out of here, just hold on."

Hannah ran to the crank, rotating it as quickly as she could. A splinter of light shone into the room, making him look up to see a crack forming above the wall. They had reached the next floor. The light basked on Lonnie's face, embracing him in a warm glow.

It feels so nice.

Hannah released the lever, bringing the elevator to another stop. "Lonnie, don't fall asleep!" Hannah gave him a shake.

Her voice grew faint in his ears. Like a scream becoming a whisper. For the first time in a long time, Lonnie felt at peace. He no longer noticed the pit in his stomach or a feeling of dread. Waves had subsided, leaving a calm ocean in their wake. And with it, he allowed his eyes to shut. Leaving behind this horrible nightmare.

Chapter 13

A Metal Purgatory

Hannah gave Lonnie a hard slap across the face. "Wake up!" she yelled. "Wake up, Lonnie, I swear to god!"

With a deep breath, he came to and forced his eyes to stay open. Hannah tried to tighten the band around his arm. "Your arm won't stop bleeding!" she said. "Damn it, the tourniquet's not working."

Through a half drunken gaze, Lonnie watched her pace around the room, pushing aside scraps of metal as if looking for something. At the opposite wall, she crouched down and ran her hands along the frame of the elevator.

"Yes!" she yipped, ripping something off the wall.

Running back to his side, he watched her drop a metal box in front of him, which, judging by the outside, seemed like it had been down here for a long time. The edges of the box looked rusted, causing the hinge to squeak as she undid the latch. Encased inside was a thin layer of dust, which she wiped away, revealing a white tear-away bag underneath. She raised the lantern to it and read the writing plastered on the face:

EMERGENCY FIRST AID KIT

Contents include: stainless steel medical scissors, Band-Aids (varying sizes), soap wipe, cotton swabs, antiseptic toilette, tweezers, bandage (1 roll), and first aid kit instruction manual.

She threw the contents onto the floor and frantically searched. "No," she growled. "Where's the sewing kit?"

Lonnie mumbled, feeling he might fade again out of consciousness when she jumped back to his side and tilted his head upright.

"Hey, stay with me!"

Her eyes grew teary as she peered around the room. Her face gave the impression that she was searching for a miracle, but after the night they'd had, that was surely a big request. Eventually, she leaned against the wall next to Lonnie, both of them probably looking like they had crawled out of the pits of hell. After a moment, though, Lonnie caught her staring back at the metal box, with curiosity building on her face.

Pulling the lantern near, she shone it down to reveal a tiny dark green bag hidden in the corner of the box. Picking it up, she pried open its Velcro strap and dumped the contents onto the ground.

"No way," she gasped.

Sitting in front of her were two flare sticks.

"Yes!" she cheered.

Lonnie grunted in response, blood still dripping down his arm.

"I got it," she announced. "Just hold on one more minute."

Hannah removed her sweatshirt and attempted to rip off one of the sleeves. "Come on," she muttered.

But the fabric was too tough for her to tear. Looking at the pile of supplies on the floor, she grabbed the medical scissors and began cutting her sweatshirt off. With the sleeve now detached, she threw the remainder of the top on the ground then rushed to wrap the sleeve around his bicep.

"Wait..." Lonnie mumbled.

She ignored him and proceeded to pull both ends upward as hard as she could, strapping them to his arm. With a finishing pull, he let out another wheeze, then went silent. The blood momentarily stopped dripping, and Hannah ripped off the previous bandage that had been caressing the wound.

Wiping away bits of blood, she saw a hole piercing through the edge of his forearm. "Oh wow." She put a hand to his cheek. "Alright, well...it's going to be okay." Raising the lantern, she grabbed a handful of medical wipes from the dirt.

Lonnie felt some warmth return to his face as the blood stopped rushing from his arm, but he knew he was far from okay. He could barely keep his focus stationary for more than a few seconds at a time.

Hannah, on the other hand, had a determined look about her. She had never seemed more confident. Like her whole life had been leading up to this moment.

Lonnie watched as she used her teeth to rip off the top of a package and pulled out a single sanitizing wipe. As she reached for his arm, he recoiled, causing her to sink her fingernails in. Pulling his arm forward, she jammed the wipe into the gash and rubbed it intensely around the wound.

He bit his tongue around a scream and tried everything in his power to get away, but she wouldn't allow it.

"Stop moving, you're going to get infected," she commanded.

He froze, taking in her words as if he were a child being told off by their parent. She continued to clean his arm, moving much faster now that he finally stopped resisting.

Ripping open another wipe, she cleaned his skin until it was all but raw, then threw the bloody wipes away. Lonnie felt sick. The smell of disinfectant floated into his nose, making the thought of hurling seem extremely pleasant. But he resisted.

Hannah picked up her sweater and proceeded to cut off her other sleeve, wrapping it around the handle of the scissors. Then with yet another wipe, she scrubbed the scissors until they shone.

"Okay then," she huffed, picking up one of the flares off the ground.

Giving a quick snap, she cracked off the end of the stick, resulting in sparks flying around the room. A red hue covered the walls as their shadows bounced along it. A tiny, deep red flame sprouted from the opening on the stick, and Hannah roasted the scissors over it. She waited until the metal turned a nice light red color, then kneeled down by Lonnie's arm and slapped the flat edge of the scissors against his wound, causing the flesh to sear.

Lonnie jolted, his eyes opening wide as he screamed.

Hannah chose to ignore it; her eyes were too focused on his arm. Her one hand held the scissors in place as the other pushed down on his chest, restraining him against the wall while using each of her knees to pin his legs to the dirt. "You need to stay still!" she yelled at him.

Going to the back side, she again pressed the scissors down tightly, causing the smell of burning flesh to fill the elevator shaft. Lonnie was in hell. Agony coated his body as he sat there helpless. He looked at her, eyes pleading for her to stop, but she continued going until he let out one final holler. With it, his head sunk down, falling unconscious.

———

Eight years ago.

The sound of shattering glass awoke Lonnie from his sleep.

What was that?

Still groggy, he tiptoed from his bedroom door, taking each step with caution. The moonlight shone in from the skylight, creating a white hue over the stairwell, and Lonnie's shadow illuminated the maroon wall as he made his way down the stairs, hugging the handrail as he went.

"Monica!" Mr. Grambell criticized from across the foyer.

"I said I was sorry," she responded.

Lonnie's curiosity drew him closer until he found himself hovering at the other end of the kitchen door.

I should go back to my room, he thought.

Instead, he pushed on the doorframe ever so slightly, his feet planted to the ground.

I really shouldn't.

Too late... He found his mother on her hands and knees, her face a crumbled mess as she cleaned chipped pieces of glass from the floor. Below her, a red stain raced across the white tile, spreading to all four corners of the room. It must have been red wine. Though judging by the gash on her palm, blood was not entirely ruled out of the mix.

An open bottle of wine sat on the island, but no glasses accompanied it aside from the one broken into a million pieces on the floor. Lonnie's mother's black funeral dress looked scuffed from her crawling on the ground, and her mascara had long since ran down her face. She might have been drunk, but it was hard to tell. Her movements were spasmodic, but this was a spasmodic-inducing kind of day.

Mr. Grambell, on the other hand, was a statue, his stiff face staring down at his disintegrating wife with anger, watching as she cleaned the mess that had now spread to the edge of the wall. His tie was loosened but still wrapped around his neck. A splotch of wine had fallen onto his white button up, but he didn't seem to care. His attention was entirely focused on Lonnie's mother.

"I can't do this," she whimpered.

"We don't have a choice," he bit back.

She raised the piece of glass towards him with malice filling her eyes. Tears dripped down her face. "You said it would be fine!"

His voice softened. "You know I have no control over it."

"My boy's dead!" She began falling to the floor.

Mr. Grambell carefully lifted the shard from her open hand as she collapsed. His eyes seemed kinder to her, like a sense of guilt had overcome him. Lonnie felt a tinge of pressure build in his chest, watching them. Without realizing, he had tugged at the edge of his pajama sleeve, curling it up within his palm.

I really should go back now.

He turned back to the stairs, ready to move, but his feet didn't follow. They couldn't. He stood glued to the doorway, his ears burning at the sound of his parents' voices.

By the time he looked back, Mrs. Grambell was once again cleaning the floors, a paper towel roll wrapped in her hand.

"Monica, stop," his father said. "We'll have someone clean it in the morning."

"No, I can clean it now," she spat back, wiping the wet

towel across the floor. But as she did so, a fragment of glass shot into her finger, causing it to bleed. She let out a yelp, pulling the gash to her lips.

"Okay, enough of this. Get up..." Mr. Grambell grabbed her arm.

"This is all too much." She ripped her arm out from his reach.

"Of course it's too much!" he shouted. "Our son is dead! Do you think I don't know that?"

She stood and brushed past him, grabbing a fresh wine glass from the cupboard. She then proceeded to pour herself a drink that instantly went down her throat.

"I mean, my god, what do I even tell people?" She almost laughed with insanity.

"We have our story," Mr. Grambell said monotonously.

She stopped drinking for a moment and just looked at him, glaring at this man like she was meeting him for the first time in her life. A stranger in her kitchen.

"I can only tell so many stories," she said quietly.

"I know. They know that." He paused long enough to take the wine glass from her and take a swig himself. "That's why they want us to send Leonard away."

"What?"

"Monica, he's a child! He can't know these things. And we can't risk you telling him."

"Wait, let's talk about this," she pleaded.

"It's already decided. We'll have his things packed in the morning. I'll make the call tonight."

Lonnie's head buzzed from all the thoughts racking his brain. Then his father started walking to the door. In a panic,

Lonnie hid around the corner of the wall as the kitchen door swung open. Lonnie held his breath as a single tear fell down his cheek, but his father didn't seem to notice him. He just continued marching up the stairs until he disappeared into his bedroom. With the door shut, Lonnie could make out a muffled conversation on the phone, but the noise was overpowered by a quiet weeping that had started in the kitchen.

Lonnie went back to the closed door, where his mother was wasting away on the floor in front of him. Snot ran down her lips, and her cheeks were a rosy red. She had returned to wiping the floor, back and forth, over and over, with the same old towel. He was about to leave her be when the wood creaked beneath him. He froze.

She looked up, her gaze meeting his between the door jamb.

A look of fear crossed over him, but she didn't seem angry. Her demeanor seemed empty. Like her insides were hollowed out and this was all that was left. Her eyes reached for him, as if to say sorry, and then she immediately went back to cleaning the floor. Never again looking back up at the doorframe.

A burning smell filled his nose as Lonnie came to.

"What's burning?" he slurred under his breath. His eyes burst open as he took another whiff. The smell was growing more foul with each gust of air, making a headache stretch across his temple.

Where is that smell coming from?

He sat up from the wall he'd been perched against as the rest of his senses slowly returned, starting with the awareness that

Hannah sat beside him, followed by an itch on his back. In an impulsive matter, he reached his arm to scratch it, sending a splitting pain through his whole body. He loudly groaned, to which Hannah's hand muzzled his mouth. "Shhh, be quiet," she whispered.

He peered over at her. She looked completely drained sitting beside him. Perspiration had gathered along her face, and blood had dried all over her clothes. Her eyes didn't even turn to face his. They were too busy watching the end of the hall.

This new room looked impeccably clean. So much so that the walls and floors carried their reflections down the hall. A greenish clear tone bathed the room from a set of fluorescent lights shining above. Doors spanned either side of the wall, each almost camouflaged except for tinted windows and little numbers plastered in the upper section of each frame. At the end of the wall, another hall stood perpendicular to theirs.

Another hall, another hell I'm in no mood to explore.

Resting his hand on the ground, Lonnie felt a puddle beneath his fingers.

Raising his hand, he saw a red liquid oozing down the sides. A trail of blood streamed around his body, spreading all the way to the opened door. Lonnie almost couldn't believe it was all his. Up until today, he didn't even think a person had that much, yet there it was all spread along the floor.

Did she drag me all the way here from the elevator? The thought was instantly snuffed out by another waft of the disgusting smell. At this point, it was beginning to burn the hairs from his nose.

My god, what is that?

He raised his hand to pinch his nostrils, but the smell only got stronger. Frazzled, he began to panic, until he noticed the fresh bandage wrapped around his arm.

Oh, it's me.

Lonnie didn't feel great, but the feeling had returned to his arm, and he was beginning to feel alive again. Or at least less dead. Hannah had saved him. Though she didn't look relieved about it. Her body seemed on edge. Like she was waiting for something. Or someone.

"What's going on?" Lonnie whispered.

She turned to him, a look of fear encapsulating her eyes.

"Hey, what's wrong—"

"Are you able to walk?" she said forcefully.

"Yes—"

"Good, then we should go." She grabbed his uninjured arm and dragged him to his feet. Her grip was strong, and she walked with a sense of urgency. Lonnie tried to stop at the first door they passed, but she continued moving, her pace steadily increasing.

"What about all the doors?" Lonnie tried turning the handle, but it didn't budge.

"I tried them already," she said bleakly.

"All of them?"

"Yes," she snapped. "Just keep moving."

Lonnie proceeded to give the next couple doors they passed a quick turn anyway. But like she said, they were locked. He frowned. What the hell was on the other side? So many doors— they had to have significance. Something important had to be behind at least one. As they drew closer to turning the corner, in a last-ditch effort, Lonnie tried another, and to his surprise, it clicked. With a push, the door swung in to reveal a pitch-black room.

"I thought you said all the doors were locked?" Lonnie pulled Hannah back toward it.

Hannah didn't respond.

"Hannah, this door is open—"

Looking back, he saw her standing frozen in the corridor, her gaze staring past the corner. Lonnie rushed over to see what she was looking at, but it wasn't necessary. He already had an idea. Weakly resonating through the walls was that metal crunching.

A black trail stained the floor in front of them, the droplets of black bile stemmed from down the hall, ending in front of one of the nearby doors.

A drop of sweat dripped down Hannah's face as she grabbed at the scratches the claws had carved into her torso. A rustling sound came from behind the closed door beside them, making them both jump. The heavy grinding grew closer and would be upon them in moments. Lonnie slid his fingers into hers, gently pulling her back around the corner. Treading quickly, they went through the open door, then shut it quietly behind them.

Darkness encapsulated the room. The place might as well have been a crypt. Regretting his decision, he listened at the door for the creature approaching, only to hear him open one nearby. Feeling for the handle, Lonnie searched in the dark for the lock.

"Come on, where is it?"

His hand carefully caressed the handle of the door until he heard a faint click. A part of him was relieved, but Hannah's grip only got tighter around his arm as the loud stomping approached outside the door, making goosebumps infest the ends of his biceps.

Thomp.

Thomp.

Growing closer with each second, it was as though the grim reaper was crossing through the hall. Lonnie cupped his mouth, trying to stop the sound of his own breath.

Thomp.

Thomp.

The sound faded away, leaving no clues as to where he went. Lonnie held his breath and waited for the monster to start again.

Where did he go?

While hearing the monster made his skin crawl, the thought of not knowing where he was made him nearly quit breathing. He could be anywhere. Despising the suspense, Lonnie took a peak through the reflective tint window when the handle suddenly started rattling.

He's here.

Lonnie bit his mouth closed so hard he nearly chopped off the tip of his tongue. Over and over, the door handle jiggled, accompanied by the sound of a rusty bolt tearing through the door jamb. He couldn't see Hannah in the dark, but by the tight grip on his hand, he knew she was just as terrified as him. Neither of them dared move a muscle.

"Just move on," he whispered. "Please."

Lonnie's lungs were as flat as month-old balloons as he held his breath, his chest sinking back into his ribs. Where could he go, what could he do? The door was nearly ripping off its hinges, but the lock continued to hold. Pins and needles ran up Lonnie's mutilated arm until he wanted to vomit from the pain. He tried to ignore it.

Hannah, on the other hand, was beginning to shake. Her

hand vibrated against his, giving him a bit of a shock. He wrapped his arm around her, letting her heartbeat pulse against his. It was moving so fast he thought it might pop.

We are going to be okay, he told himself.

But part of him knew he was lying.

To Lonnie's surprise, the door finally stopped shaking. With a disgruntled stride, the loud stomping resumed, making its way to the next door. A little longer, and a bit further down the hall, he could hear more locks rattling, one after the other, as if the monster was determined to try every last one.

Feeling confident he was out of earshot, Lonnie began looking for the light switch.

"What are you doing?" Hannah whispered as his elbow jabbed into her rib.

"Help me find the switch."

Both their hands decorated the wall, moving swiftly through the dark. Lonnie's brushed against something solid, which made a quiet metallic sound. He ran his hand along it, finding it had a hollow interior.

Is this a bookcase?

Before Lonnie could reach inside, he heard a muffled click sound.

"I found it," Hannah cheered.

Rows of light strips lit up the room in front of them, revealing dirty white walls with dull ceiling tiles. A brown carpet spanned the floor that looked like it hadn't been cleaned in years. Cobwebs grew up the walls, especially residing in the corners of the ceiling. The room was bigger than he expected, more long than wide, with metal shelves spanning down two of the walls, each full to their brim with manila folders and card-board boxes.

"What is all this?"

Hannah shrugged, seemingly uninterested, and proceeded to walk past them to the far side of the room. Lonnie's curiosity was peaked. This was the first clue he had gotten the whole time he'd been here. Maybe the folders had the answers he was looking for. Looking closer, he noticed little letters spread across the shelves, starting with A and ending with Z. It was alphabetical. Excitedly, he plucked a folder from the closest shelf and read the title:

Hunter Apris: Medical Record 2010-2017

Inside he found blood reports, body percentages, DNA ratios, genealogy, and information on just about every medical visit this man had had his entire life.

Are we in a hospital?

He grabbed a couple more files randomly from the top two rows, again reading off the titles:

Hunter Apris: School Record 1981-1995
Hunter Apris: Work History 1995-2017
Hunter Apris: Phone Call Registry 2016-2017

Lonnie was beginning to feel uncomfortable. On the same shelf, he crouched down and grabbed another bundle of files.

Hunter Apris: Flight/Travel Records 1995-2017

Opening it, he found ticket receipts and flight information. Seemingly every flight this man ever took. The plane arrival times, the time of departure. Even manifests for the other passengers on the plane. Everything down to the room number the guy stayed in at the hotel. If this man moved, someone had marked it and recorded it. Lonnie was speechless. Was this the CIA? The FBI? Where could he possibly be? A bit dazed, he turned to the next file in his stack:

DECEASED

The word immediately caught his eye in a bold red font. Beneath it, read:

Nicole Apris: Dental Records 1970-1997

He stared at the name for a moment. It was a new name, but the same last name.

They must be related.

Grabbing a couple more of her folders, he noticed they all had that same red word stamped across the top. Like they wanted it solidified that she had passed. Finally, he found the file he was looking for:

Nicole Apris: Family History 1997

As he scrolled through, his finger ran down the list, page after page, until he saw what he was looking for. Page three, there it was:

Hunter Apris: First Cousin

Confused, he took a step back. His brain tried to wrap itself around what he was looking at. A whole shelf dedicated to two people. What was the reason?

"Hannah, these files... They don't make any sense." When she didn't respond, he turned to see her hugging the side of the wall. He raised a brow. "What are you doing?"

"There has to be another way out of here," she huffed, cramming her head behind the stacks of bookcases.

"I highly doubt it."

"There has to be, because I refuse to go back out that door."

Lonnie started to argue, but he stopped himself. Searching for a door seemed to give Hannah something to do. Or at least something that was distracting her. He moved on, returning his attention back to the hundreds of rows of folders.

Suddenly, an idea hit him. "I wonder..." he muttered.

Making his way down the aisle, he found himself stopping

in front of the G section. He swiped through the files with his fingers, then stopped. He found what he was looking for. Printed neatly on the tab of the folder was:

Grambell

This was it. He was so close to the answers. He slid the file from the shelf, then gasped. There, in big bright letters, was that word again.

DECEASED

But it wasn't attached to his name. Taking another glance, he confirmed what he had thought he saw. On the cover of the file read:

Benjamin Grambell: Student Record 1998-2015

He exhaled. "Hannah, I need you to see this."

"I'm a little busy," she scolded, throwing files on the floor to reach her hand behind them.

"I don't understand." He leaned against the shelf. "This is crazy."

He couldn't stop himself from pulling out a couple more folders. Each more invasive than the last. Each digging deeper into the life of his dead brother, revealing things even Lonnie didn't know. But someone sure did.

After swiping through a couple more files, a feeling of dread grew until he found what he feared. There was his name as well:

Leonard Grambell: Dreyaird Academy Therapy Record

"Dreyaird Academy Therapy Record," he mumbled.

Without even opening it, Lonnie could already see notes spewing out from the sides of the folder. He flipped to the first page:

Leonard Grambell: Therapy Session Report: 5/17/2023

Lonnie has grown more irritable as of late, growing impatient faster and refusing to do his therapy exercises. In the past, this resulted from a refusal from his parents to visit the campus. And with his graduation approaching, it is a possibility for his sudden change in temper.

His attachment issues coupled with his pre-existing GAD will bear a difficult challenge for him leaving school next month. However, he will be attending university with his two friends, so we hope that will anchor him home.

"What is this?" he said with a heavy tone.

Lonnie scratched at his wrist. A raw feeling was gnawing at his skin. He flipped a couple pages.

Leonard Grambell: Therapy Session Report: 1/03/2023

Lonnie typically goes to his friend's home for winter break, however, this year he decided to join his girlfriend's family on vacation. He refused to talk about the experience afterward, other than saying he wish he had just gone to Jamie's.

Lonnie read a couple more reports, his blood boiling over more with each page. His fingers were now racing through the papers, flipping through each faster than the last. Every page was lined with handwritten anecdotes, random observations, his interests, his hobbies, his life... His whole life was written out straight from his own mouth to the page. In anger, he threw the file on the floor, causing papers to fly every which way. Then he was back at the cabinet, pulling out a never-ending stream of files, each finding its way to the floor.

Leonard Grambell: Medical Records 2005-2023
Leonard Grambell: Household Staff Registry 2023

***Leonard Grambell: Dreyaird Academy Housing
Forms 2015-2023***

Leonard Grambell: Internal Reports 2022-2023

He paused, holding the last one between his hands. It was
thin, no more than a stack of pages thick. but he felt drawn to
it. Curious, he began peeling back the cover page when a loud
crash came from the other side of the room. Startled, he turned
to see files relocated all over the floor as if hit by a cyclone. A
bookcase was lying face down on the ground with Hannah's
hands tightly holding the edge.

"What are you doing!" he hissed.

"I found a door!" she cheered. "Help me open it."

"Okay, but can you do it quiet—" He stopped.

Looking past Hannah, he noticed the flat metal door with a
little window baked into the wall where the bookshelf once
stood. He watched as she reached for the handle and tugged the
door open, but it swung less than a foot before getting caught
against the bookcase now barricading the edge.

"Lonnie, hurry. Help me lift it!"

Lonnie took a glance at the file in his hand, then carefully
folded up the papers inside, tucking them into his pants pocket.
He then ran over, grabbing the other end of the shelf with his
one good arm. The sound of grinding footsteps quickly
returned in the hall, as if the creature was running. He had
heard them. With a slam, the monster threw himself against the
door, causing it to creak. Chills ran down Lonnie's back.

Going in front of the door, he dug his hand under the
bookcase and began lifting it. Then, falling into a crouch, he
tucked his back under the shelf and used his body as a jack lift
until the shelf was high enough for the door to open wider. On
the other side of the room, dents began to form on the front

entrance. Before long, the thing had managed to pry back the doorframe and stick his soulless face in. The long metal claws slid in like a gentle spider and slowly felt along the door until they reached the lock.

"Open the door now!" Lonnie yelled.

Letting go of her section of the bookshelf, Hannah pried open the door just enough to slide in. Behind Lonnie, a lock sound clicked, followed by the door flying open. Toxic metal stank up the room as heavy footsteps scuffed along the floor. Lonnie looked at Hannah and tried to move but couldn't.

He was trapped. Pushing harder, he began to edge his way out from under the bookcase inch by inch. Except the creature was coming too fast. He wouldn't make it in time. The closer he got to being free, the closer the monster got to carving into him. Soon, he could feel the sparks ricocheting off the monster's rotary mouth. Lonnie shut his eyes. Maybe his sacrifice would at least give Hannah enough time to get away.

"Lonnie!" she yelled.

His eyelids sprang back open just in time to see a hand reach out from behind the door. With one last shove to the bookcase, he reached for it. Grabbing his good arm, Hannah yanked him through, causing a loud thud to echo behind them. He turned around to see the monster through the thick, clear square panel of the metal door. The creature stood where Lonnie had just been, his body sandwiched between the bookcase and the door, with barely enough room to reach out his clawed arm. Lonnie blinked for a moment as he stared at the thing, realizing that in his fractured face, Lonnie could make out a sense of helplessness. A part of him felt like he should help the poor thing, but that thought passed as quickly as Hannah locked the door. Her footsteps echoed down the hall as she walked away in silence, and Lonnie followed.

After a few minutes, Lonnie glanced over at her. Hannah looked different. Mainly her eyes. Behind them was torture and anger. Things that Lonnie had never seen her wear. She was shattered. And as he stared at her, he began to think about what Jamie had said to him in the tunnel.

Where had she been those two days?

Chapter 14

The Redhead

Four months earlier.

Lonnie laughed. "You can't be serious."

"What do you mean?" Hannah smiled.

"That's disgusting," he teased. In front of them, a pepperoni pizza sat on the table, steam still rising from crust. Hannah held a slice in her hand, dressing the top with a thick layer of mustard and ranch, both combining to form a light brown hue across the surface area of the cheese.

"Maybe to you it's gross, but—"

"Maybe to everyone, everywhere." He chuckled.

She aimed a condescending stare at him, still raising the pizza to her face. Behind her, a band played on stage, sprucing up lovely renditions of beloved songs from the past. Holding the pizza precariously over her open mouth, Hannah gave him a sly cock of the head, then promptly shoved it toward his face.

"Alright, prove me wrong."

"I will not be," he pushed her arm back, "touching that abomination."

Lonnie blocked his mouth with his hands. Rising from her

chair, Hannah proceeded to run around to the other side of the table and whilst blocking him in his chair with one hand, she held the pizza outstretched with the other. "Try it, damn it!"

"No!"

"Oh my gosh, you're such a baby," she said. "Just try it."

"I'll scream!" He stared her down. "I'll do it, I swear."

"I don't believe you." She squinted her eyes.

Giving her an arrogant smile, he leaned back and opened his mouth in a mocking gesture. Except before he knew it, Hannah shoved the pizza into his mouth and gagged him, forcing him to bite down. Once he did, she walked victoriously to her chair and sat down, light beaming from her eyes.

Lonnie turned red. Forced to chew, he stared at her with venomous eyes until he became distracted by her angelic face. Framing it, her hair was strapped back into a ponytail, but the curls still managed to find a way loose, which she twirled around her finger. She watched him intensely, looking for some kind of reaction. And as he chewed the last bite, he smiled.

"It's good, right?" She nodded her head.

Lonnie laughed, dropping his head to the table and giving her a dramatic show. "Dang it, it's..." He smiled. "Yeah, it's really good."

"I told you!" She held the pizza up in the air, causing drips of must-ranch to drip on the table.

"Fine, you told me," he mocked. "Now will you please help me eat this giant pizza?"

She finally took a bite, and Lonnie grabbed his own slice and put it on his plate. But he couldn't help watching her. The enjoyment on her face as she ate her pizza was thrilling. She was thrilling. He didn't even mind that he finished another glass of water trying to wash that disgusting taste from his mouth.

As if on cue, the band started playing a song that Lonnie remembered fondly from his childhood. It was on a day trip he took with his family a long time ago. They drove themselves, which was something they rarely did, but that day, Mr. Grambell insisted. And as they drove to the boardwalk, his father had turned on the radio to an uplifting voice that serenaded the car. His mother said it was an oldie, but all Lonnie could think of was how catchy it was. His brother must have known the song because he started singing it. Looking up to him, Lonnie started singing as well, pretending he knew any of the words. His parents laughed in a warm way that he liked.

Listening to it with Hannah over pizza, Lonnie grew emotional. His eyes got puffy as a lump formed in the back of his throat, but suddenly Hannah's gentle hand rested on his. He looked down, embarrassed. But when he glanced back up, instead of pitying eyes, he saw a collected stare. She smiled and took another bite of her heinous pizza.

They walked out of the restaurant leisurely in the cool dusk air. Hannah's hand wrapped in his as they shared a joke.

"So, where do you want to go now?" she casually asked.

"I love you," he announced.

She didn't say a word, which was new terrain for her. Lonnie usually would be second-guessing himself in a situation like this, but he couldn't help feeling happy he said it. Because he meant it, and he wanted her to know. After a flash of confusion drained from her face, she finally stopped and granted him the warmest smile with glazed over eyes and blushed cheeks. She leaned in and offered him a kiss.

Lonnie had never been in love before, but somehow in this moment, he found himself sharing a breath with someone extraordinary, and he didn't want it to end. Grabbing her coat from his arm, he helped her put it on before grabbing her hand. With a twirl, she spun around it, making a stage of the sidewalk. Then they continued their walk down the block, bright smiles planted on both faces.

Present day.

As Lonnie strode behind Hannah, he noticed a small limp when she walked. The shirt sleeve he had given her was still wrapped around her leg, but it had grown bloody and damp.

Has she had this limp the whole time? Why did it take me so long to notice?

"Hannah, your leg..."

"It's fine," she said, still facing forward. "I'm fine."

"You don't seem fine," he interjected.

"Okay, then I'm not fine."

"What?" He frowned.

"Just drop it."

He reached out for her hand. "Hannah, c'mon, just stop for a second and talk to me."

Rotating on the balls of her heels, she faced him dead on. Strands of her hair dripped down her face, and dirt had begun to mix with shallow tears that had dried around her eyes. She stared at him, an intensity running through her.

"You want me to talk to you...fine. I am a mess, okay? I have never been more terrified in my entire life." She poked him in the chest. "I have been hunted and mauled, I watched you bleed out in front of me, my leg was ripped to shreds, and I was kept in a cage. Everything is wrong."

"Jamie said they took you from the cage."

"Yeah..." She paused, her voice quieting. "But I preferred the cage."

"Where did they take you?"

Her eyes turned away, unable to match his pleading stare.

"Hannah!"

Suddenly a static noise resonated from the other end of the room. Ignoring his question, she briskly walked over, leaving Lonnie speechless.

I guess that conversation is over.

He followed her down the narrow hall that shortly funneled out into a big square room. Much like the filing room, it lacked tidiness and upkeep. But instead of files and cabinets, there was only a little desk and chair in the corner. Hannah seemed disinterested by it. Instead, she beelined it toward the big steel door in the corner of the wall. Lonnie, on the other hand, decided to have a seat on the rolling chair with its fabric spewing out foam from tiny holes chewed in it by rats.

The static sound came again, drawing him to the top of the desk. On it were six stacked monitors along with a keyboard, speaker, and intercom. For a moment, the monitors flashed a black-and-white fuzz before going black again.

Must be broken, Lonnie thought.

Without a better idea, Lonnie began playing with them, mashing keys on the keyboard and giving the side of the monitor a good slap. Which again caused the static to appear, if only briefly. There were a bunch of CRT TVs with wide backs and tiny square screens. They had to be at least twenty years old. The intercom was even older. His hand grazed along it, stopping on top of the large white button on the base, which he felt a need to click.

Buzz.

Surprised, he let go, causing the buzzing to stop. Hannah turned around for a second, a sense of shock on her face. He met her gaze before leaning into the microphone, pushing down the button again as she watched.

Buzz.

"Hello?" he said hesitantly.

The quiet buzzing filled the silence. A bit disappointed, he tried again.

"Hello...is anyone there?"

He waited another moment before taking his hand off the button. He didn't honestly know if he wanted anyone to answer. What would he even say to them? And what if the people who imprisoned him answered? He looked to Hannah, who seemed antsy to leave. Her hand clenched the edge of the door handle, but Lonnie felt he should try just once more.

Buzz.

"Hello. My name is Lonnie Grambell. We are...um...trapped, and we need help," he stuttered, trying to wrap his mind around what else to say. "Is anyone there? Hello, please answer if—"

"Lonnie, this is a waste of time; we need to get moving," Hannah whined.

"Yeah, you're right, sorry." Lonnie pulled himself from the chair as Hannah pried the door open to expose the same hallway they had started in.

Great. As Lonnie approached the doorframe, he suddenly heard a noise approaching from outside. Before he could think, a metal blur passed in front of him, and claws wrapped around Hannah's waist and lifted her off the ground. In a second, they were both gone, leaving only her scream to fill the length of the hallway.

"Hannah!" Lonnie yelled, rushing for the door. But before he could get through, it slammed shut, locking upon impact with the wall. Lonnie pried at the handle, but it wouldn't budge.

He cursed. With his good hand, he punched against the metal frame until his knuckle was raw. Then he moved to kicking it with his feet until they went numb.

"Please!" he begged.

His face grew hot as he threw himself against the door. But then he remembered the other door. In a panic, he hobbled over to unlock the handle and give it a pull.

It didn't move.

"What?" he cried out. "Let me out. Just, please, just take me instead!"

He dropped his head against the door, the cool aluminum pressing against his forehead. For a second it reminded him of that silver box he had been in. What was only earlier that day now felt like weeks ago. He abruptly looked around the room, a fear growing in his gut.

It is just going to be one silver box after another? When is it going to stop?

He sank to the floor, the emotional toll growing so much his chest began to hurt.

I am a good person. I don't deserve this.

Suddenly the static came again from the computers, but this time Lonnie didn't flinch. Remaining on the ground, he let the noise continue until it eventually stopped, just like he assumed would happen. Just like before.

"Hello?" a shrill voice said from across the room.

Lonnie raised his head.

"Is anyone there?" the voice asked through the radio static.

That voice.

Lonnie pulled himself from the wall, quickly making his way to the monitors. As he sat in the chair, he grabbed the intercom. "Jamie?" he whispered. "Is that you?"

A resting buzz filled the speakers. Lonnie didn't dare move, his heart beating a hole through his chest.

"Lonnie?" the voice questioned.

A tear fell from Lonnie's eye as he listened to his friend's weakened voice. Jamie was alive.

"Jamie, where are you?" he pleaded. "Where are they keeping you?"

"Why are you here—" Feedback chopped through his words. "You need to go!"

"What, I'm not going to leave you!"

"No!" Jamie shouted. "You don't understand!"

Lonnie gripped the intercom tighter as his hands started to tremble.

"You're doing exactly what they want! Please go now," Jamie demanded.

"Just tell me what's going on, please."

Crash.

A loud slam shot from the speaker, sending a ping in Lonnie's ear. He flinched.

"It's too late, they're back!"

"Who's back?"

The buzzing noise stopped. Lonnie waited for a second, but no response came.

"Jamie, please! Where are you? And what do I do?" Lonnie began to sob into his wrist as a feeling of hopelessness nested in his head.

Jamie was alive, and he couldn't save him. Hell, he couldn't even find him.

What did he mean, it's what they want me to do?

Suddenly a bright white light shone out from one of the computer screens. Stunned, Lonnie pulled himself from his wallowing to stare.

"Oh my god," he gasped.

On the screen was a tiny brick room with windowless walls. Coats of paint had once covered the facade, but now it peeled off in strips. In the corner of the room was an intercom tucked behind a thick pane of glass. And in the center sat Jamie, his face fifty different shades of red and his wrists torn to shreds by the shackles resting on them. He looked so delicate in the center of the floor. His body withered like a flower trying to push its way through a crack in the asphalt.

"Jamie!" Lonnie yelled once more into the intercom.

Jamie could not hear him or, if he could, he chose not to acknowledge it. Lonnie extended his arms over the keyboard, trying every combination of buttons he could think to click. But subconsciously, he knew it wouldn't do anything. It probably wasn't even connected. But it made him feel like he was doing something, aside from rotting away in yet another room.

Another screen turned on, revealing an identical cell-like room. Only this one was empty. Lonnie watched it, confused. The buzzing returned to the intercom, but Lonnie had a gut feeling not to grab it. Sitting hypnotically, he watched the door come to a stop at full swing. Followed by the most hollowing scream.

Lonnie flinched.

Looking closer at the computer screen, he saw a bundle of green cloaks striding into the room. In their arms was Hannah, her body convulsing as she tried to pry herself from their grip. They proceeded to walk her to the center of the room, where they forced her to kneel by two empty shackles chained to the floor. Lonnie tried to watch, but the door on the video had begun to block a significant chunk of the screen.

What he could see, however, was that Hannah looked enraged. Her teeth flared out as she spit violent words. The first shackle had been placed on her left arm when she decided to slam it into one of the green-cloaked men's heads. A loud thud sounded from the speaker, but he didn't go down. With a hasty swing, the man struck her on the face. Holding her arm down, the other cloaked being shackled her to the floor. With both hands tied, Hannah flung her body forward, trying everything in her might to get to the open door, but she was stuck. The cloaked men slowly vacated the small room by walking along the outer edge. With her outstretched hands, Hannah tried to grab them, but they were just out of reach. Until eventually they made their way through the door, leaving her alone in the cell.

"You promised!" she screamed, as the door closed behind them.

Her anger quickly melted as she took a survey of the room. The setting of her circumstance must have set in because her furrowed brows sank only to be replaced almost instantly with pleading eyes. She looked toward the camera, her face getting as close to it as the shackles would allow.

"You're liars!" She pulled at her shackles. "You lied—"

The audio cut.

Lonnie's hands nervously tapped the desk as a silenced Hannah continued to yell at the camera.

What is she talking about? And who is she talking to?

In that moment, Lonnie felt something pinch against his thigh. Reaching into his pocket, he pulled out the papers from the other room. He opened them.

"Internal Reports," he read aloud.

Report #1: Date: 8/20/2022

First time seeing Lonnie today. First impressions: a bit awkward, but in a nice way. Doesn't talk very much in social settings and has very few friends. Does not have much confidence and seems inherently easy to motivate.

Report #2: Date: 10/24/2022

Lonnie feels like his parents tried to get rid of him, which is why he thinks he is at this school. I have no evidence to believe he assumes an alternative reason. Lonnie is applying to colleges, his main objective is Johns Hopkins University, which he hopes to attend with his best friend Jamie.

Lonnie flipped through a couple pages.

Report #12: Date: 3/7/2023

Lonnie has been accepted into Johns Hopkins University. He plans on attending in the fall. Jamie has offered to let him stay at his house for the summer, might become a problem.

Lonnie tried to think of an appropriate response, but he couldn't even wrap his head around it. The rest of the files were records, data, logs...but this. This felt more personal. Someone had been stalking him for almost a year, and he had no idea. He had never felt more violated and couldn't help thinking, *why me?* Why did they even care about his insignificant life or the way he lived it?

He felt sick.

"Hello..." A voice sounded through the speaker, snapping

him from his mental flux. "Hello there, Lonnie," the distorted voice said malevolently. "Quite a night you've had, isn't it?"

"Why are you doing this to me?" Lonnie asked. "Why did you take my friends?"

"I imagine you have a lot of questions bouncing around that head of yours, but I'm afraid we don't have enough time for answers."

"What does that mean?"

A third screen lit up on the desk, revealing an overhead shot of Lonnie sitting in the chair. Startled, he turned around to see another tiny camera planted squarely in the corner of the ceiling. His blood began to boil.

"This is sick!" Lonnie blurted. "You realize that, right?"

"No, it's necessary," the voice bellowed. "It's all necessary."

The sound of water falling from a faucet took over the speaker. Confused, Lonnie looked to the corner of the screen to see water spilling into his friends' rooms. A small hole in the ceiling deposited gallons in seconds along the cell floor. His friends tried to wiggle free from their shackles, but they'd soon be held under the rising water.

"Stop this, please!" Lonnie shouted to the intercom.

Water was already beginning to pool around their ankles, eliciting pure terror riddled across their faces. He watched as they continued trying to break free from their shackles, but what good would that do? It would only postpone the inevitable. The door was locked from the outside. Lonnie again smacked the keyboard, hoping by some dumb luck that a combination of buttons would unlock the door.

"Lonnie," the voice mocked.

"What!" he said, frazzled, sweat bouncing off his nose.

"You need to choose now."

"Choose? I don't understand?"

But he did understand...or at least a part of him did. Because the second he heard those words, his heart had already ripped in half. His teeth grinded together as he watched his friends continue to struggle.

"Jamie is on the left. Hannah on the right. Decision is yours."

Lonnie clicked on the intercom, but as he tried to shout, he found his voice had disappeared. Enraged, he threw the mic onto the floor, lifting his foot to crush it, when the voice momentarily reappeared. "Better get going," the person boasted.

The line went dead, and an unlocking sound came from the tall metal door. Surprised, Lonnie turned around to find the door no longer glued to the wall.

If it had been a few minutes earlier he would've run from the room. But now he was finding himself prying his feet off the floor with each step he made.

"Why are you doing this?" he yelled toward the camera dangling from the ceiling. "I'm sick of this mouse maze! What do you actually want from me?"

If anyone should be in one of those rooms, it should be me, he thought.

But it wasn't him.

He pulled back the metal door with a quick thrust, revealing the now empty hallway. He could practically feel his girlfriend's scream still lingering in the air like a ghost. Before he knew it, his legs had started running. Where they were going was still a mystery, but he decided to trust the primal part of his brain.

The smell of death hugged the walls like a mausoleum

mixed with the thick scent of bleach. A harrowing cry suddenly resonated through a door from a couple yards away. It echoed alongside a faint clanging of metal. Had the cry been Hannah's? Or maybe Jamie's? Carefully, he approached the door where the noise had resonated. Its doorframe was marked with the number sixty-seven above a tinted window. Reaching over, he pried it open only to find himself face-to-face with a pitch-black room.

"Hello?" he whispered.

Out of the darkness, the crying noise began again, this time more clearly primal and not human. In front of him he saw two red circles cutting through the black. He jumped back against the door. But whatever it was stood still, watching him.

Okay, so clearly not Hannah or Jamie.

He should leave while he still had the chance, but he couldn't. His feet remained planted to the floor. Moving his palm along the wall, he searched until he found the light switch.

Click, click, click.

With a flicker, the lights powered on, revealing a metal bar a mere few feet from his face. The bars spanned to the ceiling, creating a cell in front of him. Looking carefully, Lonnie tried to see what was inside, but the lights didn't reach the back of the room, leaving a shadowy corner for the thing with the red eyes to hide in. Lonnie stepped closer to the cage.

Slowly, the red glow moved out of the shadow until the creature's frame illuminated under the ceiling lights. Lonnie stared.

Similar to the monster in the tunnels, this man had been disfigured, his pieces taken out and replaced with new ones. Even still, he seemed much more put together than the other one. Instead of metal tubes for eyes, they appeared human, aside from the fact they had glowing red irises. The sides of his mouth had been infused with shards of metal sharp enough that they cut his lips every time he closed his jaw. This left dry blood stained along his cheeks and teeth. Lonnie winced. It was horrible. Disgusting. Tragic. He peered closer at its arms and legs, which had patches of metal growing under the skin, causing it to stretch and tear. The wounds oozed out a black paste around the man's remaining skin that stood pale in contrast, like it hadn't seen sunlight in years. His body was wrapped in the same beige jumpsuit as the other creature, but this time with the number sixty-seven sewn into the sleeve.

What the hell? Who would do something like this?

The sight made him want to throw up. Lonnie looked around and noticed a file hanging by a clipboard on the side of the cage. Keeping his gaze on the creature, he grabbed the file and backed slowly away from the bars.

Nanotech Implantation in Human Genetics
Subject #67
Active Experiments:
Cataract Reversal Treatment - Outcome: Success
Side Effects: Distorted Pigmentation, Bioluminescence
Skin UV Resistance - Outcome: Success
Side Effects: Dries out skin, lightened pigmentation
Joint Strengthening - Outcome: Success
Side Effects: Extreme density shift in bone, too much tension in muscle leading to tears.

The list went on and on for pages, each test worse than the last.

"Why are they doing this to you?" Lonnie muttered.

The creature turned to Lonnie and threw himself against the bars, causing Lonnie to jump back against the door. The monster let out a heartbreaking yell, forming blood along the edges of his mouth. Reaching for the door, Lonnie caught him in the corner of his eye. The monster's hands hung from the bars as he continued to let out a muffled wail. Lonnie let go of the door, suddenly feeling drawn back to the cage.

As they looked at each other eye to eye, it became apparent that he had a metal collar strapped around his neck. Moving closer to the bars, Lonnie could see the faint burn marks it had made in the skin. Dried tears stained the monster's cheeks, mixing with the bloody gashes. Pity overtook Lonnie until, without thinking, he reached his hand out against the monster's face, making him jerk back.

"Whoever you were, you didn't deserve this," Lonnie said. "Nobody deserves this."

He took back his hand as another loud scream tore from the monster's mouth, causing blood to spit out. The collar began vibrating against his neck, and almost instantaneously, the monster dropped to the floor. He crawled back into the shadow, leaving a thin trail of blood drips in his wake.

"I'm sorry."

Feeling overwhelmed, Lonnie put back the folder and began to leave when he suddenly noticed the camera resting above him. In a fit of rage, he looked the camera right in the lens, imagining his eyes burning holes through it and into whomever was watching. He then opened the door and left. Only looking back briefly to see those sad red eyes watching from the dark.

This is hell.

Lonnie started running again. And with each door he passed, he could see the numbers on the doors continue to rise.

69, 70, 71...

How many are there?

Lonnie could hear the faintest cries reaching out to him from each door he passed. He wanted to help them all, but he kept on moving, letting their noises drift past him until he reached the end of the corridor, where two giant metal doors stood on either side of him.

Left or right...left or right?

"Help!" Jamie and Hannah suddenly screamed, gurgling on water in between breaths. Lonnie jerked around in confusion and noticed a speaker planted above him in the wall. He lunged forward to bang on the wall in front of him.

"I won't choose one over the other!" he yelled.

He tried to cover his ears, but it didn't help. Their voices ripped right through his hands and into his head as the sound of water sloshing over the speaker made their voices fade in and out.

"Stop! Turn it off, please!" he screamed into the void.

But if anything, that only seemed to make it grow louder. Crouching down, he began to hyperventilate against the wall, his mind growing foggy.

"I'm sorry..." he whispered.

Sitting there on the ground, Lonnie noticed a black fire extinguisher tucked into the wall. With hesitation, he plucked it from its rack and carried it over to the speaker. His arm burned from the effort, but he smacked at it. A small dent formed on the edge, but the audio continued. Letting his rage consume him, he continued bashing the wall, ripping the speaker apart until it was only a pile of wires sticking out between shards of plywood.

The audio abruptly cut, giving him a second of quiet. Taking a breath, he composed himself while staring at the mess in the wall he just created.

"What is that?" he whispered to himself.

Just below the speaker, a bit of the wall chipped away, revealing a dark gap in the plaster. Lonnie took the extinguisher and jammed it into the hole. He then pulled at the pieces of plywood until he had enough room to see inside.

From the bit of light shining in from the hall, he could make out a large boiler tank. Pulling back more pieces of wood, he kept prying away until the gap was big enough to crawl through.

"Oh my gosh..."

Pipes were positioned all around the space, each threading into the walls. And next to them was a boiler and electrical box. Feeling hopeful, Lonnie approached the pipes and, laying the extinguisher down on the floor, stared at the vast quantity of knobs.

Which one do I turn?

He chose one, but the sound of water only increased through the pipes. Panicked, Lonnie turned it back, but it didn't stop. The flow wouldn't decrease. He began to turn more knobs, but nothing worked. In frustration, he flipped around to search the room for a clue of what to do, but all he saw along the walls were more pipes tucked away, row after row. It would take him forever to figure out which one to switch.

"Forget this!"

Picking up the fire extinguisher, he began swinging at the pipes, then watched as they burst before him. He smiled as the floor began to flood. Invigorated, he kept hitting, breaking them apart one by one. Eventually, he stuck his ear against the wall and laughed when he realized that the sound of the faucet had stopped in the conjoining room. Except, looking down, the water in here had already reached his knees.

"Oh shoot," he gasped, noticing the electrical box at his hip.

He waded his way back to the hole as fast as he could and crawled through, throwing himself onto the now wet floor. As soon as he regained his balance, he ran to one of the doors, pulling at the handle. But it didn't budge. Sprinting over to the other one, he gave it a pull as well. Same result.

"What the hell!"

Behind him, Lonnie suddenly heard an electric spark. He peered back through the hole long enough to see the water now overlapping the electrical box.

Oh crap.

He broke into a sprint to a piece of dry ground. Behind him, the power box blew from behind the wall, sending a flash of electricity sparking through the water and burning out the lights. A moment of darkness filled the hall, which was quickly overlaid by a red backup light and the smell of burning copper. Looking up, he saw that the once active cameras had gone dormant along the walls.

The power went out.

He chuckled with relief. But his smile quickly faded as a thought popped into his head. He jumped to his feet.

"Wait!"

But it was too late. An unlocking sound came from the doors, sending a wave of water crashing through the hallway. Lonnie was lifted off his feet as he went tumbling back. Bracing his hands and feet against the floor, he tried to hold himself upright as the water beat over him, but he found it more and more difficult with each second. His fingers cramped as they were each individually pried from the slick surface, but he held his own, never taking his eyes off the open doors in front of him.

Finally, the water stopped coming, and he scraped himself off the ground. Immediately running to an open door, he saw pools of water spread across the floor inside, and in the center, a mess of red hair tangled on the ground. Hannah lay spread out on the brick. Wounds on her wrists bled from the force of the water pulling her against her shackled restraints. Lonnie slid across the ground to her side.

"Hey...hey. You're okay," he comforted her.

"Lonnie?" She tried to pull her face off the floor.

"Don't try to talk; just catch your breath." He put his head to hers as she shivered from the freezing water.

"I'm so sorry," she stuttered under her breath, her face contorting.

"It's alright. It's going to be okay. Let's go get Jamie."

Her foggy eyes suddenly cleared as she stared at him in utter confusion.

"Get Jamie?" she heaved.

Lonnie ignored her as he tugged at the shackle on her wrist.

How am I going to get this off?

Scanning the room, he noticed a loose brick ejecting from the wall. He stood up, leaving Hannah drenched in the center of the floor.

"Where are you going?" she asked.

"Hold out your hand as far out as you can," he demanded. Digging his finger into the wet mortar, he carved out the edges, slowly wiggling the brick out until he held it in his hand. With one big swing, he smashed it into the base of the chain and snapped it from the plate. He then proceeded to do it again with the other. Hannah wrapped her arm around his neck, and he dragged her out of the watery vault.

"What happened?" she asked, looking at the remnants of the wall with the hole ripped through it.

"Don't worry about it." Looking down the hallway, Lonnie noted that the previously closed doors were now spread wide open. More importantly, the animal noises from within were growing louder.

"What's that?" Hannah asked.

"We have to hurry," Lonnie said sternly, quickly pulling Hannah into the next room.

There they found Jamie, lying face down on the ground.

"Jamie!" Lonnie panicked. Kneeling down on the ground, he felt for a pulse on Jamie's neck.

Nothing.

"No!" he cried out.

"Oh, Lonnie." Hannah laid her hand on his cheek.

He pulled his face away. "No!" He sniffled. "Help me flip him."

Reaching under his back, they managed to lift his arm, which he had somehow managed to rip free from the shackle.

Lonnie laid his friend flat on his back and started pushing down on his chest over and over.

"Come on!" He tilted Jamie's head back and blew two puffs through his lips, then continued again on his chest. Lonnie didn't know any more than what he had seen in the movies, but he continued beating on Jamie's breastbone. About a minute passed, and Lonnie's hurt arm grew numb, but he continued going. The animal noises were becoming deafening, but he blocked them out. All he cared about was his friend.

Why did I go right?

The thought carved a hole in him as he pushed into his

friend's chest, again and again, the guilt rising inside him. Why did he go to the right first?

Hannah began to tug at Lonnie's arm.

"Lonnie, we can't stay here." Based on her tone, she'd just figured out what was behind the now open doors.

"Just give me another second!"

"Lonnie, please, he's gone. It's awful, but we need to go or we'll be next."

Lonnie ignored her, once again pulling Jamie's head back. He pressed his lips against his, giving him another big puff of air.

Euch!

Jamie's body suddenly convulsed and expelled a small pond of water from his mouth. Lonnie grinned from ear to ear as he turned him on his side.

"You're alive!" Lonnie hugged Jamie's back, to which Jamie rested his hand onto Lonnie's shoulder and coughed.

"Am I?"

Taking one of the water-loosened bricks from the wall, Lonnie slammed it against the remaining chain on Jamie's wrist, shattering it in half. Just as he did, the red light went out, replaced by that familiar fluorescent white. A low buzzing resonated from the speaker.

"Crap." Lonnie huffed. "Hannah, help me get Jamie up."

Slam.

Lonnie turned around to see the metal door had closed, shutting them in Jamie's cell, the electronic beep sounding as the automatic lock turned within the wall.

"What the—?" he mumbled.

Looking around the tiny room, he quickly noticed Hannah had disappeared.

"Hannah, what are you doing?" Lonnie yelled to the other side of the door to the hallway.

"I'm sorry," a voice squealed back.

"Open the door, Hannah!" he yelled.

"I can't. I'm really sorry. I can't risk it!"

"Risk what? Hannah, open the door right now!" Lonnie pounded on the metal.

"What's going on?" Jamie sighed.

Lonnie gave the metal door another hit before giving up and sitting down next to Jamie. His ears were burning red, and his voice growled under his breath. "She locked us in," he spat.

"Why would she—" Jamie weakly tried to lift himself off the ground.

"Wait, stop. Here, let me help." Lonnie propped up his arm behind Jamie's back. "I don't know why. All I know is we are trapped."

"We're not trapped."

Lonnie stared at Jamie as if he was crazy. "What do you mean? The door is locked from the outside. There's no way to unlock it from here."

Jamie let out another nasty cough as he pointed to one of the brick walls. "I saw one of them leave through there," he huffed.

"Are you serious?" Lonnie rested his hands on Jamie's shoulders.

Jamie raised his bruised wrists out in front of him. "I tried to reach it earlier, but I couldn't get my other cuff off in time."

Lonnie got up to feel his way along the wall. "Did you see how they opened it?"

"I think it had something to do with that lighter brick on the end."

Lonnie rested his hand on the light-colored brick before pushing aggressively into the wall. It didn't budge.

Shoot.

Running his hand along it more slowly, he felt a tiny ridge sticking out of the wall. With his index finger, he straddled it and gave a gentle pull.

Click.

Lonnie looked back to Jamie with a grin as he pulled out the secret door from the wall.

Chapter 15

Behind the Mask

The door slid closed behind them, leaving Jamie and Lonnie in a dusty cavity of the wall. Drips of water fell from the ceiling, forming shallow puddles along the dirt. The walkway was so small they had to shuffle horizontally in order for their shoulders to fit.

"Ack!" Lonnie ducked. A giant spiderweb stuck to him like wet paper. He waved his hands in the air, trying to brush it off, but eventually gave up.

"Do you see that?" Jamie pointed.

Attached to the right edge of the cavity was a metal rung ladder. Above it hung a shallow light, sticking out from a square cut into the ceiling.

"Here, you go first," Lonnie said.

Lifting him with his good arm, Lonnie helped Jamie onto the ladder. Still dazed, he wobbled a bit but ultimately pulled himself up to the top. Giving a hard push, the ceiling opened, bathing them both in a white light.

"Come on," Jamie whispered.

Seeing that it wasn't locked, Lonnie followed suit on the

ladder, managing to drag himself up with the little strength he had left in his arm. Jamie gave him a tug through the trapdoor opening.

"Thanks," Lonnie muttered, sprawling to his back in a sweat.

As the trapdoor closed behind them, an elegant rug hid it from view.

Jamie traced his hand over its elaborate pattern. "What is this place—"

But before he could finish his thought, growing voices floated from down the hall.

"Hide," Lonnie chirped.

The two dove behind an oddly shaped white object, trying their best not to make a sound. Peering around the corner, they watched as a squadron of green-cloaked men glided briskly by and into the orthogonal hallway. They appeared to be in a hurry. As they passed, the boys ducked their heads behind their blockade, and while Jamie continued to peek through, Lonnie studied the marble in front of them. After a moment, he reached out his hand to follow the curves with his finger. *Is this a dress?*

Taking a step back, he found himself eye level with a pair of carved marble breasts and an almost silk like textured dress wrapped around them. They led up to a half missing head. A single blank eye stared down at him. Where the rest of the face should be was a hole; its edges connected with a faint receding crack that traveled all the way to her protruding chin.

"Where are we?" he whispered.

Seeing that the cloaked people had scattered, Lonnie crept from his hiding spot and into the center of the room.

"What the? What is this place?"

Delicate oil paintings lined the finished wood walls, each cradled in a regal gold frame with a tiny white plaque positioned next to it. Scattered about the rest of the room were hand-carved marble and concrete statues, all at least a few centuries old. Each posed in a way that made the room resemble a snapshot of a ballroom. Spread between the statues, display cases sat on gold-trimmed podiums, their contents ranging from priceless historical documents to gemstone-encrusted Fabergé eggs.

Lonnie inched his way farther toward a piece that specifically drew his attention. It was a painting of a house. A tiny little cube with a few windows and a petite chimney spout sat in the middle of the canvas. All around it were waves. Horrible, destructive, stormy waves, each crashing around and covering it in a basin of water. The paint had begun to chip from the four walls, and shingles had already fallen from the roof. But through a little broken window, Lonnie could make out a family. Two boys and a happy set of parents. They were sitting so gently at a dining room table, living blissfully unbothered as they ate their supper, even as absolute hell circled just outside their door. Lonnie felt his nose begin to quiver as he stared at the family. What would his family have been if his brother hadn't died and Lonnie was never sent away? He imagined his parents laughing at a joke his brother had made, and he felt happy, even as the tiny glass windows cracked.

But that isn't my family. Not even at our best.

Continuing his hazy gaze, his eyes wandered to the camera located just above on the wall. It hung limp, its red light dimmed to a dull maroon.

Did the cameras never turn back on?

This drew a smile on his face. He turned to Jamie. "Hey, I think the cameras are still dead."

But Jamie was too far away to hear him, hiding behind the statue with an expression locked in a permanent shock. Which was a fair reaction for someone who had just resurrected from the dead. Lonnie strode over and knelt down next to him, subtly putting his hand on his shoulder. They didn't say anything more, but he knew the feeling was reciprocated. Jamie's face was red, as if he was choking on his emotions, and Lonnie, too, was finding it increasingly hard to remember the jovial person he once knew.

Maybe I did kill him after all. Or at least the parts that mattered.

As he comforted Jamie, he stared off to the end of the room. His eyes locked on a marble staircase against the end of the wall, almost camouflaged behind the glamour and marvel of the museum-like room. Lonnie hesitated, giving another glance to the fried cameras on the ceiling. For the moment, he felt safe, but how much longer could that last?

What do I have to lose...

"Come on!" Lonnie pulled at Jamie's sleeve.

"Where are we going?" Jamie whined.

"We're going up." He pointed to the stairs. "We're getting out of here."

Jamie planted himself on the ground, his wary eyes wandering across the floor. "You're an idiot if you think it would be that easy," he snapped.

Lonnie watched the pure terror behind every bat of Jamie's eyelids, but oddly enough, for the first time, he didn't feel afraid. Maybe he had reached his capacity for fear, or maybe he just felt he had nothing left to lose.

"We'd be idiots not to try."

Jamie choked. "I don't want to die."

"Well, you already did." Lonnie let out a quiet giggle. "So what do you really have to lose?"

Jamie went silent. As he stood there thinking about it, a hysterical laugh cracked from his lips, and without another word, he led the way to the stairs. Lonnie followed swiftly behind him, briefly stopping at the base to peek down the hall. A propped open door resided at the end, revealing a wall of monitors, each showing a static screen overlaid by the words:

NO SIGNAL

The previous squad of green cloaks stood around it, each of their hands tucked between torn wires spewing from the control panel. Sparks flew from the mess, followed by random curses from the men as they faced tiny shocks from the wires.

I guess that electric box did more damage than I thought.

Lonnie made his way up to meet Jamie at the top of the stairs.

"Wait, hold on," Jamie whispered, lifting his hand.

Faint voices carried from the floor above, forcing Lonnie and Jamie to slam themselves as flat as they could against the stairwell wall. With their backs tucked into the shadowy corner, they watched a pair of green cloaks retire to the center of the floor, their faces hidden behind cowls and green masks with white slits where eyes should be.

"I never agreed to this," the first cloak scoffed.

"I know, I know. It was never supposed to get this involved—"

"You said it was a guarantee, Diane—"

Slapping him across the face, the one named Diane yelled, "Don't use my name here! My god!"

"Sorry. I got stressed."

"Just get a grip; we need to get this under control."

Suddenly another person approached from a nearby door, seemingly out of breath. "Any sign of him yet?" they panted.

"No," the other two responded in unison.

"Well, find him, dammit!" The one addressing them rubbed at the vein popping above his nose. "He is growing impatient."

"Understood, but the cameras still aren't running."

"Then use your eyes!" the man spat. "Go, now!"

The two hurried away as the one green cloak stood at the top of the stairs, his hands gently resting on his face as he let out a deep sigh.

Squeak.

Lonnie turned to see Jamie's eyes widen at his wet shoe, its mark scuffed against the marble step. The green cloak turned to them, his white beady eyes staring out at them like an owl. Lonnie's heart nearly crawled up through his throat.

Why isn't he doing anything?

He moved closer, eyes looking back and forth as if searching for the source of the noise. The boys stay pressed within the shadow, hoping as he grew nearer that their slight camouflage would shield them. When the man reached a foot or so away, his whiskey odor practically dripped onto Lonnie's feet, and Jamie tugged at Lonnie's arm.

The man moved his head into the shadows but was suddenly stopped by a muffled voice chirping from his cloaked pocket. Pausing, he lifted his cowl up to reveal a tiny radio tucked to his waist.

"The girl was spotted in the southeast stairwell; report to all floor exit points immediately," the voice strained.

Hannah.

The man recoiled and ran down the hall, his shoes echoing as he went, growing quieter with each second until the noise disappeared. Lonnie and Jamie both let out a sigh of relief and crawled out from the corner of the stairwell. Climbing the rest of the way to the top, they emerged into the center of a cylindrical red velvet foyer. A single hall cut through the middle, which Lonnie had just watched the cloaked men pass through. And on the other end was a handful of doors forming a semicircle along the wall.

"What now?" Jamie said.

"Find an exit."

Jamie pressed his ear to the farthest door, with Lonnie following suit across the way. The door was colder than he expected, almost as if it led into a walk-in cooler.

What's in here?

Curious, Lonnie reached for the door handle. His hand began to shake when a muffled voice spoke from behind the door. It sounded agitated, as did whoever they were speaking to. Their argument stayed quiet at first, but soon enough they broke into a full-on screaming match. Turning, Lonnie ran as quietly as he could to Jamie, then found the nearest unlocked door and shoved them both inside. Leaving the door cracked an inch, he pressed his eye to the opening to keep watch on the empty hall.

The cold door he had been listening at burst open, filling the foyer with screaming. A single green cloak walked out, and the bottom half of the woman's face who wore it looked flustered. Her words were barely coherent as another voice barked something out at her. Lonnie watched the second figure make his way into the light. He was dressed differently from her. Different from everyone, actually. While the others wore forest green, he wore emerald, and his face mask looked like a crown wrapping around his head with red slits before his eyes. His hands wore black gloves, and his cloak split off toward the ground like suit flaps. He conveyed so much power in his words, Lonnie almost felt inclined to open the door, but he caught himself.

"Find him now!" the man commanded, his voice sharp like tacks.

"Yes, sir." The lady ran, the sound of a sniffle slipping from her nose. And with that, the emerald cloak briefly inspected the rest of the hall before returning to his room.

Lonnie shut his door fully and turned the lock built into the knob, not taking any chances.

"Okay, we should be safe—" Lonnie turned to Jamie, but he was nowhere to be found.

"Jamie?" he whispered.

In front of him, rows of leather chairs were arranged in a semi-circle around the room, each paired with a tiny round table and some variation of whiskey or champagne spread among them. By the back wall stood a bar, stocked to the ceiling with more alcohol than Lonnie had ever seen, the counter of which overflowed with glasses, some still filled with ice cubes. Facing the front of the lounge was a tiny square screen hanging in the center of a wall of paintings. The screen was mainly black, but in the center a single line of text stood out in white:

00:44:36

Then it blinked:

00:44:35

Then:

00:44:34

Is that a timer?

Lonnie didn't know what it meant, but the zero was getting closer with each second.

We need to get out of here now.

Below the screen, three circular lamps sat mounted to the wall. Two of which were shining a bright red, while the far right was a docile gray.

What does it mean?

Lonnie gave the dark one a quick kick, but it remained off. "I don't like this one bit," he muttered. "Jamie, where are you?" He scanned the room, but Jamie was nowhere to be found.

"Jamie," he whispered louder.

Unsure what to do, he hugged the wall farthest from the locked door and watched it with a growing sense of unease.

Jamie, you better show up soon.

He scooted back into a shadow only to feel something jab him in the back.

Spinning around, he came face-to-face with a parchment framed in the most beautiful gold frame. It looked like it had to be hundreds of years old at least, with the ink so deeply embedded in the picture that a single touch would shred the paper into nothing. From the top, it read in an elegant cursive:

The House Rules

1. A champion must be of kin to the House.

2. A champion must sacrifice their mind, body, and heart.

3. The title of House is granted to all whose lifeblood is wrought.

4. A House ritual must be completed in a third of day.

5. A House champion is not to be limited by youth, sex, or role.

6. The champion must spill the blood of a beloved.

7. The life of a champion may not be taken by their own hand.

8. A fallen champion shall gain the House nought.

9. Once a ritual has started, a body must be claimed before it can finish.

10. Break a rule, face a plague.

"What is this?" He squinted, reading it over again until the words were locked into his skull. Lonnie tried to come up with a logical reason for why it was there, but as he gazed once more around the room, it became quite clear. The memory of two blaring sirens echoed in his head as he stared at the pair of illuminated red orbs on the wall. A thin stench of iron seemed to season the air, and he was reminded of the prick of blood still blotted on his finger. He didn't know why this was happening, but one thought now filled his brain.

Am I the champion?

A tap of the shoulder from behind jostled Lonnie out of his head. Behind him stood Jamie, holding two green cloaks and what appeared to be masks.

"Here, put this on." He threw a set to Lonnie.

Still startled, Lonnie held out the robe and mask in front of him. Then, he slid the mask properly over his face. "Where did you get these?"

"I found a closet full of them over there." Jamie pointed to a door on the left of the room tucked near the bar counter.

"This is a terrible idea."

"Do you have a better one?"

Lonnie did not. Biting his tongue, he proceeded to throw on the cloak and cowl, still eyeing the parchment from the corner of his vision. Lonnie debated if he should tell Jamie about what he found, but it probably would only make Jamie more anxious.

"Alright, let's go," he declared.

Jamie unlocked the door, allowing them to peek out into the foyer. "It's empty."

"Here we go then," Lonnie huffed nervously.

As they slipped into the hallway, Lonnie caught a final glimpse of the timer in the distance before quietly shutting the door behind them.

00:40:34

Forty minutes. Does that mean I just need to stay alive for forty more minutes? But what happens after?

Jamie beckoned Lonnie to follow, and the two dashed down the hall in their stolen robes.

This is idiotic, Lonnie thought.

A door creaked behind them, which caught Lonnie by surprise. Trying not to spiral, he attempted to turn toward the person with grace. *Better to meet them face-on than seem suspicious.* But before he saw who'd opened the door, he felt the cold bony touch of a hand graze his shoulder.

"Hey!" the voice yelled.

Lonnie jumped into a spin and found himself face-to-face with the emerald-cloaked man.

He froze. *Oh god.*

Lonnie did everything in his might to stop his legs from buckling to the floor, including digging his heels into the carpet fibers so he wouldn't run away. The man said something else, but it just sounded like ringing in Lonnie's ears. He glanced at Jamie, who had stopped in his tracks as well. He stared back at the two of them, probably deciding whether or not he should make a run for it while he had the chance.

"I said why are you two over here?" the man repeated, now speaking directly into Lonnie's face.

Lonnie opened his mouth to reply, but he couldn't stop his teeth from chattering long enough to form a word. He turned to Jamie, who looked equally speechless.

"We—" Lonnie blurted.

The man waved his hand. "It doesn't matter. Come on. I need your help!"

Without waiting for a response, he propped back open the freezing cold door Lonnie had previously tried to open and ushered them through it. Lonnie and Jamie shared a glance.

"Hey, I said let's go," the emerald-cloaked man barked.

Lonnie wanted to bolt down the hall, but people would be on them in seconds. Instead, he begrudgingly entered the room. *Why is it so cold?* The inside had to be thirty degrees. As they walked in, frozen air wafted up their noses, chilling the hairs and making them sniffle.

Black tiles wrapped around the room as well as the floor, giving it a sleek appearance. Lonnie assumed it was meant to look chic and extravagant, but all he could see it as was some kind of sick, modern dungeon. To his right, the wall had been cut to make it stick out like steps. Almost like bleachers at a sporting match. Except this room didn't have a TV. Or champagne. It was bare. Well, almost bare. On the largest wall, he saw that same symbol from the top of the pocket watch, this time drawn in the lightest white, outlining the same protruding heads of five men, each sewn together at the spine and lashing out in agony. Lonnie approached it before jumping at the sight of his own cloaked reflection bouncing off the black tile. He reached up and slid his hand over the edge of his mask. The thing was slicing into the side of his temple.

205

"You, come here." The man pointed at Lonnie. He stood at the far side of the room, by a bowl resting gently on a small pillar.

Lonnie winced as he strode over. The smell was vile.

Inside the bowl sloshed a dark, bergundy-colored liquid.

Holding a book in one hand and a small vial in the other, the older man read silently. As his lips moved, he began pouring the bottle into the bowl and proceeded to mix the concoction.

"Now help me lift it," he commanded.

Without thinking, Lonnie gave a confused glance to Jamie before he grabbed the end. Following the man's lead, Lonnie lifted the bowl from the pillar. The thing felt much heavier than expected.

"Into the divot," the man prompted.

Noticing a small dip between the floor and wall, Lonnie leaned down to pour it in, watching as the thick liquid crawled its way along the hole. When it reached the edge of the room, it made a sharp turn and moved along until the entire perimeter of the floor had been covered in the strange goo.

Is this why it's so cold?

"Perfect," the man said calmly. "You can both grab a seat."

Hesitantly, they both sat at the bottom of the tile stairs, their backs stiff as they shared a gaze. Though Lonnie couldn't see Jamie's eyes, he knew they both were wondering the same thing.

Should we have made a run for it when we had the chance?

The man returned to reading his book, every so often making slight glances to spots around the room, like he was checking things off in his head. As he gripped the book in his arm, Lonnie realized just how old it looked. Like the parchment on the wall, it was decaying at the edges. The outside was forged out of leather, with cracks forming along the binding, and the pages were made of dusty yellow paper that looked brittle and ancient. The man truly seemed entranced by it.

"What is he reading?" Lonnie whispered to Jamie.

But before his friend could answer, the door opened, letting in a stream of people in cloaks.

"Come in, take a seat." The man gestured.

Before Lonnie knew it, a group of at least forty people had positioned themselves around them on the stairs. A sinking feeling filled his gut about what was about to happen. People crowded up next to him, causing him to become almost immobilized, his shoulders tightly locked between Jamie and another.

Everyone stayed eerily quiet as they sat. With the flick of a switch on the wall, the edges of the floor began to glow a low light, reflecting off the disgusting liquid and shining an almost red hue onto the walls. Lonnie felt Jamie's body tense against his, and he wondered what the guy next to him must be thinking.

The door opened once again, letting in a stream of light, and there, beneath that light, stood Hannah. Her arms were restrained by two much bigger men with absurdly sized cloaks. One had a gash on the side of his jaw, and the other sported a matching one on his arm through his torn sleeve. If Lonnie had to guess, those weren't the only marks Hannah made on the men. Waiting for their cue, the two dragged her to the podium. From their pockets they produced a small rope that they used to fasten her arms and legs to a hook on the wall. A gag bound her mouth, though she looked like she had tried aggressively to gnaw it off. Clearly to no success.

Lonnie wanted to help her, yet at the same time a ping of

anger stirred inside him. He had saved her from drowning, and she left him caged in that room.

Maybe she had a good reason for it.

Still reading his book, the emerald-cloaked man glanced up occasionally as they tied Hannah to the wall. Then as they finished, he raised his arm to the crowd.

"Great, thank you." He applauded. With a sharp tilt of his head, he looked out at the crowd, grazing over them before briefly stopping to look Lonnie in the eyes. He smirked, which made the unease in Lonnie's stomach lurch.

"Can someone please bring these two up to the front?" He pointed to Lonnie and Jamie.

"What?" Lonnie's heart skipped a beat.

Within seconds, hands grabbed onto their bodies, each clawing at their skin, trying to drag them to the front of the room.

"Stop!" Lonnie shouted, trying to throw them off.

They just kept coming though, weighing on him like a suffocating cloud. One person grabbed his head, ripping the mask clear from his face. He reached out for it, but the crowd had already consumed it. He felt vulnerable being lifted from his seat, but his thrashing paid him no good. With at least two hands holding each limb, it was like dredging through cement.

"Wait!" the man bellowed.

Lonnie raised his gaze to see the emerald-cloaked man still staring at him. His head cocked to the side.

"Keep him there." He gestured at Lonnie. "I just need the other one."

Relief flooded Lonnie as they planted him back into his seat, but it immediately changed to horror at Jamie's screams as they strong-armed him up to the wall. Like Hannah, they tied up his limbs and threw a gag around his mouth, muffling his violent hollering. Lonnie sat, too terrified to speak. As the restraining hands began to loosen, he couldn't help looking to the door. It was cracked slightly ajar and only a few feet away.

A loud slam shook him as the man's book hit the podium. "Right, then. Let us carry on, shall we?" The man began removing his mask and cowl from atop his head.

The audience watched as he dropped them both to the floor, revealing his wispy silver hair and stretched lines across his face. Lonnie's eyes widened with shock as Mr. Blythorne stood at the front of the room, his piercing eyes set on Lonnie.

"You seem surprised," he remarked, slowly removing his gloves and cloak to reveal an emerald three-piece suit.

Lonnie shook his head in bewilderment. "Why are you doing this to us?"

Mr. Blythorne lowered his gaze briefly to look at his watch before approaching Lonnie. His face turned into a prideful grin.

"I want you to know that you're doing quite well." He chuckled. "Quite a wild card you are. We read your files, but you never really know what to expect from all that."

Striding back toward the bowl, he produced a blade from his back pocket and pricked his pointer finger. Then bending over, he let the blood drip down his wrist and into the moat of goo.

"Am I your champion?" Lonnie blurted.

"Ah, you read the parchment!" Blythorne smiled, pulling back up to his feet. "You are much smarter than you give yourself credit for."

"But why? Why did you pick me?"

"Oh, I wish I could take credit for that, but I didn't pick you."

Lonnie glanced around in anger. "Then who did?"

"You're focusing on the wrong things, boy. You should be overjoyed. You don't realize how few people get this close to the end!"

Lonnie's spine tingled at the man's sudden optimism, stated with that pearly grin strapped to his face. "The end of what?"

"The trials of course."

Lonnie thought back to when he found Jamie. How they had thanked him for his sacrifice in the trials. *This man is insane.* He glared. "I don't understand. You've been trying to kill me, but now you're glad I'm alive?"

The man let out another chuckle.

"No, no, we never wanted you to die. Quite the opposite in fact. It's in all of our best interest if you live."

"Fine. Then just let me go," Lonnie growled. "Let me and my friends leave."

Blythorne tipped his head as if Lonnie were a naughty child. "Sadly, you still have one final trial to finish."

"What the hell! I don't care about your stupid trials. Just let us go!" Lonnie yelled.

The man stared in silence at Lonnie as if he were speaking another language. After a moment, he gave a nod to the crowd, and the other cloaked figures began removing their garments. First their headpieces, followed by their oversized cloaks, revealing dashing suits and dresses topped with diamond necklaces and watches.

As Lonnie watched them, he saw a few people he recognized from the party. People he'd noticed dancing and smoking cigarettes on the terrace.

The more he looked, the more flashbacks of faces from the party hit him. *Crap. Have I been in the house this entire time?*

And for how long?

Every hour that had passed during the ordeal felt like a day, but he couldn't be sure. It was impossible to guess if the sun had even risen yet from the evening he'd arrived.

What time is it really?

With all the cloaks and linens on the floor, Lonnie took another scan of the audience, where he briefly caught Mike's gaze. His brow furrowed as they exchanged stares, but Mike refused to look away. In fact, the man gave him a stern look, as if telling him it was all going to be okay. Lonnie noted he still wore the same suit from earlier in the cigar lounge. It just seemed more scuffed now, and upon closer inspection, his finger, along with the rest of the crowd, had that same prick of blood on it as his own.

Lonnie wanted to beg for his help, but he knew that wouldn't happen. Instead, he turned away and kept scrolling through the people, his eyes scanning each person, one at a time, imprinting their faces on the ridges of his brain. As he reached the end of the row, a cry erupted from his lips. A few feet down from him, two people sat in the farthest corner of the stands. And even though their heads were turned to the side, he could still make them out, the recognizable curves of their faces and their expensive clothes draped across their bodies.

His parents.

He shook his head. *No.* He laid a hand across his stomach at the insatiable ache cramping across his abs. His arm, his hands, his brain...everything felt raw. His father flickered a glance, then dropped his gaze, every part of his expression filled with shame. Self-loathing wafted off him; Lonnie could almost smell it, like cheap cologne. Beside him, Lonnie's mother sat brushing tears from her cheeks as quickly as they fell.

He glared at his parents in disgust. "What the hell is wrong with you?" He shook his head in disbelief before turning to include the others in the room. "You're all sick! What, do you do this just for fun? You're just too rich and bored and starved of entertainment?"

"Enough," Mr. Blythorne commanded, the grin no longer on his face.

"No, tell me! Tell me what this is all for—what any of this is for, you piece of—"

A hand slapped him across the face, jolting him into speechlessness. Blood boiling, Lonnie attempted to stand and retaliate but was pulled down again by a parade of hands.

"You need to understand that we don't do this for our enjoyment," Blythorne said.

"Then why?" Lonnie snarled. He looked again to his mother, her face now blotched with drunken tears.

How could she do this to me? How could she be a part of this?

Mr. Blythorne laid his hand against the mural on the way and ran his hands delicately against the connected spine.

"These trials aren't a game. They are an offering... An offering to them."

He turned back to Lonnie, who sat speechless, taken aback by what he had just heard.

His face must have told it all, because Mr. Blythorne continued, "You think we're insane. That's fine. We didn't believe either at first. Not until we realized what they can do."

Lonnie looked past the man to Jamie, who appeared to be trying to shred his rope restraints against a notch in the wall.

He's going to get himself killed.

Blythorne opened the book to show Lonnie the image he'd seen a number of times by now—but this time the five men were separated and surrounded by a mixture of symbols and text Lonnie couldn't seem to make out. Mr. Blythorne continued speaking. "We do not know their given names, but the oldest transcription refers to them as The Gods of Grandeur. They arrived just after cities began to grow. Five brothers sent to Earth by their father to maintain civilization. They were to be balance-keepers and judges. But without guidance, they took to their own ideas of how they would accomplish such a feat, each drawing from their own ideals they sought in others."

Mr. Blythorne first pointed at the scrawny one plastered in the mural on the wall. "Penury, the Giver. He thought his endless wealth was the answer, so he gave it away. He distributed it to every city he crossed, fueling them with more money and crops than they could ever imagine. And he was proud. He thought they could prosper without the weight of survival hanging over their heads. But he was wrong. People grew envious and prideful. Fighting each other for the wealth they shared, taking more than they needed and burning the rest, eventually resulting in no winners and cities reduced to nothing."

He next pointed to the stocky man directly above Penury on the mural. "Avarice, the Collector. Avarice was the complete opposite of his brother. He thought it smart to hold his wealth and wait for the perfect champion to present his generosity upon. But nobody could ever be perfect enough for him. Cities would grovel for his attention with offerings and worship, but it was never enough. Each time ultimately left them worse than before he arrived.

"Donor, the Pure." He pointed at the man with the cut-out eyes. "The blind son, the golden boy. Void of judgment, he gave to everyone he encountered. His kind heart, unbeknownst to him, led him to trust the monsters he had hoped to rid, giving them the power to take cities.

"Finally, Glory and Honor, the Warriors." He pointed to the twins on either end of the mural, each holding a small dagger in their hands. "The twins thought differently from their brothers. They didn't think people deserved free fortune at all. Instead, they thought humankind should fight for it. The winner of which would then get the brothers' aid. But each time the smoke had cleared and the wars ended, no winner stood to claim their prize. It was hundreds of years of chaos, and their father knew it. So, one day he decided he'd had enough. On the night of their last meeting, he took a needle and sewed their spines together as though fabric. Binding them as one, never again letting them give or take, unless agreed upon by all."

"And this is what they all agreed upon?" Lonnie asked, mystified by the tale he was just told.

"Yes."

"I see." Lonnie snorted, getting another look at Jamie ruffling his rope.

Checking his watch again, Mr. Blythorne suddenly grew impatient. "Right. And now it's time for you to choose."

"Choose?" Lonnie frowned. But he knew. The line had branded itself to his brain.

The champion must spill the blood of a beloved.

The air grew chilly beneath Blythorne's long glare. Then slowly from his back pocket he pulled out a cloth and began wiping his bloody blade clean.

Lonnie gave Jamie another glance. His rope had begun to strip.

I need to stall them.

"Did your gods also agree to those creatures downstairs?" Lonnie asked loudly. "Are they champions as well?"

Mr. Blythorne almost laughed. "No, of course not. They're my genetic research. What is having all the fortune in the world if it can't save you from the cruelty of age? I thought, what if I could fix it? What if I used nanotechnology to rewrite DNA on a genetic level? You could stop your skin from wrinkling, strengthen your bones, replace your cells at a rate unlike any other."

"Clearly you haven't figured it out," Lonnie said, looking around, sarcasm thick in his tone.

His mother let out a small gasp, which only made Lonnie more angry. To the point he almost felt giddy. "What you're doing down there is disgusting!" Lonnie spit at them.

"And yet, your father and his peers didn't seem to think so when they helped me start the program," Mr. Blythorne said bluntly. "They thought it was actually quite groundbreaking."

In that moment, Lonnie felt his father's eyes drill through the back of his head, but he didn't give him the satisfaction of a second glance. Instead, he turned to Mike, expecting an avoidant stare, but rather than remorse, he found a determined twinkle in the man's eye.

Why is he looking at me like that?

"Here we go." Mr. Blythorne strode over and forced the knife into Lonnie's clasped hand.

Lonnie shook his head in horror. "I'm not going to do that."

"I can't make you choose." Blythorne pointed first to Hannah, then Jamie. "But if you can't pick one of them, then we'll have to choose you. In which case," he lifted his hands to indicate the rest of the room, "all of this was for nothing."

"Nobody needs to die," Lonnie whispered.

"Someone always needs to. That's just the way this works. It's how it's always worked." He briefly checked his watch.

"Because a book says so?" Lonnie sniffed.

"I—" Mr. Blythorne stumbled as the door cracked open, catching the room's occupants by surprise. Through it, a woman emerged wearing a dark green suit. Unlike the rest of them, she didn't cover herself in a mask and cloak. Rather, her hair was tied back into a tight bun, revealing all the sharp features of her face. A clacking sound bounced off the floor as she approached Mr. Blythorne.

"Hello, Patrick." She rested her hand on his shoulder.

He glared at the woman. "I have everything under control, Ophelia," he muttered.

"I'm sure you do, but I'll take it from here. Have a seat," she said sternly.

"But it's—"

She raised her arm, cutting off the words spewing from his mouth. Then she gestured him toward the stairwell. He obeyed without another word.

"Do you know who I am?" she asked, now facing Lonnie.

He gave her a hard look, not sure why it mattered whether he knew her or not. But the features did look familiar. After a moment, it clicked.

"Mrs. Blythorne?"

Chapter 16

Where Secrets Lie

It took Lonnie a minute to process this woman with the tied-down hair and minimalist suit being the same as the party hostess who wore the pageant hair and elegant red velvet dress. Even her bright smile had been replaced by a cold, unsettling, and blank expression.

"You look different from the party," he said icily.

"The party was just a show. We surround ourselves with all those ungrateful people to remind us that we are different. They will never truly understand the cost of true wealth. Because, believe me, if they did, they surely would never pay it." She sighed. "Now—"

"I'm not going to choose," Lonnie interrupted.

She furrowed her eyebrows in a disdained expression. Her wrinkle lines flowed right into place, as if this was a typical look she wore. Then on the turn of a dime, she cracked a sentimental smile. "My father first showed me and my older siblings this book when we were just children," she said, picking up the book and rubbing her hand along the outer edge of the leather. "It can seem overwhelming, the burden of sacrificing the people you love. But that's what all of this," she swung her arm to encompass the lavish room, "requires. Riches require blood. To get rich, and to stay rich, one must be sacrificed to satisfy the rest." As she spoke, her voice softened, and she stroked the book again as if no longer speaking to Lonnie but to her weird religious god instead. "That's why we bring in new people. People like your father. People like you. And we share the burden. A different family sacrifices every year." She looked up and gave him a genuine grin. "Sure, we all lose something. But the gain is for the greater good."

As she spoke, Lonnie peered at Jamie over her shoulder. He was still concentrating on his rope.

Oh, for hell's sake! Hurry up, Jamie.

"These trials require delicacy," Mrs. Blythorne continued, absorbed in her cult-speak. "They don't just want your death, they want you to shed the pieces of your soul and expose them so they may see you are truly worthy of their admiration! Your mind, your body, your heart—they want it all, they yearn for it all!" She reached out a hand to pet his face, but he jerked away. She nodded. "And right now, they are still missing your heart."

With a snap of her fingers, the people surrounding Lonnie pushed him forward. Grabbing his arm, Mrs. Blythorne dragged him over to stand in front of his friends. Still clenching the knife in his hands, Lonnie glanced at the woman's abdomen. The thought of jamming it in flitted through his mind. Lifting his gaze, he smirked, but her face showed a lack of fear.

"You shouldn't waste your time with such idiotic thoughts," she snapped. "Now tell me, whose life do you value more, your friends' or your own?"

Dropping his gaze from her, Lonnie scrambled to come up

with a plan. His mind raced through one idea after another, but nothing he landed on would end well. Slowly, he approached his friends, both of whom sat shackled to the wall. Hannah's eyes bugged as she tried desperately to remove the bondage from her mouth. Jamie, however, was rather calm. Or maybe his mind was just elsewhere. He sat on the floor, without so much as flinching a muscle.

What do I do?

He could feel all eyes in the room fixed on him, the silence leaving space for his heartbeat to bleed into his eardrums. He twisted the knife in his hand, letting the sharp edge graze across his palm. "I just have to know," he said, "why did you pick me?"

Mrs. Blythorne let out a slight chuckle. "We don't pick."

"Well then who did?"

"Who do you think?" she said, directing her gaze to Hannah's weltering face.

Hannah let out a muffled scream as the words hung in the air. She tugged at her rope, her face growing redder by the second. Tears streamed down her cheeks, smearing two-day-old mascara down onto her lips.

"You're lying," Lonnie snapped, though he couldn't decide if he actually believed that. Hannah now shared the same guilty expression plastered across his parents' faces just on the other side of the room.

Distracted, he moved the blade and nicked his finger, sending drops of blood along the floor. Rattled, he approached Hannah. With a tug, he pulled the cloth from her mouth and dropped it around her neck. "Is that true?" he choked.

Her eyes darted back and forth, looking for how to answer, before she suddenly strained as close to him as she could reach.

"Lonnie," she sobbed out. "Please."

"Why?" He stared at her in disbelief. "Why would you do that? How could you do that... I don't understand."

"Lon—"

A crash resonated from the outside hallway, causing everyone to turn to the door.

"Someone go check what happened," Mrs. Blythorne demanded.

Two bigger gentlemen removed themselves from the stairs and made their way to the door. They opened it and stepped out into the hallway. From inside, everyone saw them survey both ends of the hall, give each other a confused look, then turn back to the room. Intrigued, Mrs. Blythorne strode over.

Lonnie suddenly heard the unmistakable sound of gears churning. His breath caught in his throat.

Oh my god.

As casually and discreetly as possible, he scooted over to Jamie, who had already managed to free one of his hands from the rope restraints and was subtly untying the other. Standing in front of him, Lonnie dropped the knife to the floor, which Jamie snagged up with his open hand. Then, using the growing sound of grinding gears as cover, Jamie sliced through the rope at his feet. While he did so, Lonnie stood still and refused to take his eyes off the hallway or the two men who still looked confused.

A chill passed through Lonnie's bones. Then the destruction hit.

A wave of disfigured bodies flung around the hallway corner. Through the doorway, Lonnie saw the creatures appear, all gears and skin and blood. Before he could blink, the monsters plucked the two men off their feet and clamped razor-sharp claws into them, shooting blood in all directions. Their dying screams haunted the corridor as the red dripping from their bodies slid over the tiles.

"What are you waiting for?" someone shouted. "Shut the door!"

As if in obedience, three men and a lady all jumped for the door and slammed it shut, then barricaded it with their bodies. Mrs. Blythorne tried to keep a calm face, but even she seemed unnerved. Her walkie-talkie materialized in her hand as she rang for help. "Why aren't their collars on!" she yelled.

The static rang until eventually a quiet, muffled voice responded, "The control panel is still fried. We lost control!"

"Damn it!" she cursed, tossing the walkie onto the floor.

Without hesitation, Mr. Blythorne joined her. He pulled a gun from the back side of his pants and aimed it toward the door. Six people now held the door, as bodies slammed against it from the other side. Suddenly, a pair of sharp talons slid through the crack in the door, slicing at the people's forearms as monster-like screams continued to echo from outside.

Welcome to hell, Lonnie thought. *It's about time you all experienced it too.*

Having freed his other limbs, Jamie bumped Lonnie and handed him the knife. Lonnie clenched it and strode over to point the tip at Hannah, anger washing over him. He'd loved her. Absolutely. Completely. She'd been family to him when his parents wouldn't. And it was all to drag him into their sick game?

"Lonnie, don't," Jamie said above the noise. He rubbed the rope burn on his wrist.

"Lonnie, wait!" Hannah squirmed up the wall.

He moved closer until the blade was inches from her neck.

Every muscle in his hand shook as dark thoughts spun through his mind.

"Please!" she begged.

Grabbing the rope tied around her wrists, he pulled her up. Then arching his hand back, he struck the blade down. She flinched, only to find he had cut her loose from her restraint. As she stood frozen in shock, Lonnie undid her leg restraint as well, fully detaching her from the wall.

"Thank you," she gasped.

"You're going to tell me everything you know," he snarled.

As she gained her footing, he quickly backed her against the wall until they were nearly mushed together. With his arms, he pinned her in so she couldn't flee. "Everything."

Jamie slid his hand between them and pried Lonnie back.

"If we stay here, it won't do you much good," he noted amid the chaos that was spiraling around them. "We need to find a way out."

A gunshot went off, causing them to jump. The door had been bent on its hinge, giving view to the flow of creatures. Lonnie blinked in horror at the abundance of them. Every genetic mashup that had lined the rooms behind the doors in the hell-pit Lonnie had just escaped from were climbing through the hall. A few had so little skin left it was hard to believe they once started as human.

Another gunshot sounded, this one from Mr. Blythorne, who stood in the center of the room, smoke spewing from his pistol even as his legs trembled, especially when the blood began to pool around his feet, creating a muggy paste.

The blood continued along the tile until it reached the far corner of the room, where Mrs. Blythorne stood with that precious religious cult book of hers tucked under her arm. She had her face pressed against the wall.

Lonnie frowned. *What is she doing?*

Suddenly the tiles unlocked from the wall, revealing a hidden door.

Another secret passage?

Mrs. Blythorne pushed the door open to reveal a dark tunnel that she promptly hustled inside. She spared a brief glance back at the room in horror before slamming the door shut.

"Come on!" Lonnie shouted.

Pushing Hannah in front of him, they slammed themselves against the wall and rubbed their hands along it.

"How did she open it?" Jamie yelled.

Behind them, the sound of the door ripping from his frame was followed by more screams as people jostled to hide or flee until they had nowhere else to go. They ran to the center of the room, cowering in fear behind Mr. Blythorne and his gun. Blythorne let off a few more shots, but they merely lodged into the creatures' metal frames or ricocheted around the room. Lonnie looked back in time to notice one had even bounced back into his shoulder just as a red silhouette spread along his green suit jacket.

"Hurry!" Lonnie slapped his hand against the wall.

"Damn it!" a voice shouted from behind.

The gun began clicking over and over as Blythorne kept pulling the trigger. He was out of bullets.

As if aware of this, the creatures' monstrous growling started up again, growing louder and louder in the frenzy.

"Here!" A man appeared by Lonnie's side and ran a calloused hand over the panel.

Click.

Lonnie turned to see Mike standing beside him.

"Go!" he yelled, pushing the kids into the room.

Behind the tile wall, a dirt tunnel materialized, the room of which sat just barely higher than Lonnie's head. Hannah and Jamie entered, with Lonnie close behind. He turned to Mike. "Why are you helping me?"

"I couldn't save my brother, but maybe I can save you. Now go!"

Before Lonnie could object, Mike started to seal the door, but one of the creatures grabbed his leg and yanked him back. Mike kicked it off and scrambled to reach the door while more piled around him. They began pulling at him, cutting at him with their bladed claws. One punctured him in the chest, but Mike kept crawling.

"Go!" he shouted again, as more approached him from behind.

"Lonnie, what are you doing? Come on!" Jamie shouted.

As Lonnie turned to leave, a flash of hair caught his eye from behind the corner of the tile stairs on the far side of the podium. It was his mother. Her face looked so haunted and innocent as they exchanged glances, and Lonnie felt a pinch in his chest. All the anger toward her suddenly felt like a dream.

"I can't leave her."

"What are you talking about?" Hannah grabbed his arm. "Lonnie, come on, we need to move!"

For the first time in years, his mother gave him a heartfelt stare that softened something inside him. The mother he remembered could fill any room she wanted, but right at this moment, she looked so small against the wall. Suddenly she cupped her lips. The word "go" formed from her mouth. Tears leapt into Lonnie's eyes.

That's my mother.

"No," he mouthed to her.

But she shook her head, allowing a look of acceptance to wash over her, giving her a beautiful glow. Lonnie tried to reenter the room, but his friends continued to pull his arm into the tunnel.

"I'm sorry," he mumbled.

Turning to follow his friends, Lonnie wiped the tears from his eyes as they hurried up a steep incline built between the walls. Darkness consumed the wall cavity aside from the faint glow stemming from something ahead. As he grappled his way up the hill, Lonnie's eyes filled so full he was finding it hard to see. Noticing his friends, he bit down on the collar of his shirt so as to quiet his grief, but the screaming from the back room continued to buzz around his head, making him want to vomit.

Just zone it out.

He made it a few more steps, but a new woman's scream suddenly cut through the noise. Something about it was so familiar. And in that moment, he just knew it was his mother's.

Without even a hesitation, Lonnie turned and grabbed a crumbled rock from beneath his shoe then slid back down the hill.

"What are you doing?" Hannah yelled.

"I have to do something!" he shouted.

When he reached the door, he found it still half open. Mike's body lay beside it, his punctured hand inches from the door panel.

"Goodbye, Mike," Lonnie whispered kindly to the man.

Dredging past him, Lonnie made his way into the room. It

had become a graveyard, with pieces of bodies ripped apart and scattered along the floor. The monsters had already vacated to the hallway, where fresh screams erupted from the other side of the wall.

Are the rest of the party guests still here? I wonder if they can hear this?

Shaking his head, Lonnie hurried to the space behind the curtain and stairs, only to find it empty. In a panic, he looked frantically around.

"Mom!" he shouted, wiping the tears with his one good hand. "Mom!" he shouted again.

He began searching the bodies along the floor, looking for one that resembled his mother. But she wasn't there. Continuing forward, he suddenly tripped, and with a hard slam, hit the tile. Pulling himself to his knees, he saw a dismembered hand by his foot. Trying to not gag, he followed it down to the wristwatch it still wore. It was his father's stainless steel blue. Its face was smashed, with the second hand finally mute and still. He let out a sigh as a wave of conflicting emotions rushed through him. Some satisfied, others guilty, but all...painful.

His mother shrieked, and looking up, Lonnie found her lying on her back, just outside the door. A creature rested on top of her, rubbing his hand along her cheek. *He's taunting her.*

"Get off her!" Lonnie ran full speed toward the door, tackling the creature into the wall. With his body plopped on top of him, he raised the rock into the air, ready to slam it down on the thing's head. But he hesitated, giving the creature enough time to jostle him off and knock Lonnie onto the ground. The rock slipped from his grip. He reached for it, but the creature had already risen and flipped around to face him.

Panic flaring, Lonnie continued shuffling his hand across

the ground, looking for his weapon until the creature kicked it away. Without anywhere to turn, Lonnie peered up at the glowing red eyes piercing down at him.

"Wait," he wanted to plead, but he froze. His lips quivering.

The creature grabbed him by the shirt to pull him up and against the wall as if he weighed nothing. Lonnie lifted his arms to block his face, listening to the ghostly groaning coming from the monster's mouth. Hopeless, he closed his eyes and waited for death to take him at last.

He'd been so close to making it through this sick place.

As he waited, the first day of college glimmered through his mind. His feet pressed on the grass while he stared up at his new residence hall. He tried to remember what fresh air felt like, but it seemed like a foreign memory. His friends were there, Hannah with her ruffled hair and Jamie with his stupid camera. They all gathered for a picture when the flash suddenly knocked him back to reality.

The metallic hand pressed against his clavicle, stapling him to the wall. He flinched, waiting for something to happen, but nothing did.

Why aren't I dead yet?

Opening his eyes, he noticed the creature just staring at him, his other claw still resting at his side. The monster looked at him with a cocked head, as if deciding what to do.

Lonnie grew annoyed by the toying. "Are you kidding me? Just do it already!" he yelled.

But the creature remained mesmerized. He dropped his gaze to the wrapped wound on Lonnie's arm, and in that moment, Lonnie recognized the sixty-seven sewn into the front of the monster's suit. Shocked, he bit his tongue. Then, raising his hand ever so carefully, he rested his hand on the creature's face, letting him nestle against his palm. His red eyes stared at Lonnie, the painful glare momentarily being replaced with peace. With a sudden thrust, the monster pulled back his arm, causing Lonnie to drop to the floor. The groaning stopped, and the beast just watched him. His feet planted on the ground, standing awkwardly as though he was awaking from a dream. Lonnie stood to his feet, dragging his mother up with him. "Come on," he whispered.

In the momentary silence, Lonnie almost thought he heard his mother say, "thank you." But it could have just been his imagination. Behind him, the other creatures had grown privy to their presence and were coming back toward the door.

"Hurry," he urged his mom.

Sidestepping the carnage, Lonnie led his mother to the tile wall. Behind them, the creatures had stopped at the hallway door, watching them carefully. Waiting for them to move. Taking a deep breath, Lonnie counted down to his mother, "Three...two...one," he whispered. "Now!"

They quickly darted to the doorway, the scuffing of their shoes sending a loud echo in the momentarily quiet room.

Behind her, the creatures jumped into a full-on sprint.

"Go!" He shoved his mother inside, then flipped around to the door. "Use your hand!"

In that split second moment before his mother lifted her palm to the wall, Lonnie caught a glimpse of the creatures' mangled faces and the blood flowing from their mouths like foam.

Thud.

He slid the door fully shut, and the sound of the monsters smacking into it reverberated through the tunnel. He could hear their fists and claws laying wreckage to the tiles.

They're going to break through.

Lonnie took off at a run, hurrying his mother amid helping her climb the dirt mound. To his surprise, it seemed lighter in the tunnel than before. Ahead of them, he caught sight of trap-door opening. Jamie and Hannah were seated on the other side, reaching their arms down to grab him.

"Hurry!" they shouted.

Grabbing his mother's uplifted hands, they pulled her through first, even as the door to the creatures sounded like it was crumbling away piece by piece. Lonnie jumped and felt the grip of their arms just before they dragged him into the light. A wave of heat bathed him, and it was possibly the best feeling he had ever known. Jamie slammed the latch closed.

"There." He let out a sigh.

Except the moaning in the tunnel beneath them grew louder, indicating the creatures broke through the first door. With a bang, the trapdoor rattled as the monsters reached it and began to beat against it.

"It's holding for the moment," Lonnie said, turning to see where the door had led them to.

A red carpet spread out across a hallway floor beneath decadent walls decorated with pieces of gold cemented on like mosaics, with black paint underneath. Moving slowly toward his friends, they waited a few moments for the moaning to eventually settle into an eerie breathing beneath the door.

Suddenly a pair of hands wrapped around Lonnie's neck, giving him a jolt. His mother hugged him, tears struggling to free themselves from her botoxed cheeks. "Thank you, sweetheart," she groveled. "You saved my life."

Her touch felt like poison against his skin. Coldly, he shifted her off himself. "Don't."

She fell to floor with a loud thud, which almost made him feel guilty, but it was quick to wash away. The fictional innocence he had seen in his mother back in the room faded as fast as it had arrived.

He shook his head. "I might not be able to let you die, but trust me when I say you're dead to me," he growled.

"Let's go," Lonnie blurted to the others.

As the fear of death lessened in his tense shoulders, Hannah stopped ahead of him, guilt sprouting all over her face like hives. A sudden headache cracked across his forehead, again bubbling up from an anger he didn't know if he could control. Stepping forward, Jamie grabbed his arm with a deathly grip. He shook his head. "Not now. The monsters won't be long behind us."

Lonnie knew he was right. Biting the inside of his cheek, he pushed past Hannah with disgust. "I need to get out of this house."

He made it only a few steps forward when his mother's scratching voice chanted behind him. "Don't blame her."

Lonnie spun around. "Don't blame her? Are you serious? That's all you have to say?" He let loose a humorless laugh.

Mrs. Grambell avoided his gaze. "She didn't have a choice."

Lonnie glared at Hannah. "What is she talking about?" he pushed.

"I don't—"

"Answer me. What aren't you telling me?"

She began to cry, but whether they were real or crocodile tears, Lonnie didn't care.

"My parents don't have any siblings, and their parents have passed," Hannah said. "So, the first year their name was chosen, all they had to choose from was themselves and their kids." She began to cry harder. "I had an older sister. She was only twelve when they sent her in, but she didn't stand a chance. Now this year was supposed to be my family's turn again, and they were going to send in my brother." She choked. "They were going to sacrifice him, just like they did to her! I couldn't go through it again."

"What the hell?" Lonnie pressed. "So it was fine if it was me and my family as long as yours was fine?"

"You don't understand. Your family's turn was going to be next year anyway. They thought you had a better chance to win than he did, so they said if I could get you to come home, they would skip his turn."

He swore. "So, all of this was a lie? Everything between us?"

"No, I love you!"

"Right. Like I can trust anything you say!" Lonnie yelled.

"Can we put a pin in this conversation, please?" Jamie pleaded, grabbing Lonnie by the shoulder. "It's not safe here; we need to go."

Hannah moved closer to gently caress Lonnie's arm with her fingers.

"I really do love you, I swear! I wasn't supposed to, but I did." She dropped her hand. "I was supposed to be your friend. Convince you to come home in time for the ritual. I'm sorry! They had my brother, and if you didn't show up, they would've thrown him in instead."

"You're sick!"

"I said I'm sorry—"

"No, you don't get to apologize. I...I have lost almost everyone in my life, and you knew that. I told you things...deep, personal things, and you twisted them and used them against me." As he spoke, he backed her against the wall, his eyes glazing over. "Look how fast they turned on you. They threw you in there right alongside me. They wanted me to kill you! How can you live knowing those are the people you stood behind? Murderers."

Her expression crumpled. "They tricked me, I didn't know. When they pulled me out of the cage and told me...I...I didn't care, I couldn't care. I was willing to take the chance."

"Take the chance that they would kill me instead of you?" Jamie butted in. "What is wrong with you?"

"I'm sorry, I didn't know all the rules. I didn't know what was going to happen. They just told me to try to keep Lonnie alive."

"You're really going to tell us you would do all that just to save your brother?"

"Yes, of course. I thought, of all people, you would understand that!" She winced beneath Lonnie's glare.

He punched his fist against the wall beside her head. Memories of his brother flooded through his head like a leaky dam. "Don't you dare talk about him!" he yelled.

His voice was so grizzly and sharp that even Jamie did a slight stumble backward. Hannah didn't seem fazed, her face remaining steady and at eye level with his, matching his gaze. "You don't even know what he did for you," she said after a moment. "What he sacrificed for you."

His gaze narrowed. "What are you talking about?"

She grasped his face, her hands melting to his skin, and pried herself off the wall to stand toe to toe with him. Her guilty conscious shedding onto the floor left nothing but a confident glare. "Don't you get it?" she blurted. "You're the reason he's dead!"

Lonnie's brain grew fuzzy, the edges of his vision shaking as he tried to hold his anger in check.

"She's just lying to you again," Jamie spat.

Behind him, Lonnie's mother sank to the floor, her legs collapsing on the carpet as she clutched her necklace chain around her neck. A primal cry came from her throat as she choked.

"She's telling the truth."

Lonnie stared at his mom. "What do you mean?"

"I can show you," she said, gesturing down the hall. "They keep records of everything."

"No offense, but I'm not following you anywhere!" Jamie snarled.

Lonnie stood frozen, the invitation gnawing on the back of his brain. "Show me," he finally muttered.

"What!" Jamie stared at him. "What if it's a trap?"

"I don't care. I am so sick and tired of being kept in the dark. I want to know. I *need* to know."

Jamie grabbed him by the arm. "You can't trust them, Lonnie," he whispered. "Let's just leave. I can sense it; we are so close."

Lonnie pulled Jamie into a hug.

"I am so sorry that I got you dragged into this," he said sincerely. "You should go. Call the police and get as far away from this house as possible."

Jamie began to argue, but Lonnie cut him off. "Go! I'll be right behind you."

"Are you kidding me?" Jamie seemed hurt. "I'm not leaving you alone with them."

"Fine, but I need to know what happened to my brother."

Jamie placed his hand on his shoulder. "Then we both go."

The gesture was so innocent, so sincere, that Lonnie practically crumbled under its weight. A sore feeling grew in the back of his throat. "Thank you."

Jamie faced Mrs. Grambell. "Alright, shall we then?"

Lonnie's mother took the lead, navigating them down the corridor, further and further from the vent in the wall. Lonnie turned back, watching the grand hallway shrink into the distance.

Why am I following her?

He shook his head, refocusing his gaze on his mother. She was limping, which drew his attention to her feet. The heel was chipped on her left shoe, causing her height to fluctuate up and down with each step. When she walked, he watched her face contort, which surprisingly made him chuckle. He couldn't figure out why...but the feeling of it brought him a surprising amount of joy.

"It's in here," his mother said. She opened a door along the wall, and an office appeared before them. Nothing dramatic, but as grand as to be expected. A large television hung flush with the wall, with a tiny new computer placed directly below it on the desk. Lonnie peeked at it, shocked by what he saw.

6:20 AM was illuminated at the bottom of the monitor.

My pocket watch hadn't been broken. It's still the morning. But then, why had the times on my phone and watch changed?

Lonnie let this thought slip away as Mrs. Grambell hobbled over to the computer and entered in the password without missing a beat. Lonnie watched her intently, his toes pointed toward the door. Hannah was rubbing her finger on the edge of her chin, which she always did when she was anxious. Jamie just glared at them both in silence. And Lonnie's mom continued typing, her shattered face silhouetted by the blue haze of the screen. She pulled up a file that read:

June 14th, 2015

She opened it and synced a video to the television. Lonnie watched her hand shake as she tried subtly to tuck it beneath the table. The screen stayed black, but the volume began to grow in the background. As if on cue, Mrs. Grambell plucked herself from the table and moved to the opposite end of the room, as far away from the screen as she possibly could be.

The monitor flickered, filling with static. With a loud beep, the screen transitioned to a room full of people. Lonnie stood staring, his mouth practically hanging from his jaw. There in the center of the room...was himself.

Chapter 17

Hand to Heart

"What is this?" Lonnie looked at his mother. "I don't understand."

In the middle of the room, his ten-year-old self sat, propped up on a chair like a doll. His eyes were shut, and he had on his favorite pajamas with stars spread across the shirt and pants.

"I don't remember any of this."

One of the members in the room placed a chair next to Lonnie in the video. An older girl was carried over and placed in it, her hair tangled into a mop and her body limp against the arms of the chair. Lonnie recognized her, but he shook his head in disbelief. It was his brother's girlfriend, Danielle.

Behind the two of them stood Ben.

His shirt was caked in sweat and tears where gashes had formed against his chest. One of his eyes had swollen shut, and the other had a nasty gash below it. He looked pale. In Ben's hand, he had something pressed to the back of younger Lonnie's head, but it was hard to make out on the screen.

"What is that?" Lonnie mumbled, unsure if he really wanted to know.

Ben shifted his stance, and light reflected off the silver object in his hand. A gun.

Lonnie put his hand to his mouth. The scene playing out on the video was beginning to make horrible, unfathomable sense.

Ben held the gun outstretched with his finger lightly around its trigger. Tears streamed out of his one good eye as he pressed it to the back of Lonnie's head. In the background, the audience cheered at him, their voices forming a choir of even chants, like crickets.

The image was blurry, but Lonnie could just make out his mother and father sitting gracefully in the second row of the makeshift stands. It was sickening.

Ben's brows trembled, and his hands seemed barely able to support the gun. Lonnie watched the television as his brother took a step back and turned his gaze directly to the camera. Directly to him, now, as he stood here watching all these years after Ben's death. Lonnie's heart flickered as his brother stared out at him, and for a moment, Lonnie saw a flash of peace grow behind his eyes.

"I'm sorry, Lonnie," he calmly muttered.

Bang.

With a quick spin of the gun, Ben had pointed it at his own head and pulled the trigger, sending his body dropping instantly to the floor.

No! Lonnie jumped forward, staring at the image of his brother on the floor beside younger Lonnie on the chair. Vomit rose in his throat. His brother chose himself—that's how he died?

He died saving me...

Tears began to leak from his eyes. He glanced around for a

trashcan to throw up in, but just then, a chilling, primal cry echoed from the screen. It was a younger Mrs. Grambell pushing through the crowd to hover over her oldest son's lifeless corpse.

Lonnie froze.

That chorus. That gunshot. The woman's scream.

All the times he'd been haunted by nightmares threatening to bubble to the surface. The therapy sessions. The med-induced dreams...

Images of his misshapen dreams came rushing back, his mind now filling the gaps with the things he had seen. The creature slamming against the large door, the smell of bleach spread throughout the green-toned hallway. He could feel now the straps of the wheelchair being guided by the cloaked figures taking him to the tile room. He could even feel the cold spot, like a patch of ice, where his brother had rested the gun to his head.

He gasped as the memories flooded in.

They were real.

He wept as he turned to his mother. "All this time, it was you. You both killed him!" He looked back to the video to see his mother tucking Ben's head between her arms and resting herself under him. His brain matter was smeared on the wall behind her as she rocked him back and forth against her chest. Mr. and Mrs. Blythorne appeared in the corner of the room, their faces petrified by the outcome they clearly hadn't expected. People finally began to rise from their seats and scramble for Ben to check him for a pulse.

Lonnie turned from the screen to his mother again. "What did you do to him? To me? Why can I only remember pieces?"

She sputtered.

"Answer me!" he seethed.

"I slipped you and the girl one of my pills," she blurted. "I didn't know how much you were supposed to give a child. I must have given you both the wrong dose—"

Lonnie was shaking now. "You're vile."

She nodded as if acknowledging it. "But you're one of the only people he loved. It wouldn't have worked with anyone else."

"Wouldn't have worked? You wanted him to kill me? Do you hear yourself right now?"

She avoided his stare, turning her face in shame.

"How could you do that to us? To him? To me? I'm your son! We were your sons." His voice cracked. "You're supposed to protect us. That's your job!"

"I know, but what was I to do?" she whined. "I didn't have a choice!"

"Everyone has a choice."

He noticed the alcohol cart sitting in the corner of the office. An array of whiskeys and wines were spread out on top, as well as a chilled bucket with a bottle of champagne lounging inside. He strode over and picked it up, then glanced down at the champagne flute resting next to it.

He couldn't help thinking of the glass his mother had given to him at the bar. The texture of it...and the taste. Bitterness surged up his throat, but he no longer felt the sharp pain in his chest. Eyes blazing, he turned to his mother, lifting the bottle into the air for her to see. "I guess it wasn't hard to make yours," he said disappointingly. With a scream, he chucked the bottle against the wall and watched it shatter into a million shards of glass. Hannah hollered in fright at his outburst and the fact that she was now soaked with champagne. Jamie, on the other hand, seemed quite pleased.

"Come on, let's go." Jamie pulled on Lonnie's collar.

Exiting to the hallway, the two boys turned to leave when they heard a faint thud emerge from somewhere behind them. It came again, and this time the muffled noise repeated from a room a couple doors down. Confused, Lonnie and Jamie slipped toward it until they had reached the wooden door. The handle stared them down like a loaded gun. Before either of them could move, another slam came from inside, making the boys hesitant but curious to pry it open.

The inside was dark, but soon a motion sensor revealed a string of lights that spanned down the lengthy room. Rococo paintings lined the walls, creating a pleasant illusion, all leading to a dead-end where a scrawny red-haired man was hanging by his arms that were shackled to chains from the ceiling.

"What the hell?" Jamie muttered.

"Oh my gosh!" Hannah cried out as she and Lonnie's mother entered behind them. "Carter!"

She pushed past Lonnie and ran to her brother. She pulled at his restraints, and when that didn't work, she tore the room apart until she found a set of keys hidden in a nearby drawer. She then riffled through them until the correct one released him. "Are you okay?" she whispered to him as he fell into her arms.

"Yes," he replied in a hoarse voice.

She hugged him again, tears streaming down her face. Her cheeks darkened like roses.

Thud.

Thud.

A violent slam reverberated from the hall.

"Okay, we should leave now," Jamie announced nervously.

"Wait." Hannah reached forward and grabbed Lonnie's hand.

Lonnie swung his arm free, creating a gap between them. Hannah pried a long, narrow shard of the champagne glass from her pocket, which made Lonnie jump back. "Woah, hold on!" he yelled defensively.

"You have to pick," she said solemnly. "You—"

"Oh my god! What is the matter with you? We found your brother, now let's go." He grabbed her hand, ripping the shard from her fingers, and began to walk. "All the people are dead. Those monsters killed everyone. Don't you see that? You're free."

She looked at him in confusion, then shook her head. "You don't understand how this works." She sighed. "Do you really think that was everyone? What about my parents? Mrs. Blythornes' siblings? All the others? The House consists of the richest people from all over the world. Do you think they would risk showing up here in person?"

A sinking feeling emerged in his stomach.

"Lonnie, when you disobey the rules, when you willingly choose to not complete the trials...terrible things will happen."

He snorted, trying to sound more certain than he was. "You can't actually believe that. They're just stories."

"It doesn't matter if I believe or not, because they do. My parents told me that when your brother broke the rules and aimed that gun at his head, companies went bankrupt in a matter of days. People's houses caught fire with them still inside, and government officials were overthrown in a night. Who do you think they blamed for that? And who do you think they will blame this time? These people won't take this lightly. They will kill you. They will kill all of us."

"That's absurd!" Lonnie didn't believe it. He *refused* to believe it.

"Damn it." She pointed at Jamie. "What do you think will happen to him if we just walk out of here right now?"

Lonnie frowned. "What do you mean?"

"You think they will let him walk away from all this, knowing what he knows now?" she accused. "You think they won't just kill him as a precaution?"

She stared at him, her big emerald eyes glistening with tears. She rested her hands on his shoulders, letting the weight of her body sink onto him. "I'm sorry, but I won't let you risk the people I love."

With a quick jerk, she threw herself towards him. Her chest smacked up against his as she wrapped her arms around his neck. Confused, he pushed her back as she let out a hollow grunt.

"What is wrong with you!"

As she stumbled back, he noticed a red circle grow on her chest. In his hands, the piece of long, pointed glass stood jutting out, caked in a thick layer of blood.

"No!" Carter yelled from where he'd dropped to the floor.

"Oh my god, no. No!" Lonnie folded beside her, carefully guiding her down against the wall. "Hey...hey... Please!... You're okay. You'll be okay, I swear. Please be okay."

Above them, Lonnie's mother and Jamie watched in horror as blood dripped onto the floor. Ignoring them, Hannah rubbed her hand gently against Lonnie's face, her eyes clouding as she looked just past him to give her sobbing brother a calming smile. Lonnie held her tightly, her blood oozing out onto his fingers as he whimpered.

"Please save my brother," she gasped in his ear.

Wiping away a tear streaking down her cheek, Lonnie glanced at Carter.

"Don't worry. I will," Lonnie promised as she closed her eyes. He leaned over her and felt the glut of tears release from his eyes until even his nose was running.

A louder thud came from the hall. This time it sounded like metal sheets slamming together.

"Was that—" Jamie started.

"We need to go, Jamie. Mom, help Carter." Lonnie knelt down and pulled Hannah's arm over his shoulder, then lifted her gently from the floor. "Just hold on, Hannah."

Pushing through the door, loud noises met them. They were coming from the trapdoor they'd climbed up through. Running down the hall, Lonnie caught a glimpse of claws piercing through the outer wall. Hobbling as fast as they could, they ran past the trapdoor and towards the ballroom. Chunks of drywall shot up from around the latch, revealing glowing eyes in various colors.

Without stopping, the group continued their way down the hallway, just as the sound of the metal hinge breaking met their ears. Following it came a chorus of crawling bodies who were throwing themselves after Lonnie and his group.

A sense of familiarity washed over Lonnie as they turned onto a hall full of shallow archways. The sight of an emerald-encrusted bathroom and tower-high library sparked a memory that felt so old yet was only the night prior. Flashbacks of the party filled his head, and he realized they had finally reached the ground floor. Spanning around the corner, they entered the now empty foyer, where windows shined life in from the outside.

"Come on! We are so close," chirped Lonnie. "The front door should be right through there."

Before they could reach it, though, the creatures emerged behind them. Lonnie slowed and turned to see the monsters. Some still had dried blood chipped on their faces, and others had holes on their bodies oozing out that black liquid. Most of their beige uniforms had been stained red or torn, revealing their pasty leather skin.

"Please, leave us alone!" Lonnie yelled at them. Releasing Hannah to Jamie, he moved to face the group. They immediately stopped in place, cocking their heads to stare at him. Slivers of daylight shone in through the windows, basking around the large space.

The creatures seemed startled. The closest huffed, then decided to approach him. Moving slowly, he got desperately close to Lonnie. So much so that his rotting breath made him woozy.

Lonnie's legs shook. Sweat formed along his forehead that he subtly wiped away in a weak attempt to hold his confidence.

The monster lifted his arm and brought the claw close to Lonnie's face, barely grazing the bottom of his chin. Lonnie held in a whimper and closed his eyes in horrible anticipation that something bad was to come.

Bang!

He peeled open his eyes to see the creature lying on the ground, a bullet hole resting between his now dull green eyes. Frantically, Lonnie raised his arms in defense while looking for the origin of the bullet.

"Lonnie!" Jamie yelled.

Lonnie turned to see Jamie beckoning him to the corner as another bullet flew through the air. Maddening groans came from the crowd of monsters as they grew agitated by the sharp noise.

Bang!

Another creature hit the floor. The smell of burning metal lifted into the air as feet shuffled nearby. Mrs. Blythorne came out from the shadows, a shotgun wielded between her hands and a string of shells wrapped around her belt. Lonnie side-stepped out of her way as she began plowing through the swarm. One after another, they fell as she reloaded her gun, then raised it time and again like a master marksman. Lonnie was both terrified and impressed by her speed, but as the number of bodies seemed to diminish, he began worrying that one of those bullets might be for him.

Seeing her distracted, he wrapped himself under Hannah's arm and led her and the others to the front door. There, Jamie and his mother took the lead in dragging Carter out, as Lonnie helped Hannah, who was still unresponsive. The outside revealed an early morning sky with the sun just rising over the horizon. Lonnie nearly tumbled down the front steps with Hannah in his arms, but he caught himself. With gentle care, he lowered her down into the grass next to her brother, then pressed his hand over her mouth.

"Her breathing is getting faint. We need to get an ambulance. Mom, give me your phone."

She patted herself down, but it was obvious from her dress' lack of pockets that it was still inside the house. "I don't have it with me," she whined.

Lonnie turned to Jamie, who revealed his dead phone. "I'm sorry," he stammered.

"But we need to save her!" Lonnie pleaded. "I can go find a phone in the house. There has to be one somewhere."

"Lonnie, you can't go back in there. It's too dangerous," Jamie said.

"Well, we have to do something!" Lonnie raised his voice. "We can't just let her die!"

They all looked to Hannah, whose chest was no longer moving. Her skin grew paler with each second, like it was turning to ice.

"I'm sorry, there is nothing we can do," Jamie said bluntly.

Lonnie turned to his mother, who gave him a pitying glare that just made him angry. Holding Hannah, Lonnie gently caressed her tangled hair, her blood staining what remained of his white dress shirt. It wasn't until that moment when he noticed the trail of blood that had followed them from the house. Specks of blood stippled down the steps of the house to her unwavering legs.

It's so much blood. It's too much blood.

Putting his hand to her neck, he listened as the beat dropped to nothing. Choking up tears, he rested her head on the ground.

"God..." he mumbled in pain.

"Hey!" Jamie bounced up, startling Lonnie. He looked up to see Jamie staring anxiously at the front door. Mrs. Blythorne now stood in front of it with a pistol aimed down at the four of them.

"We finished your trials," Lonnie spit out at her. "Can't you see that?" He gestured to his girlfriend's cooling corpse.

Mrs. Blythorne lowered the gun, giving a subtle smile. "Very well," she stated, pleased.

"So can we leave?"

"Of course not. You're members of the House now."

"I'd rather die than be a part of this," Lonnie snarled.

"I see." She aimed the gun again. "Well, I can't have you leave with what you know, then."

Lonnie placed his body in front of Jamie, a rush of confidence shielding him from the terror of a flying bullet. He waited for the usual pit to appear in his chest, but it never did. If anything, he felt strong.

Why am I doing this?

Just as he heard her undo the safety, a pair of claws shot through her abdomen, shooting out and wrapping up to the front of her face. Mrs. Blythorne gasped and coughed up blood, spitting it out onto the steps as it flowed ferociously from her opened gut. Cocking her head, she turned to see one of the creatures lying on the ground. Its chest was riddled with bullet holes, and its green eyes flickered on and off. Pulling its claw from her body, she stumbled a few feet before toppling down the steps, landing in a crude way on the bottom stair.

Lonnie stared, wiping the sweat from his hands and onto his pants.

Behind him, a yellowish-orange glow shone down onto the staircase, giving a nice shadow as the sun finished rising, spreading colors across the sky like a wildfire. Lonnie almost cried at the sight of it, thinking of how he had taken all of the world for granted.

A muffled grunt came from the top of the stairs as creatures began crawling out onto the stairwell, each oozing bile and organs out on the ground. They didn't stop moving though, each managing to spread themselves out on the concrete. They held their torn up faces to the sun, letting it shine on their exposed bone.

Many of them ceased moving, letting their corpses rot along the staircase. The rest continued basking in the sunlight.

They deserved so much better.

Lonnie took a seat on the grass and stared up at the house. He hadn't seen it in the daylight before. The facade was sculpted in a way that made each window and door look mysterious and inviting, and each column was chiseled with patience and precision. The sun reflected off the walls, making it a steamy flavor of orange, with bits of pink illuminating the archways. It was quite a beautiful place.

Whoever would have believed how ugly it was on the inside?

Chapter 18

The People We Become at Parties

One year later.

Lonnie rattled his pencil back and forth across the desk, his hand briskly rubbing a deep scar that was peeking out of his outstretched sleeve. He eyed the clock on the wall, watching the hand tick forward second by second. Classmates around him clutched their necks, wiping their perspiration onto the floor.

"And that is time, everyone," a voice called.

Looking up from his exam, Lonnie took note of the professor rapping the corner of his desk with his ruler.

"You can set all your tests here, then you're free to go. Enjoy your summers, and I'll see you back here next year," he boasted.

Lonnie rose from his seat and carried his test tightly in his grip. With a sense of urgency, he walked down the steps of the lecture hall, trying to display a calm energy toward his peers. After dropping off his test, he exited out into the courtyard and let the sweltering sun wrap around him like a cozy fire.

"Hey, Lonnie." A student waved to him midway across the walkway.

"Hey! Have a good summer." He gave a smile.

Lonnie broke into a brisk pace and made his way down the parade of steps. A girl walked past, her face beaming at the sight of him.

"Hey, have a good summer, alright?" She beamed.

"Thanks, you too." With a quick peek back at her, he continued forward. Not until he'd made it around the bend did he let himself slow into a calming stroll, eventually stopping in front of a big cement block that read:

Johns Hopkins University

He jumped atop it and kicked his feet off the edge as he looked at the campus.

Ring.

Pulling his phone from his pocket, his smile faded. "Hey, are you almost here?" Lonnie looked out at the street.

"Yeah, just turning down the road," Jamie replied.

Lonnie cupped his eyes. "Oh wait, I see you."

A sleek black Lexus manifested in front of him, rolling up quite stylishly until pulling to a firm stop. Lonnie hopped from the sign and staggered across the grass to the car. Jamie rolled down the passenger window.

"Hey," he muttered.

Lonnie rested his arms on the sill, staring intently at Jamie. His already faint smile reeled back another degree as wrinkles subtly appeared around his eyes. "You ready for this?"

Jamie let out a huff. "Nope."

"Do you have the—" Lonnie started.

"Yeah, they're in the back."

"Right. Let's get on with it then." Lonnie nodded.

Once Lonnie climbed in, Jamie pulled the car from the curb and turned around the loop. Lonnie leaned out his window to see the masonry facade that occupied his whole view. Bushels of buildings filled the horizon, the sun peeking out from behind, shrouding them in a golden silhouette.

As he watched his school fade in the distance, he couldn't help thinking of the year he'd just survived. He spent the rest of last summer at Mr. and Mrs. Harken's house with Jamie. Of course, they couldn't say what really happened at the party they'd attended. How would they even start to explain it? Instead, they said they were mugged in the city and that Lonnie didn't feel comfortable with his parents. It seemed to be enough of an explanation to satisfy everyone.

Looking back, though, the feeling of that summer was hard for Lonnie to explain. The trauma of it all weighed down on him like bricks. The image of Hannah's corpse in his arms, the experiments, the trials. But for some reason that he couldn't explain, he also felt lighter than he ever had before. Maybe it was now knowing the answers to the questions he always wondered about, like how his brother died, or why his parents didn't want him to be a part of their life. Or maybe it was just that his meds had stopped triggering those horrific dreams. He couldn't be sure the exact reason, but that summer he had grown optimistic about his future.

How naive I was.

Lonnie received the first letter on the morning of college move-in day. As he and Jamie arrived at their new dorm, they were greeted by its unwavering presence propped against the nightstand. Lonnie didn't even need to open it to know who it had come from. The familiar black wax seal was enough to send an itch down his back. As he held the green envelope, the symbol seemed so obvious to him now. It wasn't a tree with human faces. Instead, he saw the etching of five men stretching out from their shared spine, their hands reaching toward the edges of the wax. Against his better judgment, Lonnie opened the envelope. The letter read:

To Leonard Grambell & Jamie Harken,

Your presence is requested at the Blythorne Annual Anniversary Gala

Date: June 14th, 2024

Time: 9 pm

Call (304) 227-3452 to confirm your attendance.

Feeling a surge of confidence, Lonnie had crumpled it into the trash. However, that wasn't the end of it. More letters continued to come, each appearing on their nightstand without a trace of how it got there. And each requesting their attendance once again. It was becoming blatantly obvious that it was not something they could ignore. Not something they were going to be allowed to put behind themselves.

Eventually, Lonnie called the number to hear a monotone voice merely respond, "We look forward to seeing you."

This stopped the letters completely for months. Until a few days ago.

Lonnie pulled the newest letter from his backpack. The seal flap hung from the envelope. He read it to himself in the car, still unable to believe what he was reading.

Jamie turned on the music, which was a nice distraction from the utter silence as hours passed and the sun drifted down across the horizon. Lonnie felt his block of confidence reducing to a fine powder. He reached into his bag and pulled out a pill bottle. Ripping off the cap, he shoved a pill into his hand and threw it down his throat.

Both boys grew silent as they faced out the front window. Lonnie again scratched at his scar until the ends of it began to hurt. He looked older now, his face less full of its youthful complexion. His forehead burrowed with defining wrinkles that no one his age should ever have to wear. He looked tired, but it was only obvious if you really cared to notice, or maybe just if you remembered what he had looked like before.

His eyes suddenly widened as something caught his attention in the distance. "There," he pointed.

Jamie followed his hand to see the big shingle roof overlaying the tree line. Its upper windows peered out like glaring eyes chasing them through the canopies. Darkness had befallen the car, making every bit of light they glimpsed feel like a jump scare.

Taking a hard turn, Jamie pulled around a grove of trees. Their branches tangled outward as though beckoning them in. The leaves had shed onto the ground, creating a crunching noise beneath the tires. Looking through the window, Lonnie watched the house flash between the gaps in the trees, its homely light guiding them along the road.

The gate had already begun to open as they approached, giving them right of way to enter the front pass. Jamie spun the car around the lot, parking in a way that revealed the front entrance before them. His hands remained on the wheel a moment, his jaw locked as he glared at the building in disgust.

Lonnie placed his hand on his friend's shoulder, which only made Jamie flinch.

"Let's go then, huh?" Lonnie pushed.

Walking around to the trunk of the car, they popped it open to reveal a pair of tuxedo suits arranged neatly in vacuum-sealed bags hanging from the trunk hook. Pulling them out, they briefly looked around the plaza full of expensive cars. Music flew from the house as people's outlines filled the windowsills. It seemed like everyone was inside. Stripping to their underwear, they threw upon themselves an ensemble of black and gold suits.

Lonnie briefly noticed himself in the car window, an angry expression looking back at him as he parted his hair with a comb. More than that, judgment seared out at him from his own eyes, one that made him feel disgust, but all he could do was try to ignore it. He tied his shoes so he could briefly avoid looking at himself. Then finally he slid the green envelope into his pocket and shut the door. Walking in pace with Jamie to the front entrance, they carefully drifted up the sparkling, white marble stairs that had been covered in bloody bodies the last time he'd seen them.

How are they so clean?

He rubbed his foot on the step, trying to imagine the trail of blood that had once flowed down them like rain runoff. But he quickly stopped when a dizzy spell threatened to overwhelm him.

"You okay?" Jamie asked at the front door.

"Yeah," Lonnie lied through his teeth.

Lonnie grabbed the handle of the front door. Some part of him imagined his hand would combust on impact, but when nothing happened, he felt rather stupid.

It's only a door, he thought.

Then again, some would say it was only a house. But that word now meant so much more than he ever realized. Pulling on the door, it slid open to reveal a lavish arrangement of hundreds of people dancing in the center of a ballroom, just on the other side of the foyer. Lonnie thought he could still smell the gun smoke in the air from Mrs. Blythorne's gun, but he could only assume it was his imagination.

"I'll wait at the bar," Lonnie huffed.

Jamie nodded. "Okay, I'll meet you there in a second."

They shared an exchange as Jamie exited out onto the balcony. Meanwhile, Lonnie worked his way to the quaint little bar at the end of the room, which was illuminated only by the occasional dancing spotlight and little lamp.

Does anyone even live in here anymore? Lonnie wondered, looking at the empty conjoined staircases across the dance floor.

The people seemed different this year. They were more spry...happier. Lonnie couldn't help wondering if it had something to do with his offering, but he found it hard to believe. He had waited for some godlike miracle to happen all summer— some stroke of good fortune to fall into his lap, some winning lottery ticket to slap him in the face while walking down the street. However, nothing came.

Was all this for nothing?

Lonnie was curious if these people also felt the trials were maddening but continued to stay a part of them out of fear of defiance. Or maybe the placebo was simply enough to make each success feel like a gift from their cultic gods, and each failure feel like the fault of someone else instead of their own. These people did quite love putting blame on anyone but themselves.

Lonnie faced the bartender, who had just finished helping a radiant couple at the other end of the bar. He looked rather pure, his eyes sweet and kind and his ears inviting for secrets. He was someone you wouldn't expect to find at a house like this. The thought made Lonnie obsessed with him.

"What can I get you?" the bartender asked softly when he approached.

"Two champagnes, please."

"Sure, just a second." He gave a dimpled smile.

The man disappeared, leaving Lonnie to watch the smitten people dancing along the floor. Smiles poured lavishly from their faces, and rhythm flowed from their hips. They danced like nobody was watching, and all Lonnie could think about was all the horrors that were right below their feet.

Is this my life now?

Lonnie thought back to the contents of the letter in his pocket. The way the words sank into his chest. The powerless feeling he experienced when he read them. He reached into his pocket to grab the paper but stopped as the bartender returned.

Clink.

"Here you go." The bartender set the two champagne flutes in front of him. Lonnie took one, swirling it uncomfortably in his hand.

Thud.

The seat next to him was suddenly occupied by a man a year or two older than Lonnie. His bleach-blonde hair was parted in a way that showed no penchant for shyness; his suit pressed so tightly to his skin that Lonnie thought his muscles might burst through the stitching. It would be a lie if Lonnie didn't feel somewhat intimidated by this guy. He gave him a smile.

"How's the party?" Lonnie probed, shifting his seat to face him.

"This is insane," the guy divulged. "Truly...my god. The size of this place, you could get lost here."

"I know."

"And did you see the performer earlier? I mean...I mean I thought that guy was dead," he whispered.

"Yeah, this place is quite interesting, isn't it?" Lonnie gazed out at the crowd. "What's your name?"

"Oh, it's Roman," the guy rambled, sticking out his hand.

Lonnie stared at the hand for a moment before reaching out his own.

"Leonard..." he said, putting on a smile. "Pleasure to meet you."

They both went silent for a second as Roman continued admiring the room. His pupils were dilating from the sheer excitement of it all. Lonnie handed him the champagne glass before grabbing his own from the counter. "Would you like some?" Lonnie offered.

Roman smiled and took it. "Sure, thanks!"

"Cheers!" Lonnie chirped.

"Cheers!"

With a swing of the wrists, they both downed their drinks, after which Roman hopped back up from his chair. "Alright, I got to get back out there." He started for the dance floor. "You coming?"

"No, that's alright. My friend is coming to meet me."

"Alright, suit yourself, man!" Roman let out a holler, making his way back into the pit of dancers. His outstretched arms rose above the rest of people, like tree trunks growing past a layer of short-cut grass. Lonnie watched him for awhile, a naive smile printed on his face.

"He looks like he is having fun." Jamie sat down beside him.

"Time of his life..." Lonnie murmured.

"Gin and tonic, please," Jamie directed to the bartender.

"One for me as well," Lonnie added.

Pushing his empty champagne flute as far away as possible, Lonnie growled, "I can't stand the taste of champagne."

"How long do you think we have to stay?"

Lonnie crinkled the envelope in his pocket, then pulled it out. He began to read the letter:

Dear Leonard Grambell and Jamie Harken,

We are honored by your attendance at this year's annual gala. However, before an official welcome can be made, we must ask of you a favor. At the bottom of the envelope, we have included a picture of this year's guest of honor. Please make sure he has a wonderful night.

We know you won't disappoint!

Lonnie reached deeper into the envelope and took out a wallet-sized photo of Roman. Then from his pocket he pulled a blister pack of white pills with one slot now empty. He shoved it back into the envelope.

"Shouldn't be long now," he responded flatly. A tear grew in the corner of his eye, but he wiped it so fast he almost scratched out his cornea.

We know you won't disappoint.

The weight that one line held on his chest grew unbearable. Lonnie knew it was a threat if they didn't perform.

It's another test.

The idea of failing it terrified him. Lonnie had tasted all the horror he could have ever fathomed last summer. He never wanted to experience that level of terror again. He frowned and wondered if this was how his parents joined all those years ago. Had they feared for their safety as well? He wondered if his father had simply gone to Hopkins to help people and got swept up in the madness of his professor. Or if his mother thought she had met a nice man only to be blindsided by a world she never wanted to be a part of.

I guess I'll never know.

He hadn't spoken to his mom since that god-awful night.

Lonnie looked at that disfigured statue below the staircase. Five men with one spine. He wanted to break it into a million pieces, but he knew he couldn't. On its torso, Lonnie spotted a drop of dried blood. He knew no one else noticed it because nobody else would be looking for it. But he did.

Will there be another drop of blood tonight?

A helpless feeling consumed him as his eyes fell on the crowd. A wave of confetti fell from the ceiling, capturing all the dancers in a glittering ring of light. They all cheered except for one guest. Darting along the edge of the crowd, Roman kept stumbling in an attempt to reach the balcony window. His feet barely supported him as he ran across the tiles and crumbled down in front of the railing. Lonnie watched from his chair.

A couple of people gasped and ran to his side, lifting his head off the ground and calling for help. The music seemed to deafen their screams into quiet whispers. Two large men emerged from a nearby room and gestured for the bystanders to pass before lifting Roman's arms over their shoulders. As quickly as he fell, the men carried him down the hall and out of sight. All while the party continued around him.

The event made Lonnie think of Hannah.

Was this how she felt that morning she said goodbye to me? he thought. *Did she feel as helpless as I do now?*

Lonnie noted that familiar pit in his stomach, but this time he didn't care anymore. He couldn't do anything about it.

"Here are your drinks, gentlemen," the bartender announced.

"Thank you," they responded.

Grabbing their gin and tonics, they took a long sip and listened to the fireworks bursting over the pool. Lonnie took a filtered breath through his teeth as he caught a little red-dotted camera positioned at him from behind the bar. His mouth forced itself into a content smile as he raised his glass toward it.

And while he sat there, a single thought replayed through his head. A saying he'd often heard but never really believed until now.

The House Always Wins.

Acknowledgments

While writing a book may seem like a battle one goes into alone, I can say proudly from experience that this couldn't be farther from the truth. To those I am about to mention, know that no matter how big a part you played, this book breathes because of you.

To my mother: Thank you for indulging in a silly dream I had and convincing me it could be a reality. I will always cherish our midnight book conversations and the joy of watching you read each chapter for the first time. Your optimism is contagious, and I hope to always have it with me.

To my editor, Mary: Your initial book review left me spellbound. Your excitement toward it was so persuasive that it washed away all my doubts and was an anchor for me during those final grueling months of editing. I can never thank you enough for the guidance and kindness you showed me during this entire process.

To my first reader, Lissett: You were the best reviewer I could have asked for. I threw this request at you with no warning, and you enthusiastically dove into the challenge. I appreciate all the notes you gave, and I full-heartedly believe this book is better off due to you. Thanks for your support and friendship.

To my cover designer, Christian: When I saw your work, I knew that I had to have you be a part of this project. The care and energy you put into your illustrations is commendable, and I am happy to unveil this one as another addition to your portfolio.

To the Hudson Theatre Coffee Shop: Thank you for allowing me to camp out inside your café for all those months of writing. The relaxed atmosphere, amazing staff, and creative energy flowing through those walls consistently inspired me to sit down and write. I couldn't have chosen a better place to create this novel.

To my proof editor, Sherie: Thank you for helping me finish the final leg of this race and making me feel confident in delivering this novel to the world.

To everyone not listed by name, thank you as well for the support you have shown me. I am grateful for each and every one of you.

Made in the USA
Las Vegas, NV
26 October 2024